The Martian Archives

J. Nadir Ryf

**Translated from the French version titled:
Les Archives de Mars**

by Grahame Spence

Trafford rev. 01/22/2011

 www.trafford.com

North America & international
toll-free: 1 888 232 4444 (USA & Canada)
phone: 250 383 6864 ♦ fax: 812 355 4082

Preface

This story is based upon ancient teachings lost in the night of time because a great number of cataclysms have afflicted the earth many times. These spiritual teachings that are extraterrestrial in origin came directly from those who colonized the planet Alma and have been ignored and modified by those who survived the many earthquakes and floods and who created a great number of sects and religions which were destroyed with time along with unnumbered wars between peoples or with the dwellers of the shadow, specifically the Luciferians.

The heroes of our story are of different races and came from different planets of our solar system. Under the direction of the avatar of that age, they separated and spread out to different places on Alma in order to survive.

At the beginning of the year 2012, the space organization sent a spacecraft to the planet Mars to discover the remains of a great civilization destroyed by wars. The survivors of those wars were forced to leave and find another planet to continue their lives. They left behind an ingenious system integrated in a giant crystal sphere handled by a few extraterrestrials to show a film in three dimensions coming directly from the akashic records of the world. Thus all the earth's inhabitants in 2012 were able to see and follow the epics and great difficulties they endured such as adaptation and fights with the demonic Luciferians who terrorized all the planets of our solar system, in the past. The Martians built beautiful cities on earth thanks to their deep knowledge of physical and metaphysical technology and two big cities appeared at that time: Poseidia on the continent called Atlantis and Muria on the continent of Lemuria. And their adventures which happened over 45 000 years ago continue further after the great catastrophe that happened after the birth of the planet Mercury. These events will be presented in the next book *The Atlantean Archives.*

3

The Martian Archives

The brothers of space, also called the brothers of the light, periodically send avatars, masters of the divine light to guide and protect us in our evolution towards the primordial light.

I am grateful to Madeleine Poirier for her professional assistance in the writing of these books.

Joseph Nadir Ryf

Preamble

It is likely that this story might appear to be rather imaginary, but it does seem possible because of ancient events relating to the earth's evolution. Some huge changes took place in the past but now, for anybody believing in the permanence of the solar system or in the fixed orbits where the earth constantly follows the same path, for them, the past must stay impenetrable and mysterious, but, if one's conception changes, the old view is torn up and the evolution of the universe appears to be a real fact that parallels the evolution of species, all in a natural order.

Since the planets were born from the sun, they spread out unceasingly. Before occupying its position known today, Alma Gaya, the earth, where we are now living, once held the position of present day Venus and later that of Mercury. The actual states of these "stars" were those of its youth. One can easily imagine the pressure exerted on them caused by the power of the sun's cosmic wind. The cosmic rays were causing constant chemical reactions, the production of gases, the formation of water, the seismic forces, the melting of ice, immersions and reappearances of land masses and the gradual cooling of the earth's crust. All these types of changes were taking place over the course of ages.

Such changes influenced life on earth; no alternative course was possible; either life and its forms were rigid and therefore would not survive all these cataclysms or they were supple and plastic and adapted themselves continually to the environment and its circumstances. However, we need to understand that innumerable individuals did not survive these disasters and there were some mass extinctions when many species perished to be wiped out forever. Those who withstood the environmental rigors in the survival process were transformed in a sudden and overwhelming manner. That is what explains the process of mutations appearing to show a series of metamorphoses going from an initial state to a final one. In this manner, new species were born in the violence of change. As for humanity itself, why would it not exist on other planets which were once on the same orbit as the earth occupies today. Nothing stops us believing that humanity itself came from the planet Mars or from even further away, Jupiter. Then, seeing the impossibility of surviving on their planet which was gradually moving further away from the sun and undergoing irreversible changes rendering life impossible, human beings decided to come and live on the newly forming planet. That would mean a planet occupying the earth's actual orbit and therefore livable for the human species being neither too close to the sun nor too far away. Thus we could be descendants of Plutonians, Neptunians, Uranians, Saturnians, Jupiterians or Martians and even later, if we are obliged to leave the earth because of transformations taking place due to its retreating from the sun, we will become Venusians. It could be that our mother sun will still give birth to other little planets on which we will continue to survive.

The fact of the earth's retreating from the sun caused slowly but surely a drop in solar radiation pressure resulting in the dissipation of the huge carapaces which were protecting the animals against their enemies and also against the strength of the sun's rays, so that adaptation continued. The passage from aquatic to land-based life happened gradually. Life can also move in the opposite direction as seen in the whales (cetaceans) that recommenced their evolution in the oceans. Evolution persists in a condition of life which lacks permanence. There exists one law which directs that each time an imbalance occurs between an individual creature and its environment, that law has repercussions on cellular activity creating an impetus for change. If, on the other hand, balance is perfect between the individual creature and its environment, there is neither impetus nor thought nor action. This means that all thought is founded on the contact between the individual and the outside world and that all imbalance leads to balance, so that we can really see that what rules an individual's status is based on its adaptation to the ambience of its environment. The exception to this applies to a being, possessing a high level of consciousness. In the latter case, the mechanisms of thought are more complicated. The individual must vibrate in resonance with its surroundings, this being a law of perfect harmony.

All the past changes that the world of Alma suffered had their records burnt up, engulfed and eliminated. The sparse records which remained concerning Atlantis and Lemuria were burnt up in the fire at the great library of Alexandria. Later, some Greek philosophers spoke about them, such as Plato, Plutarch, Socrates, Pythagoras and Solon. Similar events happened on other planets. History continually repeats itself.

My history is based on the visions followed by personal studies and on the works of Professor Louis Jacot, but, as nothing can be proved in our era and because the past is now too remote, everything enters the realm of science-fiction. In our day, modern technology has made a connection with the actual facts of the matter thanks to research, computers and the sending-out of space probes.

The universe is constantly changing and the world is always in a state of evolution. Time and space are always present but remain fictional entities. I recall Jules Verne who anticipated in his vision the future of his epoch. Mankind must live constantly viewing in totality the works of God and must have a grasp of the beauty and harmony of creation which has as its starting point the loving of his or her fellow being.

On Earth, in our time, a more advanced technology has allowed astronomers to study outer space in more detail and for a number of years the planet Mars has challenged the interest of the experts. We want to know why the red planet which seemed once to have had life on its surface is now a desert. We have, perhaps, a faint memory of spending our life on Mars which (from now on in this story) will be called Mara. Huge sums of money have been absorbed by this research as well as in the goal of reaching Mars in order to obtain an explanation of its mysteries or perhaps recovering a trace of our ancient parentage. We will not doubt that

Adam and Eve could have existed but the question of when and where remains.

The European Space Agency sent the *Mars Express* (space probe) which should have reached Mars in 2003 with its Lander *Beagle 2*. NASA has been able to create equipment for checking whether water remains on the planet but that will only be in 2008. That expedition named *Exo Mars* will include an automatic robot containing a specialized laboratory. At this point, our story has its beginning.

Mars is 56 million km from the earth at its closest approach and this is something which only happens every 50 000 years and then it shines like the star Sirius. Its features include four seasons, Mount Olympus a gigantic extinct volcano and the Valles Marinaris and a series of immense canyons 7 km deep extending up to a length of 5 000 km. There are two polar caps which were viewed by the space probe *Mariner IV* which made the trip in 1965. The *Viking* probe in 1995 sent back photographs showing red sand. This is due to extensive erosion and constant sweeping of the planet by storms which cover everything with sand much like the Sahara desert. Mars has two satellites called *Deimos* and *Phobos*, possesses a core of iron 1500 km deep, a crust 100 km thick and a mantle of silicates. Its surface temperature varies between 21°C in the daytime and -110 °C at night. It rotates on its axis once every 25 hours.

Well known as they are, these facts were very different when Mars was in the same orbit which the Earth now occupies. In its remote past, Mars was like the Earth carrying a beautiful human civilization. Alas, there came a time when a moving-out from the sun and a prolonged war totally ravaged it and it needed the presence of a divine incarnation before its fall in order to save humanity. This divine Messiah without whom the human race could not have survived was the Sun-God taking the name of Lemoria. Thanks to this first Avatar, human beings were able to continue their evolution over the ages. It is of importance to me personally that I had the opportunity to meet the Avatar of the world of today who lives in India and who serves as my guide and also influenced the birth of this book. What is interesting in this story is that it may evoke in our mind many memories of other well known stories such as *Star Wars*, *The Planet of the Apes*, *Jurassic Park*, (Extraterrestrial) *E.T.*, *The Lord of the Rings* and the magic of Harry Potter as well as all the children's stories we know and love. All this in a great episode which is our establishment on earth. Let us now be guided by our imagination and let us travel together in that fantastic past where our entire destiny was played out.

Chapter I

Landing on Mars (Mara)

Infinite space is at the same time, a pitiless tomb and the eternal cradle of all forms of life. It is in the fathomless borders of the microcosm where light filters everywhere to create force that can take forms through the unique medium of the creative powers of the universe. This mysterious light having the huge potential of the power of love comes directly from the central sun, the divine mother. The rays of this soul of all worlds now shed its silvery light on the latest probe to be sent in the direction of Mars. The preparation for sending the probe was organized in minute detail and the months passed in space were without incident. Now on earth the descent sequence to the red planet was started and the activation of the special landing sequence which was intended to report on all trips made so as to inform NASA and all research centers of new discoveries to be made.

All the electronic equipment was set in operation, the red planet was now in view, the computers were calculating the distance still remaining. Since everything was automated, one instrument gave its data to others and evaluations were made systematically. In approaching the gravitational field of the planet, the strength of its gravitational attraction increased and became sufficiently strong that the craft was forced to brake its descent. It is more than twenty years since NASA and ESA (European Space Agency) sent different kinds of probes to photograph the red planet, but now, we have advanced enough in our technology to take samples of soil for automatic analysis on-site and have the results sent to earth right away by a direct data link. We have realized that Mars was a verdant planet in the past, well supplied with lakes, rivers and seas.

The vehicle carried by the spacecraft is a complex mobile laboratory designed to negotiate the hills and valleys of Mars. The spacecraft, after passing through different atmospheric layers, reversed itself and used its rocket motors together with the deployment of its large landing legs to make its touch-down as soft as possible. The chosen site was a flat area close to an immense canyon in the southern hemisphere near a kind of giant dome seeming to be made of tinted glass in different colors which, from afar, gives the impression of a giant octopus because of the central dome being linked to other cupolas by huge channels of the same tinted glass. This is as if the inhabitants of Mars were living underground as troglodytes.

After a fairly long time, the automatic Lander glided to the ground and the vehicle (having detached itself) started to move slowly towards the canyon nearest to the first of the large cupolas. It was strongly evident that these cupolas were constructed by the hands of men. It remained to find out what would be the Martians' reception of these intrusions coming from Earth.

However, on Earth, the film of these events was being watched. It was certain now that there had been human life on Mars. It remained to determine what condition it was in. All were very keen, curious, but also astonished and delighted at the same time. The vehicle was now directing itself without any obstacle the length of a crevasse, moving around immense hillocks of red sand and passing through a forest of uprooted trees and others still planted but with their bark burnt and hardened, stately as a forest of petrified wood. The dome of tinted glass was immense. Its centre must have been at least three hundred meters high. Three large tunnels also covered with glass came out from it; two of them linking to one of the other domes far off.

The Lander was now in front of a huge door, oval shaped. At that moment, the lights around the door started to operate and high-pitched sounds were heard. Slowly, the door started to slide open noiselessly revealing an opening. One could say that the Lander from earth knew how to enter these huge mysterious passages on the planet Mars but the real mystery was still to come.

Anxiously, we asked ourselves if these beings were welcoming or if they would destroy the vehicle. Under an open sky, it was easy to control the vehicle from a distance but if it reached the interior of the glass building could the radio waves still reach it, could they keep all its complex laboratory instrumentation operating, in the situation where all the energy would be provided by the probe and the sun rays.

Long minutes passed to see what would happen. The red, blue and yellow colored lights which illuminated the top of the door went out. Then sounds coming from a voice could be heard. It resembled the tone of voice speaking inside a closed vase with a guttural sound in an incomprehensible language. At last, out came a small creature. He was standing on a flying platform about five feet above the floor. He had a control panel in front of him. He very much resembled E.T. (of the movie) the small well-known extraterrestrial. He made signals that the vehicle should enter. It was decided, anyway, to enter the dome and the vehicle was guided to a pressurized chamber upon which, the great door closed again. One of the big mechanical arms of the vehicle signalled the "Martian" to approach and he started to communicate in several different earth languages in order to find out which would be the best for understanding, we responded with English. Then the little creature started laughing with a staccato sound like a little English dwarf who sounded as though he were in a closed vase and making signs said: "Come, come follow me" and climbed once more on to his platform as a second door opened. The vehicle now followed him and moved ahead through a large hall to the end which lay in the middle of the large dome. It led us in front of a giant sphere of glass transparent like crystal and then said: "There are only 13 of us, inhabitants of Mara, who live here. We are the creation of the Marians who fashioned our genes to give us the strength necessary to remain as guardians on the planet. We are able to survive in the climate of Mara. Our creators could not have survived whether they lived on Mara or inside it. On account of our last war, they left Mara more than 50 000 years ago. We stayed on to be the guardians. We reproduce ourselves, in turn for the role, every 500 years when our bodies expire. We have visited the Earth, your planet, several times already to see where our ancestors went but we cannot settle there because of the bacteria which are present and because of the difference in our organism. When you came down with your spacecraft we could have disintegrated you into dust with our defensive weapons, but we refrained, knowing that you came from the planet Earth with a desire only to acquire knowledge. Such an event was predicted to us quite a long time ago. For a long time now, we have been receiving all the messages which you transmitted in order to communicate with other planets and galaxies, but apart from our visits to Earth without attracting attention, we did not want to communicate with other planets because of the sudden attack by the Saturians more than 50 000 years ago. We did not wish for other contacts but in your case, we made an exception. We need to inform you what was happening on Mara in those times. You should now direct your camera towards the center of that giant sphere so that you can see before you a parade of all the Marian history and the reason why its inhabitants left the planet for Alma, the Earth.

You are going to relive all of their adventures as they have been told to us, from now up to the time of the last deluge on Alma when all our equipment was buried. This film is derived from the akashic record and is in three dimensions. So, you are going to become acquainted with your ancestors who populated your planet and the difficulties which they overcame in order to ensure their survival in the physical world. We are now going to ensure that your equipment has sufficient power by making a transfer that will avoid any possible technical failure. "Are you ready?" From Earth, the reply was "yes, we are ready; everything will be recorded on Earth by our own equipment." Three Marians having the same size as E.T. approached and moved the control levers so that the sphere which was twelve feet high started to rotate while dividing its interior into fragments and then images could be seen forming themselves in three dimensions. Suddenly, a large person having a tanned appearance came into view. It was a man resembling in size the ancient Egyptians with black hair, a well-trimmed beard and a small moustache. He wore golden metal shoulder pads for protection with ornaments on his chest displaying a symbolic emblem of a Marian religious order of the brotherhood of light, a circle of gold carrying in its centre a four-petalled flower having the color of garnet in the middle of which was a smaller yellow disc containing a gold letter M. That symbolized the highest ranking official of Mara. The same letter was also evident on the escutcheon of his belt, this being also of pure gold. At his right side hung a weapon in the form of a three-sided knife in white steel with a handle decorated with sparkling gold stars. We learned later, that this device could emit a white ray capable of disintegrating gelatinous substances, even flesh. He wore black pants and calf-covering boots of a supple material resembling leather. On his head shone a golden helmet with a black disc above the forehead carrying the same golden letter M and golden wrist-bands with the same golden letter M covered his forearms.

He started to speak to an invisible audience, evidently ourselves, on Earth. Let us not forget that this happened about 50 000 years ago. He also spoke in a guttural voice in his own tongue, then, suddenly switched to English and we heard him say "Welcome, welcome! We have an important message to pass on to you visitors. It concerns our history and perhaps yours also. The beings who welcomed you are the guardians of our old home Mara. They can survive because of the cito genes which we implanted in them. We are the Marians of four different family roots which came from the other planets of our solar system. They also have several times suffered exile and it is that kind of event which has created our different races. I am professor Adamos and here is my partner Evena."

A woman with long black hair and slightly shorter in build came towards him. She wore on her forehead a golden headband with the same Marian emblem. He then continued. "Our ancestors came from the planet Satur and thousands of years ago left for planet Mara because of its retreat from the sun. Normally, we communicate using a system of hieroglyphics, but the discoveries of our guardians in the future now allow you to listen in your own language. This is so that you can really understand our problem; I need to tell you about the evolution of all the planets in our solar system."

Evena began to speak while extending her hands as if presenting a picture and said: "See here the most impressive type of theatre, life's most beautiful, which shows the birth of the sun as a daily curtain-raiser when each morning it wakes us from our sleep to invite us to enjoy its light and life. Now, can you see that all is based on the universal dynamic principle emitted from the Sun of Suns, the Mother Sun. Nothing is static, such an impression is only an illusion. We know that all forces are in contact one with another, nothing is limited, all that exists affects the visible world as well as the invisible one. As we have already said, our exodus from the planet became necessary for the survival of the human species in its physical manifestation. My spouse is going to project for you the images which will make you understand the retreat of the planets from the sun and the consequences arising from it."

"So look at this," said Adamos. "You see that the sun appears at the centre of the crystal sphere. One might think that between the sun and the planets, the space is empty but that is not the case. What we call the sun and the planets are only the basic structure but around them lies a sea of energy. It is invisible to the eye but it certainly exists. Everything works together much like clockwork. The wheels that you are seeing as an example are always two forces put in contact linked by their axes forming couples turning inversely one to the other. In our own case, the sun is not limited by its physical size this being barely its kernel. Its influence spreads out to the planets. That is what is called the solar perisphere. You can see here an ellipse and at its centre, the physical sun. In fact, we are bathing in the sun. The solar system is not a collection of balls separated by a void, it contains the planets as if in an egg and the whole system rotates in a collective movement like a huge whirlpool. It rather resembles a fruit. Let us take the example of a peach: in the middle is a kernel, the sun and around it is the flesh containing the planets. The sun itself rotates about its axis in twenty five days at present. Our planet Mara is 227 million km from the sun and orbits in 687 actual days but that was not the case 40 000 years ago when it was nearer the sun. Each planet gets its speed from its surroundings because the whole system is moving from the centre to the periphery. Look, in this great solar whirlpool, there does not exist a single movement which defines a closed orbit. All the planets, therefore, resemble a spiral, progressively increasing their distance from the sun. Rigidity or the perpetual maintenance of a planetary carrousel does not exist because the universe in all its parts is evolving and the planets around all stars are distancing themselves from their solar origin as if attracted magnetically by another invisible sun. The effect of the separation changes the degree of the pressure felt by each planet. The planet is subjected to a very large pressure when it is close to its sun and it is held at the same time as in a vice lacking its own rotation and is very slow. Such is the case of the planet Mercury which is 58 million km from the sun and completes an orbit in 88 days. That is today, since 40 000 years ago Mercury was not born. When a planet distances itself from the sun, we have the effect of a wheel whose brake is applied gently. It begins to turn slowly then over time a little faster and with better regulation. Each planet is born from the sun its mother and distances itself like a child leaving its mother's breast. In undergoing the solar pressure, the more the distance increases, the more the pressure diminishes. This has the effect of hardening its core and consequently increasing its density.

The centrifugal force is a particular direction taken and is inversely proportional to the pressure taken in a circulatory sense. That causes the planet not to maintain its distance from the sun, and, because of its elliptical orbit, it moves faster when it is nearer the sun than it does when it is further away. Thus the planetary movement follows the conditions of the circulatory movement which is always more rapid near the centre than at the periphery."

Evena was making designs on a white board describing these moving spheres while Adamos was taking a break. These two people possessed beautiful facial expressions and refined and elegant body movements.

Adamos continued his speech. "The sun itself is enclosed within a galaxy from which it is moving out. What concerns us in Mara (Mars) is the external solar pressure slowly decreasing year after year which causes the central part of the planet to dilate. It is no longer the biosphere where all the life-giving elements were in harmony when this was Mara on the elliptic orbit where the planet Alma Gaya (the Earth) is now positioned. Another reason is the disastrous war which we suffered due to the invasion of the Saturians, who, under the negative influence of the Luciferian spirits came from Satur's satellite *Rhea* where they had established their base to attack and invade us."

Evena now made appear the scenes of the apocalyptic war.

"The Saturians had found through their research that a mineral compound called Tefton possessed the property of intense energy when included in an alloy with a compressed crystal and the planet Mara possessed the greatest quantity. Satur had almost none of it and we the Marians did not want to use it in our trade with the Saturians because of the dangers of using the yellow energy for destructive purposes. The Saturians decided to go to war and steal all the Tefton which they were coveting and, despite the attempts at conciliation by those of their citizens who were of good intentions, they prepared to move against us."

We saw appear on the screen the battle of Thelema on the planet Mara. The fast deployment of the airborne forces coming from Satur had burnt the whole of the Marian surface with their chemical laser-rays from Tefton combined with two super reactive elements, hydrogen and fluorine. Without warning, the Saturians possessed by the demonic Luciferian spirit had decided to decimate the planet Mara.

They were technically more advanced with their war machine than the Marians and they coveted the red planet in order to steal its natural resources. The twenty seven capital cities were devastated. The large city of Thelema was going to fall into the hands of the Saturians who were intent on their next coveted principal objective, the sacred cosmic pillar, holder of the great cosmic energy.

Before the invasion, the war leader, Colonel Molox said in addressing the Moloxians: "Moloxians, we are ready to attack Mara. You know that the Marians are of the red race. Their blood contains iron and copper and they are good warriors but since our brothers Saturians emigrated to Mara, thousands of years have passed. In bringing our technology there, they also took up the religion of light enfeebling them and also making them followers of the inner beauty of love and compassion. Our ultimate goal is to recover the sacred cosmic pillar which they took with them because, in so doing, they took away our power in the physical universe on the pretext that we were following the Luciferian way. Sad to say, that is probably true from their point of view but they cannot take away our rights and we have to take back the pillar at the price of their lives. We need it for the ceremony of adoration to our god Moloch and our goddess of evil, Cyra."

Following this message, the immense armada left *Rhea* with its thousand flying craft like discs all armed with the yellow ray symbol of destruction and with the terrible gas Tefton. The Luciferians had total control over the majority of the Saturians since their great defeat in another war. This involved the invasion of the Satur planetary system in the past and the colonization of its satellites *Phobos* and *Rhea*. It was there that most of their arsenal was produced. Colonel Molox was a bloodthirsty and cruel being, his spirit entirely at the mercy of the Luciferians causing him to feel invincible. This coupled with his total adoration of the androgynic goddess Cyra of monstrous appearance made him strong and bestial.

On the occasion of his last Molochian rite, the goddess appeared to him in flesh and bone. She was big with a fine dark face and the body of a beast. She ordered the seizing of the lingam, the pillar of light. "We must overcome these ignoble sons of the light and must use our strength on them and make them our slaves. Be sure to follow Molox, he will lead you to victory. We have supported you with a terrible weapon, the Tefton, which, projected by your laser beams will burn everything in its path so that nothing will grow for many centuries on this planet; life will also disappear. Go! My protection goes with you." On hearing these words from his goddess the wild boar-like appearance of Molox was filled with contentment. Before setting out for war, his goddess had said that she would protect him. Nothing serious could affect him and that was what he needed most. With that, the diabolical armada launched itself into space on the great quest towards Mara in order to destroy it.

Chapter II

The battle of Thelema

Adamos continued: "We were at the mercy of the Saturians and we defended our planet with tenacity to our deaths but it was the avatar Lemoria who delivered us from conquest by them thanks to his supernatural powers. At first, we were decimated by the enemy but thanks to his intervention, this extremely destructive war was ended.

It was the solar avatar who appeared on Mara just before the final attack which was going to destroy everything. This was when the final order had gone from the headquarters of the airborne fleet to use the disintegrator rays with Tefton to burn everything. Suddenly, we saw him, his companion close behind him. A luminous circle of terrifying intensity surrounded the invaders. The Saturian armada turned on their heads. The two of them were standing on the largest building at the centre of a large terrace when Votour, leader of the airborne attack, saw them and gave the order to raze the city together with all the inhabitants who had taken refuge there. At that exact moment, Lemoria raised his right hand to the heavens. He was holding a flame which gave out twisting fires in a spiral of light. A huge green ray, negative in nature, went from the clear sky into the gloom and expanded with the speed of light. Then the whole armada composed of the one hundred and forty-five spacecraft remaining which had not yet been destroyed, instantly disappeared as if hit by a thunderbolt. Lemoria lowered his arms and descended the large stairs around which the crowd had gathered. Addressing all of them, he said: *"Your prayers have been heard by the Lord Creator of this world and he has forbidden the extinction of your race because you have a mission to accomplish in the future and we have come to help you enter this new age for humanity's advancement!"*

Hardly had he completed his sentence when Molox who was on the ground with his army around the great pyramid covered with onyx plates went towards it. He was preparing to steal the holy lingam inside it when suddenly Lemoria and his companion appeared. Molox had not yet noticed the disappearance of his aerial forces because he had given the order to save the city centre with the great pyramid. Lemoria shouted to him, *"Molox, stop!"* The bloodthirsty Molox, completely surprised, paused a moment and demanded to know how this man knew his name, when, growling, he advanced brandishing his fiery sword. On seeing this and the meanness of Molox, Lemoria lifted his right arm and Lemuria who was leaning on his back lifted her left arm. Lemoria pointed his right finger up to the sky and a flaming crown started to rotate around both of their hands. He advanced towards Molox, the chief of the Molochs. He held in his left hand the conch-shell, a universal symbol and cried out: *"Get back Molox; you are defying the forces of heaven, return to the place from which you came."* Molox, who did not recognize him, laughed and brandishing his sword cried bitterly: *"You think you can frighten me. I have with me all the devils of hell reborn and I am going to annihilate you, your wife, and all the inhabitants of this planet."* Then he fired his weapon which spouted flames towards Lemoria who repeated his command: *"For the last time Molox, go back"*, but the bloodthirsty Molox in a fury did not want to listen. He advanced with his army of demons. Then Lemoria pointed his finger towards the mass of Saturian demons, a crown of fire left his finger and the men fell to their knees flaming like fiery torches, ending finally as little piles of cinders. Molox, seeing that, made off running, and disappeared into space. Lemoria had spared him but nobody knew why.

Lemoria made us aware that he had visited the world Alma Gaya several times by teleporting himself and said to them: *"I incarnate myself from time to time in order to help in the advancement of humanity. My brothers and sisters of Mara, your planet is actually now at its perihelion, the closest approach to the orbit of Alma the distance*

21

being 40 million km. In order to survive the disaster of this war, you will have to live underground like troglodytes. The air is thin and there is no longer water on the surface. It will be necessary for you to leave Mara for the Earth within a short time. I know that you have finished the construction of your special interplanetary spacecraft, the Gyrosphere, and I see that it is working very well. Alma has not yet reached a mature state where it can receive human life, but I will look after that. In spite of having a very dense core, the planet right up to the present, has gases and very little water. At this time, its icy polar caps are forming as well as its continents. Like the other planets, it separated from the sun and started to move away. It is slowly settling itself into the right orbit. Not so long ago (speaking in terms of thousands of years) it was at the same distance from the sun when Venus was born a short time ago. The planet itself does not rotate and shows always the same side to the sun while the other is plunged in the shadow of an icy night. Alma, the earth, as it was later located at the distance of the planet Venus continued moving out in a spiral, then the pressure got less and the planet expanded from its interior causing crustal collisions which resulted in volcanic eruptions. During that time, life did appear in all its various forms."

***

While on earth at NASA headquarters, via the spherical crystal screen, one could see pictures of all that had happened to the earth in the beginning. *"See,"* said Lemoria, *"the heaviest elements are expelled from their origin at the same time as others appear explosively, thrown out in an immense boiling pot, all pushed by the same radioactivity which exists in the sun. Since the expansion is general, nothing escapes it. So it is not only that the earth increases in volume starting from its interior but to all that activity are added external effects such as crustal forces making their own adjustments. In this manner, Alma is getting ready for its future of supporting life in all its varieties of forms and species and colors. This is being prepared at the same time as the movement away from the sun as well as the planet's rotation slowly starting up."*

"You know", continued Lemoria, "your planet Mara has suffered greatly as it distanced itself from the sun and even more due to this war in which the Saturians invaded your planet forced by the guidance of the Luciferians' evil spirit. Those events totally upset the life currents and cycles and the normal mixing of gases. They also destroyed all vegetable and animal life as well as the insect world. Your food, air to breathe, and water to drink is consequently, totally lost to you. It is therefore necessary to construct an enclosed biosphere for you in order to protect you and allow you to survive. Life is becoming more difficult and accidents are a daily occurrence. You will have to start the pumps right away to get water from deep underground. The thousands of nuclear explosions which you suffered have burnt the soil which is now no longer fertile as well as annihilating ninety percent of your population. It is a disaster!

The effects of the red rays have been to remove 60% of the reserves of oxygen and drinking water. Survivors in other cities whether Marian or Saturian have succumbed to suffocation and dehydration due to a stifling dry heat lasting for 60 days followed by extreme cold. Now the proliferation of bacteria which can live without oxygen increases unceasingly causing widespread sickness. From the big central dome which I am going to make for you now, you will have to construct tunnels of glass in a tubular shape and below the contaminated soil where you will be able to grow vegetables and fruits for your survival. As you dig these underground facilities, you will find water but with the destruction of the planet the nights will become longer and colder. You should therefore prepare to leave Mara for the planet Alma Gaya. There are amongst you descendants of the people from Satur and Jupita who emigrated to Mara 800 000 years ago. I am giving you two years to prepare for this migration and I will return with Lemuria to help you during and after this great voyage."

The film continued on the crystal sphere and Lemoria followed by Lemuria could be seen leaving the terrace of the great pyramid of onyx and heading for the central square. The people went with them and there his companion leaned against his back. He faced the rising sun and extended his right arm with Lemuria extending in turn her left arm, towards the pyramid in the direction of the sacred lingam. The side of the pyramid was transparent like glass, and suddenly a lightning sparked from the centre of the lingam across from the pyramid to encircle Lemuria's left arm and then went out from Lemoria's right hand. He then made, with a gesture of his hand, an immense circle around the city of Thelema and from his hand radiated a golden light. Then from particles of this light now materialized an innumerable quantity of luminous cell-like snowflakes in a huge storm which fell in front of the astounded eyes of the thousands of Marian inhabitants and they then saw a dome rise resembling an immense colored glass all around them, 10 km in circumference and about 300 m high. Ten huge doors appeared each with a complex opening mechanism. There were currents of air and it seemed that the heat that was suffocating before it adjusted itself. Other openings were visible for the evacuation of air. Turbines were included which operated to integrate the energy system. *"You are now set up to survive the terrible war and you can now take over control but I warn you to stop reproducing your species. The few of you who will be leaving for the world of Alma should not have children before they leave. If any choose to do so they will only breed monsters,"* concluded Lemoria.

At these words, the avatar of the age of the Turtle departed, with his companion, from the view of the last survivors of Mara. Only some of the very old had heard avatar Lemoria speak. Some great masters had the privilege of seeing him during their prayers and understood that he was the personification of the god Shnu. This time, he appeared to them in the form of a large man with a bronzed complexion, black eyes and a large forehead having a bump between his two eyes at the location of the third eye. Avatar Lemoria had the capability of changing his bodily form and could appear smaller or larger, younger or older. The colors of his skin and eyes could be different on occasion and when he was in contact with the holy lingam, his skin changed from a brown color to a violet-blue, then he became totally spiritual. He had the power to transcend the material worlds and often disappeared for a long time. His spouse, incorporated in him, was his double in transcendent power. They were one indivisible. They could give life and take it back. Marvel now at the power of the two beings who came to save the human race on the planet Mara. And so finished the discourse of Adamos and Evena.

***

Meanwhile, back on Earth, the scientists and theologians were trying to understand the sense of everything that they were seeing and hearing. They were asking themselves who these supernormal beings could be, the avatar Lemoria and his companion. It all appeared to be a fantastic story, quite outside their system of beliefs. However, the possibility of the earth being colonized by extraterrestrials especially humans from our solar system seemed perfectly possible. These archives from Mars were quite natural. Nobody doubted what had happened, even the man in the street. On the contrary, for the mass of people now living on earth, it answered a thousand questions on the origins of man. When a planet is in the favorable cycle of the wave of life, its inhabitants live in an earthly paradise. Food is abundant and life is easy. Alas, it is the nature of man and his desires which change the conditions of life and often render it impossible. So even a paradise can become a hell. In imperfection, perfection is hidden and it is up to man to find it.

Another large man with a beard and skin the color of ebony made his appearance on the screen. "I greet you," he said with a smile showing his shining white teeth. "My name is Afrika. I am descended from an ancient civilization on Jupita and I joined the expedition of Dr Adamos in order to aid all the members of our clan find a new world for our descendants. My specialization as a chemist will be useful for our task. As you know, the biggest problem for our planet is the lack of oxygen caused by the war. The trees and all the other vegetables have perished and all the surface water is swallowed up by the soil. The rest has evaporated into space because of the massive bombardments. This disturbance in the balance of hydrogen and oxygen caused by the last war has dangerously affected our lives and the same for all nature down to the smallest particles of atoms with their electrons.

When the structure of their cycle is upset, life becomes largely impossible. Happily, we are able to remedy the situation by living underground thanks to the refuges and to the pressurized passages made by Lemoria but we are still at the mercy of accidental events.

In our researches for methods of survival, we discovered new avenues in nuclear physics. We are able to create, reproduce or control cosmic rays. It is thus that the white ray creates and gives life, the red ray heats and burns things to ashes, the green one based on chlorophyll sooths and heals, the blue ray harmonizes and calms the spirit, the yellow increases the life energy, but combined with the black ray, it becomes the destructive one which is connected to the black sun of antimatter. If it is combined with the negative indigo ray, it destroys matter totally. Its energy, thus concentrated, is our ultimate armament against the threat of danger. We had to use it against the Saturians with the permission of Avatar Lemoria. The Saturians had already destroyed the majority of all our colonies, except those that were established to safeguard life on our planet thanks to cities constructed underground. They used their nuclear weapons with Tefton. In spying on us they were capable of concentrating the red ray together with the yellow one and in the last war they burnt up the little life which remained on the surface of Mara. It was necessary to wipe them out but these were only the Saturians influenced by the spirit of evil who attacked us, the others who fought against the Luciferian spirits came to us with peace and understanding. For the rest, Lord Lemoria and his companion came from Satur where they harmonized their spirits before coming to our rescue, and it was through him that we were able to use the indigo ray. It was they who made us understand why, and the reason for these attacks against our people and our planet. So here is what we have been able to understand. The good Saturians are those which left their planet at the moment when (as it happened on Mara) its exit from the sun caused great coldness and serious drops in temperature. They were vegetarian by nature and had developed amongst themselves love and understanding. It was this that distanced them from the other inhabitants of Satur who were carnivorous by nature and aggressive. They survived the disasters well but the moving out of the planet also affected their spirits and their minds, above all those of the meat eaters. A character balanced between goodness and materialism deteriorates more easily, because, in approaching the black sun, they receive more of its influence and become gradually destructive. The black sun absorbs matter and destroys it by massive contraction. So as you can see, things repeat themselves from people to people and from planet to planet.

During their evolution in the past, the Luciferians inhabiting planet Lucifer had suffered all their natural transformations. They should have become self-realized on Neptuna but because of diabolical influences succumbed to black magic and the noxious influences of the black sun. No longer living in a physical body they continued their existence as discarnate spirits in the lower astral when their planet exploded. The influences of the black sun spread across the Luciferian spirit which is invisible to the naked eye, but can be seen only by the third eye. Being invisible it is capable of infiltrating right into the genes of its victims. The planet Lucifer which separated itself from contact with the black sun kept its spirit intact for a long time, but its polarity became negative and highly egocentric, later only serving to promote evil. The Luciferians were inhabitants of the planet Lucifer, one of the firstborn from the sun. This planet, after moving away to the extreme distance, was finally attracted by the black sun which nourished itself from it and broke up its matter in a slow final disintegration. Being the first planet to be born from the sun, it possessed an intense vital planetary energy and was brilliant like the sun. Its powerful solar spirit was called Lux-Si-Fer, the double of the solar light. The beings which inhabited it had great intelligence, but became extremely egocentric at the end. Their evolution was slow and the majority fell into the shadow of negative forces when their planet later expanded out of the solar realm.

The more a planet approaches the black sun, the more its surviving spirits become demoniac, resembling the black sun which has a function that is extremely egocentric, taking all lives, fortunes, matter, nourishing themselves from them and destroying them, becoming the negative god in action called Shva. On the other hand, the white sun gives everything in return, it is called Shram, that which creates. It has a vital and pure ray, which creates all forms and lives; it is doubled in the invisible and becomes Shnu, that which maintains life in its creation. It is the source of equilibrium. Its intelligence penetrates all creation and balances it, then it splits itself and becomes Shva the black sun of the anti-matter. These entities which are considered as gods are an integral part of all life in the cosmos. The more we are close to the white sun the more our psyche is filled with light due to the loving influence of the supreme mother. The beings that move away from the sun are jealous of those which are impregnated by the light and profit from the times when they can take it by force. The light has several forms; it is the vital energy to survive as much as in the physical shape as in the spiritual because it is that which supports life. When the planet is located on its vital biological orbit, equilibrium is created in all forms taking on life. It finds itself between the solar influences where life is harmonious and the cycles are balanced and its other extreme, the negative. The central point between the two forces is called the eye of God. In that state of consciousness we are aware of the love of God in our life. In that state, nature is an earthly paradise for an extended period of time; the etheric and astral planes have a beneficial influence. Nevertheless it is necessary to be constantly on guard keeping the spirit in a state of goodness, beauty and love and not to allow anything negative to infiltrate thoughts, creating disorder. Such are the rules to follow to overcome the illusion of the world of duality (the good and the bad). If we deviate minutely from this life-principal rule, we become aware of the presence of the beings of the Luciferian world. These were beings who fought in the remote past for the glory of the light and the truth up till the end but could not leave their planet before they arrived at the gates of the black sun which finally absorbed them. Such are the events which forced the Luciferians to deviate into black magic and they were our ancestors, but what concerns us now are all the reasons which forced us to leave Mara and go and live on Alma when, the way things were, our biological system needed to undergo great transformations. And it seemed that this was foreseen in the secret codes of creation that follow the law of the three Gods. On the other hand, those who overcame fatality became the angels.

In our voyage, we will be taking with us our research and energy laboratories hoping that they will not be demolished by possible disturbances. See now, I am finishing my presentation and I now introduce to you professor Atalanta who is the commander of this expedition and who will give you further information about us."

Another large man bronzed with a thick moustache and blue eyes made his appearance. He was accompanied by a beautiful young woman with emerald blue eyes and red hair. He said, making a welcoming gesture to his audience: "Now it is my turn to address you. My brothers and sisters of Mara our dear planet, it is true that we are really well informed of the consequences and resigned to live on the planet Alma, but it is a serious adventure which we are taking on. It is far from being a simple voyage. There are difficulties from all points of view which we have to overcome, and perhaps even at the cost of our lives. As you know, our brotherhood of light has determined that it was the time to put ourselves to the test and the old ones did not want to leave Mara. There are only forty of us chosen for this unique exodus. In truth, we know that such a thing has already been done in the remote past and we are confident for the future. Here, life has become practically impossible, which is no longer natural and we are too dependent on artificial factors to maintain it. We are forced to live below ground like worms because of a fierce cold and dryness without respite. Thanks to our technology, we will be staying continually in contact with you and we will keep you up to date with all changes which might arise as much as our lives will permit. We are going to take with us Linga II by which we can communicate with Linga I as well as with the cosmic heart of the universe. Also we will not be affected by the uncertainty of fear. As for the rest, Lemoria, our high priest will be with us.

Linga I is a sacred pillar oblong, being six feet high and of pure diamond, supported on a plinth elevated two feet in rock crystal. Nobody on Mara knew who had created this giant lingam. It was of a perfect transparency and at its centre had a circumference of three feet, within its centre one could make out two other lingams: the first a beautiful dark yellow with orange sparkles, the other, smaller in size, was bluish and slightly reddish at its centre, it all resembled the flame of a candle and when the attendants were dancing around it and the priests were reciting their mantric-prayers, it became brilliant like the sun. You could not keep your eyes on it. In its centre was a small continuously glowing red light. When the white flame was alight, it released an immense amount of heat with very great radiance. One felt that enormous power was released from this pillar and felt an impulse to worship it. All the same Lemoria used to say *"Do not worship it; it is only an instrument in the service of God and humanity."* Linga I was installed in the stone body of a giant sphinx. That was its temple contained in an immense pyramid transparent like glass. The granite rock had the form of a giant sphinx, the rock being in the form of a resting lion and it was topped by a human head wearing a helmet like that used by an astronaut. That symbolized human evolution coming from the animals then experiencing human life in order to rise to divinity. A whole philosophy was contained in that image. The lingam was the light of the soul, pure and immortal, the jewel of Mara. It was there that, before leaving, we will have a special departure ceremony. One of the main reasons why the Saturians attacked us was to get their hands on the holy Lingam. They tried every trick possible to capture it and we had to hide it. We think that Linga I was created by the seven great sages, messengers of the universe coming from distant galaxies or from the star Sirius to help mankind in their solar evolution, meaning their return to the "sun" from which they originated. By their thoughts, gestures and mantric chants, they compounded the elements out of the cosmos and gave them the form of this immense lingam. They left a teaching for the conduct of life and disappeared as suddenly as they had arrived. Now, every day, when the sun is at its zenith, one can hear the sound of creation, OM vibrate strongly at first then gradually diminishing one hundred and eight times originating from the holy lingam causing the whole building to vibrate like an echo for at least fifteen minutes.

Everywhere we go, we will keep in contact with the great cosmic heart because of its vibration of love which makes us live and it is thanks to the Lingam II which is a copy of the first one that we are taking with us to Alma. We cannot live only by the benefits of the fruits of planet Alma, our spirit linked with our soul must be bathed by the light of the creator at the centre of the cosmic heart. Our heart must itself harmonize with that thing without which there is no reason to exist. We are lucky to have with us the avatar Lemoria who represents the cosmic deity. He is our spiritual guide for the new solar era. We are going now to continue the message from our archives with Professor Zanga and his partner Zaraya. Both of them are working on researches into the nature of things."

Zanga and his partner made their appearance on the screen. He was a man with yellow colored skin and slanting eyes having smaller stature which his partner also possessed. He spoke with a sharper voice. "I am also a botanist, he said and it was in my mind to be able to contribute together with my spouse to the development of agriculture on Alma. We are taking with us a large number of vegetable seeds as well as the seeds of cereals, flowers, fruit trees and nut trees from our greenhouse. Some had already been brought by our ancestors from Myso (the planet Neptuna) in the course of their stay on Satur and later on Mara. Then there are species of plants which we have crossed and genetically modified. Thanks to that activity, plants which were for a long time harmful became edible."

Zanga showed pictures on the screen of a large variety of diverse plants that they were going to be able to plant as well as the gardens which would be ready to receive them.

"For that it was necessary to save at the last possible moment the vital seeds for nourishing survival before the murderous wars started. The experience showed that we could live by taking the radiations of the positive green ray but only for a short time. We had to take, as quickly as possible, the food sources produced the most abundantly by nature and also those elements which would maintain our health in balance. We were able to irradiate this food with the green ray to increase its potential energy. We have some domestic animals with us that we were able to save from disaster such as cats, dogs, some birds, some fish and a quantity of frozen embryos which will provide us with animal bodies when appropriate. We are vegetarians and count on staying that way on Alma, all of which depends on the conditions there. The fact that our planet is 45 000 000 km from Alma (the shortest distance for 60 000 years) will reduce the length of our voyage. We are going not for curiosity but above all because of necessity. We suspect that other human forms exist on Alma. Master Lemoria who has, in the astral, visited many parts of the planet has seen them. He says that they are small and hairy like a different species, the apes, who live in trees except that the humans live in caves. He believes that they are of an aggressive nature, that they often live in packs, others, much larger live in the mountainous regions. Some of the hairy men use poisoned darts made from a tree. He says that he has also seen huge trees and others having creepers which grow like the tentacles of a huge octopus. Yet another species of creeper are sticky with a very acidic substance capable of causing burns. The ape-men taken and killed by the creeper are eaten by the plant which sucks all their life-protein through thousands of tiny pores. There are still giant animals that remain from the past. Alma presents a multitude of dangers which we have to face in the soil, water and air.

Up to now, our means of reproduction are limited. We base them on the quality of life and of a character that already eliminates all negative elements at the moment of conception and after, during pregnancy, by a careful control of genes. Whatever is harmful is removed. We are in the habit of removing feeble bodies in order to obtain ones which are strong and resistant (to disease), but we have learnt that great spirits capable of helping the evolution of society on the physical, mental and spiritual planes prefer to return into weaker bodies. Minds cause illumination when entering a weaker physical body and it would not help to concentrate only on a strong physical race, the same goes for women.

A woman on Mara possesses identical capabilities to a man. We know that a type of reincarnation exists and that dead people continue to live on another plane in which they can be contacted. Finally, in an important communication, the spirit of one of our forefathers who was very important in his physical life, told us through our spirit-videoscope where we can see his picture reflected in a large crystal sphere. *"I am very happy that you have decided to follow our advice and emigrate to the planet Alma. We had to do the same thing in the past in order to settle on Mara. That is man's destiny. It is going to allow a large number of us to reincarnate, something which is necessary to enable us to experience the physical life on a new planet and pay our karmic debts. We are keeping in contact with you and even though we are invisible to you we are able to help you in thousands of ways."*

"Take with you as many vegetable seeds as possible as well as the sperm of some animals. At this moment, Alma is populated with monsters but that will be changing in the future. Alma is capable of becoming a paradise of wonderful life forms; it is even more supportive of life than was our own planet Mara in its beginning." And so he ended his comments and recommendations.

The appearance we observed on the cosmic crystal sphere was of the round and reddish face and abdomen of E.T. our guide on the planet Mara who, with his small, sweet nasal voice said: "Now we are in process of making you see the tremendous odyssey of Captain Adamos on the new planet Alma. The images which you are about to see and those which follow are sent from a flying remote-camera which can operate independently and automatically, and is capable of surveying scenes without being affected by its external environment. It transmits everything it views to us, down to each exact detail. This is the mystery of the akashic records!"

Suddenly, on the earth, at NASA's control centre, there were crackling noises, an alarm sounded, and a red light came on. The guardian interrupted his transmission and asked "Hello earth, are you having problems with the signal?" From earth came the response "No, it isn't that but we have technicians who have a question for you. We want to know if these are films recorded on tape which you are showing to us." "Oh no, replied the guardian but ask the same question again mentally with strength to Professor Lemoria in an instant and he will answer you."

On earth there was even more astonishment "but how? Everything happened 45000 years ago, it's impossible." "I understand your doubt, said the guardian with a smile, you believe that the past is past but this concept is incorrect. The past present and future are all one. Try to call mentally to Professor Lemoria and you will see. I am restoring the connection."

There were some shades of color in the crystal sphere and after a second the face of Lemoria could be seen, with his quiet smile. After a short pause he addressed the earthlings. Facing the NASA equipment he made a gesture and replied: *"I can communicate directly with you since I am outside time and space. The pictures which you are seeing and which are being transmitted to you as being viewed on the sphere come from the past. So much is true. I have established a special form of direct communication with the events of the past so that you can receive them in the present. Yes, effectively it is stored on the tape of time which is called the akashic record similar to magnetic tapes and printed in the aura of Alma, the earth. Every event which happens at every instant in the world, on the ground or in the sky belongs to the planet and forms part of its evolution and is stored in it.*

Yourselves, each one of you, has an astral light-body which records all the thoughts, gestures and actions which belong to you and give you your karma. Nothing can escape it. It is important for you to be aware of this fact. It is a reason why we are reliving the events of the past. It is up to you to avoid the problems which you are causing on the earth by your present actions. By a policy based on a mistaken materialistic philosophy you are causing the loss of your own and thousands of other lives in other lands. So, further, you are preventing the reincarnation of thousands of souls ready to return to earth to help you with putting things in order."

"Professor Lemoria, can we communicate more often with you in the future?"

"For now, it is an exception. I have other tasks to do. You are going to receive help through another avatar. I have decided to reincarnate myself to help humanity in this difficult time, you have my promise."

On Earth, everybody looked at each other puzzled and wondered if all that had happened was not a dream.

"This Lemoria," said somebody, "is he God?"

On the large sphere appeared another luminous sphere surrounded by a dozen smaller spheres which circled around it. The voice of Lemoria made itself heard again.

"What you are seeing at this moment is the unique image from the celestial akashic camera which records everything happening on earth without exception."

After this mysterious image had disappeared, another one appeared. It was that of a particular spaceship departing from its base and with a spherical shape resembling a pear or a light bulb around which rotated a ring of ultra light metal. When it was under way, there were openings for windows and other openings to let out the currents of ionic energy. About forty people couples chosen for their physical and moral characteristics climbed on board using a kind of escalator in the form of a spiral ladder.

The NASA technicians were wondering how such a machine could fly. Unfortunately, no explanation followed the pictures. It could only be said that in the past, techniques still unknown today were being used. Some people spoke of an electromagnetic gyroscope. It was clearly in view that below that ring there were openings for propulsion jets. The blue-tinted metal seemed also to be of a special kind. The glass appeared to be made of the same material as that used for the large domes on Mara and which had a metallic reflection which you can see through.

A large brown man with black eyes stopped in front of the camera. It was Captain Adamos with his spouse at his side. They introduced themselves again. His spouse was called Evena. "We are ready for the departure", they said and both of them raised their hand by way of a salute. Evena said, smiling "look; now you are the witnesses of our cosmic adventure. Fortunately, we have talented people in our team" and she indicated Adamos. "My spouse, for example, has flown in space a great deal; he is qualified by many years of experience. Further, he is the direct descendent of Prince Amos his great-grand-father who saved the planet Mara from a disaster caused by the Luciferians coming from the planet Satur.

He was also the general who led his army against them in a campaign which led to their expulsion from our planet. Prince Amos had divine powers originating directly from the galaxy in Andromeda, the golden sun where the number of men is reduced to 108, all being sages who have attained the highest level of divine spirituality meaning that they are in total unity with The One. They no longer have sexual relations because they have become androgynous. Their spouses became part of themselves!

Thus, a very long time ago, Amos was transported into our solar system having seen it in a dream and having become aware of the difficulties encountered in individual human evolution amongst its inhabitants caused by the negative influence of the Luciferians. He was moved by the situation and even more when he saw the tearful face of a beautiful woman who was feeling great sadness. He was conscious of being transported in time towards her. He recognized her immediately for in the remote past, they were living together on Sandoma in Andromeda, their mother planet. This was a woman, who after many reincarnations was suddenly placed in the solar system on planet Mara and that also found herself in the biosphere where Alma the earth is now in this era. She was locked into the life-after-life wheel of reincarnations and by this, a long way from ultimate reality. She had arrived there through negative influences that controlled her, but there was a reason for this.

Prince Amos, took account of the fact that the love which he had for "Androgyna", (that was her name then) was eternal and he had to go and find her in order to save her wherever she was. The only thing was, Amos by reincarnating into a body of flesh and blood was forced to lose a great part of his divine powers and it was a great sacrifice to make, giving himself another karma to endure, but this was known by the divine intelligence.

Thus Amos, guided by a deep love had no hesitation and that is why he appeared suddenly in front of her. In that life, she carried the name of Princess Aïn. She had hidden herself in the royal palace in the mountain of Zara, guided by an occult force. Hunted and wounded, she had become very weak and was ready to die, and then, reviving, she saw him coming towards her. In the depths of her being she felt that she knew this man. He was not dressed like the others and he had a warm smile of kindness. When she held his hands, Aïn revived, full of hope. Thus they renewed their acquaintance and thus restarted their life together. Amos, with the help of the gods, fought off the Luciferians already in that period of our history.

Today, we have Adamos, the expedition's captain who possesses the spirit of his great-grandfather and myself, now carrying the name Evena, who was the Princess Aïn in a past life. Thus our destiny is to be bound together again. I believe that our different appearances are part of the game of the life and in them the game of love is also played out. Destiny is a chain of things and events lived in the past which are reborn from cycle to cycle in an eternal play anywhere in the cosmic world.

The exodus of our race to Alma the earth, forms part of the continual renewal and that is played out on other planets on other solar systems throughout the universe. This knowledge in itself is the real secret of the gods."

Following these words, Evena took a break from talking to us and climbed up into the spaceship, the *Gyrosphere*, and slowly the door shut tightly behind her. The craft shook silently and rose into the orange sky of the sunrise. Slowly, the two rings turned in opposite senses, one to the other, faster and faster. After some time, the spaceship disappeared from view to the technicians of Alma in a cloud of red dust and became only a speck on the horizon. The *Gyrosphere* had left Mara for the beginning of an extraordinary adventure on the planet Alma the earth.

Chapter III

Alma the Promised Land

It took several months of travel through space to arrive in view of Alma; happily this was achieved without serious incident. The *Gyrosphere*, because of its size was built for safety in travel as well as speed. Because of the constant sweeping of the electromagnetic currents, it could pass through a shower of meteorites without being affected. The plan which had been decided upon was to found a clan or tribe of the four races at the four corners of the globe and these would first be based on a mountain sufficiently high to provide a safe haven, and also as remote as possible from volcanoes likely to erupt as well as dangerous animals such as dinosaurs. The place to land was on a mountain located in a huge continent touching both Asia and South America which was given the name Lemuria because it was there that Lemoria had decided to locate his first headquarters and communications centre.

On this mountain the first city called Muria was built and it was there that the *Gyrosphere* rested. They constructed huge platforms there in the form of marine animals which served as points of reference for landing the *Gyrosphere*. For a great number of years, the spaceship was used for travel between continents and to the centre of Lemuria. No one could be sure of the planet's future, for there were still changes to take place. Alma was still young and unstable and would remain so up until the time when its surface could attain a perfect equilibrium. Our pioneers having set foot on the ground were very aware of these difficulties and were ready to face up to them.

Adamos warned everybody on-board. "Brothers and sisters, here everything is based on adaptation to our environment and that is part of our inner being, as much in our spirit as in our body. The latter was not born on this planet and, as a result, we will face some consequences. There are, here, bacteria to which we have never been exposed. It will take time and a few generations to create a perfect balance within ourselves. Gradually, we must expose our bodies to the fruits of Alma. None of us must eat or drink anything unless it is first exposed to the integrator ray. We brought this with us and it is capable of revealing the composition and quality of plant and fruits to be consumed. We are forced to make distinctions between which potential foods are good or bad on this planet because we can be seriously affected by what we eat. We have our eyes to see with, our nose to smell with and ears to hear with. All the powers of our senses must be on alert in this new world. Whoever does not know how to adapt may perish, that is the law of survival.

We have the advantage of our intuition, but, we will all also have to use the range of our sophisticated instruments which can be helpful to us, and never forget, the Luciferian spirit is on the lookout everywhere in our solar system and, in particular, here on Alma, a young planet in the process of evolution. They create the bad to balance the good, and, at certain moments which depend on the place and the zodiacal influence are effective beyond expectations. They attack everywhere they sense a weakness either in us or at some other place. Our intelligence lets us anticipate what may happen and prevent such things ahead of time. These faculties we must use with our greatest wisdom. We will also have to fight against evil beings controlled by them."

At these words, Adamos gestured towards Lemoria saying: "I believe our spiritual guide has something to tell us." Lemoria rose to his feet and addressing his people said: *"I have flown many times over the place where we are now located which surrounds this mountain called Machu by us and, over there on that immense plain, there are tropical trees quite different in form from those on Mara where no more remain. Tomorrow, we are going to a large plateau where I think we can establish ourselves. We are going to found a city to be named Muria in memory of the city of Mura on Mara. For today we will stay here until all is ready over there. In the valley and the plain are many risks, and as we have just arrived, we are not yet ready to face all dangers which we are soon to encounter. I propose to wait for a period of about three days before descending and exploring the region. Does everyone agree?"*

All hands were raised in common accord. The five leaders and their spouses formed a council to decide how matters should be organized. In case of difficulties, each one of the ten knew how to operate the *Gyrosphere* and its automated system. All of them possessed, in addition, a good knowledge of the use of the available weapons they took with them.

A short time passed and Adamos was satisfied with the way things were progressing. Water had been found in the form of a beautiful mountain stream flowing from a snow-covered summit. This beautiful snow, unknown on Mara was a good beginning because our remaining resources were seriously diminished. Here on Alma, the day was very long and so was the night. The absence of the sun lasted several days (of the length experienced on Mara). In the evenings, we were hearing wild clamours and cries coming from the giant beasts in the valleys. One of us gave a cry of fear because a giant bat had just flown over its head. Such a bat could have a wingspan of six feet. The climate was very hot and humid but not a dry heat surpassing two hundred degrees as on Mara. The automatic ladder was raised and everybody was then on board the spacecraft. We prepared ourselves to spend a long night there. For the moment, we were in a shelter. The persistent silence was sometimes broken by the noises resulting from earth tremors. One of these, longer than the others, made the *Gyrosphere* lean to one side and the engine had to be started in order to put it straight. Nobody slept a wink so as to be ready for any eventuality.

At that time, the nights were long. It took Alma six regular days to make one complete rotation which now, in our own era, takes twenty-four hours. During these long nights, there were a large number of animal predators hunting their prey. A large number of active volcanoes in the region which were currently in eruption illuminated the darkness by their glowing rivers of molten lava and the trees that they set on fire. The noises caused by such events as well as other unidentifiable noises at a great distance gave the overall effect of an apocalyptic landscape.

Since the time was slow in passing compared to the time on Mara and the bodies of the spaceship's crew were unaccustomed to this change, Adamos formed study circles in which everybody took part. It was a valuable opportunity to prepare for facing up to their new life.

"This evening," he said, "I propose to initiate a discussion on the nature of waves. Ask me any questions which you might have. We are going to define what a wave is." Someone asked: "Adamos, is a wave made of vibrations?"

"Effectively yes, one could say that it is like a wave in water where the molecules don't get displaced. What makes the wave is the line which connects at the same time a multitude of contiguous particles sustaining a pressure in a particular direction of propagation. In the same way that matter is only an aspect of force the same as a wave is only the appearance of an oscillatory pattern coming from a shock in an ambient medium. Forces of collision communicate the pressure from one to the next and it is this transmission from one to the other which constitutes wave motion. And here, we have to get accustomed to water, that means rivers, lakes or oceans."

"So that is the nature of vibration."

"That is so, each particle which is colliding with another produces on the next one a pressure which disseminates in a particular direction, but if that particle encounters resistance, there will be a counter-pressure. This resistance could occur as much in a vertical as in a horizontal direction. We are going to meet all of these phenomena on Alma because there are bodies of water covering large areas which we are going to have to cross whether a lake or a sea and for which we will have to build a boat. A boat floats on the water due to its buoyancy and the resistance it causes. On descending from our mountain we are going to meet streams and torrents. There are masses of water which descend violently from the mountains and which carve out their channels through the rocks producing boulders. Nobody amongst us knows how to swim, therefore we will have to be careful especially on tsunamis. Those are giant waves of water."

A woman asked: "Are we influenced by the evolution on Alma?"

"Yes, because everything evolves. Everything on earth depends on the sun. By the constant distancing of the planet from the sun, the solar pressure which is radiated from the latter diminishes. This produces an expansion of the atomic systems translating itself by the expulsion of elements; this causes radioactivity. This disintegration at the top level of bodies is only the crowning bouquet of a range of phenomena acting at all levels because no system can escape the general dilation. One could say that evolution is operational through the dislocation of atomic systems and so their structure gradually becomes simplified because their density diminishes. This means that the volume of bodies increases and the earth grows bigger in accordance with this phenomenon. Even the electron suffers dilation being itself similar to the sun, a sphere in rotation; it transforms itself by the expulsion of particles."

"Dr Adamos," she persisted, "can you explain to me why you and your companion as well as the other couples who are assisting you are so different from us? You possess powers over nature and the elements which we do not have."

"That is true, we have been initiated through the transmission of divine power from our holy lingam by Lemoria and his companion Lemuria who are themselves divine beings incarnated on Mara to guide us in this adventure, but we have only received a tiny part of these divine powers. We have to obtain them by our own transformation. As for yourselves, by following your own spiritual advancement you will be certain to be initiated one day. Each one has this privilege and each one this same right but you have to deserve it."

"Is it the case that the nature of bodies on Alma is the same as we have on Mara?"

"Yes, but on Mara, because such great changes were produced over time, many bodies were modified and were forced to undergo serious mutations which affected our life and health. Here it is different, we have to take into account these new elements and acquire a new mastery of our environment. That is why I'm talking to you about matter because we live with it and we have to understand its function. We therefore have to start to understand these bodies. In reality you have to notice when I speak of vibrations it is the case of the extraordinary moment when the divine sound OM is spread out over space and the new creation of God has taken form."

Adamos continued. "Is it not true that the state of a body is determined according to the constituent particles and their links with each other? In each atom the electrons circulate around the nucleus. It is this electrical motion which gives a gas its force of expansion and pushes atoms, one against another to move them around. Almost all bodies are formed of atoms which are linked together by their ionic and covalent bonds two by two. It is that which constitutes molecules and each has a movement which is a rotation particular to itself not being related to those of its neighbors. It is not the definition of particles in movement which determines the state of the body but rather the independence of rotational movements. It could be a gaseous state in spite of the union of atoms and molecules."

"Adamos, can you tell us how liquids are formed?"

"I certainly can, one could say that alongside molecules of which the architecture is compatible with the movement of rotation there are those of which the structure is very simple. An example is the molecule of water which, according to the conditions of temperature and pressure passes from the gaseous state to the liquid one. In this state molecules are rubbing one against others mutually braking each other and being moved in very agitated packets, for the passage from one state to the other is always made suddenly."

"And now tell us how solid bodies are formed?"

"In solid bodies, particles fit together one into another so that none of them enjoys its own movement anymore. Certain connections are more identical and certain "fits" more resistant than others. In simple bodies, the assembly of atoms is such that one cannot distinguish molecular groups. In diamond, the hardest and purest, one cannot determine the molecule of carbon. Solid bodies are assemblies of elements which have their diverse movements which, in opposing each other, produce immobility. The result is that neither the molecules nor the electrons are moved one with respect to the other. That is why we and our children are going to live in an era really different from that on Mara.

So, everything is going to depend on our knowledge and what means we use to implement the law of our universe. Such a thing also depends on our adaptation to the environment. We will, for example, have to create the calendar and as the rotation of the planet is at this moment very much slower, we cannot use the sun as a marker. Recall that our satellites orbited around our old planet much quicker than the rotation of Mara. Here on Alma the moon which has been ejected from the planet, orbits very much faster than Alma can turn on its own axis. For this reason we will have to use the moon as a calendar because neither the rotation of Alma nor its orbital time can serve as a basis at the present moment. Later the planet will turn faster on its axis as was predicted by Lord Lemoria. This was when he saw a vision of a giant meteor colliding with the earth producing this change. From that time on we will be able to use a solar calendar. Right now it is the satellite which can serve as a marking point. Here, presently, we are subject to very long seasons of a dry burning heat then to other long periods of humidity and rainfall which are followed by deluges. You see why we have to stay in the mountains especially during the winter. At the beginning, we will have to live in caves until Lemoria changes things as he let us know previously. The caves can be transformed to make them more habitable, then we will descend into the plains to construct towns and cities, but right now Alma is still very unstable.

I have next to me Doctor Zanga who is going to enlighten us about the satellite, the moon, which is going to serve us as a calendar."

Zanga approached the great horseshoe-shaped desk of the conference hall of the spacecraft and spoke to the men and women present.

"I am also ready to answer your questions about whatever is important to our studies of the situation. This will be with the help of my companion. I must state that we are not yet very advanced because our excursions on this planet have not yet started. We arrived a short time ago on Alma which is in great turmoil between the glaciations on one side and intermittent squalls on the other, also between other extremes as between on one hand the ground burned by its prolonged exposure to the sun and, on the other, the ground hardened by the cold, hidden by the nights and all that because of the rotation of the planet on its axis which is still slow. We have to adapt to the circumstance, there is really no choice in the matter."

"Tell us Zanga why Alma has finally taken a more rapid rotation on its axis for thousands of years and how that was achieved?"

"A good question my brother! Well here is my theory. We think that at the moment when the satellite of Alma was born and then was ejected from the sea, it caused an enormous push which gave a huge propulsive force to the equator which affected the whole planet, a little like a mother who is giving her child to the world needs to push it out. The moon removed itself from the terrestrial gravitation and after having created an attractive and repulsive magnetic force resembles an enormous ball held by an elastic band to the mother world which caused a sudden acceleration of Alma on its axis. That permitted Alma to reach a primary period of stability. The moon came out of the interior of the world of Alma Gaya, its belly. Before the earth was unstable and storms were daily events and for a long time before our arrival the Lord Lemoria did what Amos had done on Mara. He concentrated the reproductive forces of Alma in its interior and from there the moon was born. The moon stabilizes the axial rotation of Alma. Without that our world would be constantly unstable and its chaotic oscillations would cause violent upsets in climate. Note that it is not the influence of other planets and their orbits which could accomplish that. The orbits of the outer planets like Jupita, Satur, Urania and Neptuna have remained stable while the inner planets Venus, Alma and Mara have chaotic trajectories because of the influence that they exercise one upon another but their orientation is stabilized by the effects of the solar tide. Without the moon, life would be unstable on Alma. The forces of gravity between the moon and the sun affect the earth's seas and oceans. All of that happens because it is not rigid but elastic. That is how the coupling of the force constituted by the gravitational attractions of the moon and the sun affects the oceans, the atmosphere and the movements of the earth's crustal plates. The moon tends, globally, to pull the earth and lift up the oceans deforming the earth into an ellipsoid form all with a very smooth action. The seas and their tides reach their maximum amplitude at full moon and new moon when the earth, the sun and the moon are aligned and fall to their minimal amplitude when the two bodies are in quadrature this happening at the times when the earth-moon and the earth-sun axes form a right angle. A similar effect applies also to the molten metal occupying the centre of the earth something which affects, as well, the circadian rhythm of all ordinary men and mankind as a whole."

"If we understand it well, the world of Alma has placed in the world of its heart, its child the moon, which becomes its satellite and which remains bound to it and that is what allows myriads of different forms of life essentially aquatic to transform and evolve. Is that the planning followed by universal intelligence?"

"Yes, most certainly, the divine mother of all the galaxies in our universe possesses the supreme desire to be manifest in taking all possible forms and her intelligence mixes with the divine consciousness in all created things. The Lord Lemoria has told us that one day a long time ago he foresaw our exodus to the world of Alma Gaya. He was seated on a large rock at Machu and in looking deeply at a place which came to be in your days called the Pacific Ocean. He spoke thus to the mother earth, saying: "Alma, this is the time to create in your womb the infant moon which is going to stabilize your terrestrial evolution and allow harmonious life to come into being. Concentrate the fire of your love in your centre and with the action of all the volcanoes in your belly, your baby will grow. When you are ready, call upon me."

And much later, Lemoria came back with Lemuria for the birth of the baby Moon. They were of a great help in its expulsion and in guiding the moon into its orbit which had to be very precise. The mental force of Lemoria is divine."

"Do you know from your calculations the number of times Alma has turned on its axis?"

"We believe that we arrived here only a few thousand years after a great deluge. From our most recent calculations Alma turns on itself in about six days. It was almost the same when our planet, the world of Mara was in its biological ellipse and that is where the world of Alma is at this moment. The ideal of a harmonious rotation for all forms of life on the surface to be in state of paradise should be twenty four hours, that being where the distance from the sun is followed in a normal elliptical orbit. At this moment we can say that the moon takes about seven days to make its orbit around the world of Alma and on that we can base our first calendar. The lunar cycle gives us one week and with that we can mark the times and cycles of many things. Only for us at this moment we have to get used to a cycle of one-day which lasts almost a week. This influences the whole of our organic circadian system that can prolong the length of our lives after one or two generations. So we can understand that the deviation from the rule which has disturbed the inclination of the earth's orbit was done with respect to the solar equator. The planet now passes the point of the spring equinox before its complete orbit and that is very soon.

So I continue, for you see here in our case the rotation completes its first half in almost six days this is compared to Mara which makes one ideal rotation of 26 hours, and the moon which makes an orbit in seven days. We think besides this that other difficulties will come because we will still have winters of great length with consequent glaciations, and because of the quantity of ice and snow which can accumulate, melt waters which will flood the planet."

"Zanga, tell us where we can establish ourselves without danger to survive the present moment?"

"Ah yes, for that we are going to follow the indications of our spiritual guide Lemoria since he possesses the extra-sensory abilities capable of guiding us out of danger at this time to avoid misfortune."

"Can you guide us on the way to cook the bulbs, roots and leaves of the plants that we are going to pick for our nourishment?" asked a woman.

"First, we are going to display in a few minutes on the table all these plants that we call vegetables as well as the fruits which we believe to be edible. We are going to separate the others which are harmful. Because there is a huge variety we will still have to study them with the green ray and patience will be necessary because the process will take some time. However, don't forget, besides the value of the mineral content, the rare elements, the proteins and the carbohydrates contained in these plants it is always the solar energy that we absorb by chlorophyll which composes them, that must be assimilated in our bodies through a form of latent energy. The fact that we enrich it with the green ray will eliminate the toxins and other poisons for us."

"Can we find a good place to found our village and the means to cultivate the ground?"

"Effectively, we have found a beautiful place to found our village, the first Marian village on the planet Alma it is near a small valley between three mountains at high altitude. The place is protected from high winds, tidal waves or floods. Tomorrow we will come out of the night to start another day and gradually we will have more light. We will be able to visit the site and perhaps even to lay the foundation of the first building with the help of Lemoria. That will take six long periods of deep concentration in the higher astral at the four cardinal points helped with powerful mantras of creation for the elements to assemble in the world of forms and create themselves in finished material."

"So, that means that we have to prepare ourselves mentally starting from now to receive the necessary vital force and create a powerful channel coming from the high astral right down to the physical world."

"Exactly, we will place the sacred lingam Linga II at the centre of our circle as Lemoria has indicated. Adamos will place himself at the east, Lemoria will rest at the centre, I will go to the north and Afrika will place himself at the south. Atalanta will be at the west and all of you will form a great circle around us and the lingam, your companions will be in line behind each of you so that we will resemble a huge wheel and we will have to enter a deep meditation during a chant of 108 OM, the divine sound of all creation."

"When have you fixed the start of this particular meditation?"

"In exactly one Marian day which corresponds to the conjunction of the planets of our solar system and those of the zodiac, that is to say galaxies situated along the equatorial band of Alma surrounding the earth, they are in a supporting mode of vibration."

"So we have right away to prepare for our meditation."

"Yes it is best to begin now."

From this moment everyone entered into their respective cabins and a great silence began. All were now ready for the great manifestation. There were six long periods when we did not eat and when all thoughts remain fixed on a single point, the first point of creation of God the emanation of the creative light of OM coming directly from Shram the creator.

***

When the memorable day arrived, Atalanta placed himself at the command post of the *Gyrosphere* and it rose gently between the mountains to travel to the small valley destined to receive them. The place chosen for the *Gyrosphere* to land was on the shore of a tranquil blue lake. It was a place dreamed of on an earth, still unknown, full of mystery and little welcoming.

After a period of time, before the rising sun appeared in the east, everyone came out of the spaceship and placed themselves in an area facing the east seated together in a great silence. After a short time the Lord Lemoria broke the silence and made the sacred lingam and pillar of light move and be placed on a pedestal right at the centre of the circle where everyone was waiting. A beautiful ray of the sun already illuminated it and it became resplendent with lights. Then Lemoria said: *"All creation is divine in its appearance we are all the channels through which God is manifesting."* Everyone placed themselves according to the rite of the creative light around Lemoria and his wife. The four guides and their spouses behind them seated themselves in front at each corner of the square and all the others were in a circle around the square, the women on one side, and the men on the other. After a series of deep meditations which lasted for an interminable time in a silent OM enveloping each one with its holy mantra, a luminous ray descended from the sun to illuminate the lingam up to seven times 108 times. In the intervals of silence, the positive vibrations increased all around the group. Lord Lemoria and his spouse were in profound meditation and suddenly we saw millions of tiny golden particles appear, falling like snowflakes around the group in meditation. As soon as these made contact with the ground they built themselves in the form of stone blocks of different sizes and a marvellous palace was observed being designed and materialized around them with a beautiful finish of white marble with gold lines, marvellous large staircases and finished off with terraces and spacious rooms having huge windows and immense carpets. There were great roofs with curled sides following the Chinese pattern. A wall high and long now surrounded the building, protecting the palace like a fortification. Inside could be seen gardens with myriads of flowers and in the centre of the great court there was the *Gyrosphere*. Now they recognized the touch of Lemuria whose hands added the harmonious beauty to the creation of her partner. Most of these flowers were still unknown on Alma.

In a large park there were fruit trees with many diverse plants. All that appeared was created almost instantly coming from the thoughts of the avatar and his spouse who imagined it all in the creative astral world. All that was accomplished in the world of matter was thanks to the triple power of the sacred lingam. Their thoughts were channelled and could manifest directly, penetrating the physical world to take form. The effect was extraordinary. When, at the end of a long moment, the creation of the marvellous palace was fixed, a current of cold air swept through the place and the light became less diffused and there was a great silence. All those who had never been present at a miracle of this nature were astounded. Some of them had already been present at such events but not one like this. Whatever had appeared illusory at the beginning had become concrete and stable. A palace of this size and beauty would have taken years and a great number of artists and workers for its construction.

The avatar began to speak. *"Dear brothers and sisters, here is a beautiful place which God has given us which is going to shelter our first city for a time as long as we will be among you and nothing will be able to destroy it. This much you know. Nothing is eternal in the forms of the world of matter and all is subject to change. We were incarnated among you in order to guide you not only in the domain of matter which is secondary but also in your spiritual evolution. After the experience of the material world your soul should be thinking about returning to its divine source. The ability to master the power of creation is given to the avatar only to prove to you that in the higher domains of thought miracles exist for they are facts of divine nature. You are now the owners of the first palace built on the planet Alma. What we have just accomplished Lemuria and I can only be accomplished with the aid of the divine Shakti with which you have all participated. It is a gift of heaven. Let us thank God and the divine power for it. Let us join in a prayer of adoration, humility and thankfulness during this sublime moment."*

Everyone closed their eyes and in pure devotion sent thoughts of love towards God. Afterwards someone asked: "Tell us Lemoria, how do you do this work in thought with Lemuria?"

"It is special for the two of us, because she and I are continually in telepathic communication. Lemuria knows what mental images I am projecting and she adds all the details to the task in hand so it is totally

completed. As in this case, which you have just seen, Lemuria with considerable artistry creates around the building gardens with ponds of water surrounded by flowers. The palace will be the centre of Alma's first city which will be called Shangi Râ, the city of the angels of the sun. The planet Alma should be conquered by the angels of light and its population should also follow principles of life in behavior filled with pure light. Lemuria and I have at our service a multitude of angels that all have different functions."

"Are there other details needed to complete this task?" he was asked.

"Most definitively, we shall have things which need manual labor. Amongst you there are artists, but the main work here is done. There is not yet equipment in the kitchens and bathrooms, there is running water everywhere and drainage and that is all. There are no windows or doors anywhere. Those things, you will have to install by your own efforts. We are going to visit the rooms and move our beds and covers from the Gyrosphere then we will move ourselves into those rooms. Everybody involved with the food preparation can go into the kitchens and start organizing this. I am going to leave the sacred lingam at the centre of the great courtyard so that anyone who at any time wishes to rest and meditate near it can do so. Later you will have to build a temple that will be a pyramid of light around it."

Everybody then stood up to visit the palace and find a room to suit themselves. So was this remarkable event accomplished on this blessed day.

Chapter IV

Posthumous meetings on Alma

As the weeks and days and nights followed each other, the brothers and sisters of light worked with devotion to build their city around the palace and create a small human society on Alma. It remained to find out if there were humans on the planet, then to find sources of food. Up to then there had not been any serious encounters with animal life.

Several women had become pregnant and a group of the youngest men got together and were keen to make an expedition to the valleys lower down the mountain. We could often hear the wild cries, mournful and howling of animals fighting each other to the death. Such sounds echoed along the sides of the mountain and right up to the summit. Atalanta was consulted on the subject. Atalanta replied: "I am not sure about the situation regarding starting an expedition, and as we are small in numbers, I think it could be dangerous to risk our lives uselessly, but we can always ask the advice of Lemoria." Lemoria, as if he had been called, appeared in the great hall smiling. *"I know that about ten of you are impatient to visit the planet. I know that they are not short-sighted, that is true, but there is no need to be careless. Several are known to be fathers and that almost two years of gestation are needed for their wives, because right now things are different in that you are adapting to another kind of evolution on Alma and in order for stability to be achieved your wives are going to need help. If, now that there are five of the most daring ones among you who will accept, Atalanta and a team will make a first expedition into the valley during the daylight period in order to determine the condition of the territory."*

Five hands went up. "We are ready," they said.

"Very well said Lemoria, you have my protection. I am going to prepare a map of the place with captain Atalanta, and we are going to prepare for our first adventure. It is useless to tell you that here we are in a safe harbour, over there it is like hell and you will have to be ready to fight for your lives, to face the dangers and hardships. Get ready for that and learn to stay on your guard, the strength of your muscles is soon going to be put to the test."

The preparations required a number of activities and equipment. Good boots were needed, also weapons for defence and storage as well as containers for water and food. Those going also needed to do physical exercises to train their muscles and give them rapid reflexes.

For their part, Zanga and his companion Zaraya had prepared an elixir of life in their laboratory which was unique and had the property of rapidly healing any wound and could rejuvenate completely the major cells of the body. This was derived from a climbing plant discovered around a giant tree which resembled a vine having exquisite flowers and violet colored fruit. Their essence combined with a leaf of a pink plant had this power of regeneration. Each person was able to carry on him a flask of this elixir. As well, they could remain in contact with the *Gyrosphere* which was parked in the courtyard of the palace.

Full of drive as usual, Atalanta kissed his wife and took the lead of the expedition. This elixir proved important for everybody because of the disruption of the circadian cycle due to the changing of the slow rotation of the planet which on account of its length affected the organism of the Marians. They started out on uneven ground and, when leaving the little valley soft and luxuriant that we now called Shangi Râ, we encountered a road of sharp stones and we had to be very careful of falling rocks. The water which flowed from the lake formed a torrent and then a waterfall which fell nearly 1000 meters down to the lower valley where giant reptiles were still swarming and there was not a practical way of getting there.

"Marzo," shouted Atalanta, "let's go and get three flying platforms. It's a waste of time to try and get down here without ropes or climbing equipment, we could break our necks."

Marzo and the others ran in the direction of the *Gyrosphere* to get from it three platforms. Now, with each two seated at the controls of their platform, they rose up, set in motion by the inverse electromagnetic currents arising from the earth which, when amplified, enabled them to rise up in the air like birds. Standing on platforms of a light construction where it was necessary to have good control because of the rapid changes of the level of speed, they could go around obstacles such as trees or pass between them. The three flew in a V formation. Atalanta in the lead, they flew over the immense cliff following the waterfall and its cataracts towards the plain.

The idea in their heads was to explore the whole region on a reconnaissance flight and to look for different types of life forms. The source of energy which drove the flying platforms was almost unlimited and handling them was very easy. Standing on the platform the driver had a control panel in front of him with all the commands available. For safety, one could not exceed the speed limit which was that of a bird in flight. There was a stabilizer for balancing the craft and to prevent it from turning over. One could therefore glide and as the energy was produced by winds of magnetic energy, the engine was light in weight.

The three always flew in a V formation, with Atalanta in the lead. They now approached the waterfall. Suddenly, there came from crevices in the rocks, probably from a nest, a gigantic bird of prey like a flying lizard which then rushed upon Atalanta, with its mouth wide open giving a savage scream and ready to plant its huge claws in Atalanta's shoulders as he tried to avoid it. Marzo who was flying right behind them brought out his weapon with the indigo ray and pointed it quickly towards the monster whose sharp teeth he could see were at the point of biting the neck of Atalanta who was almost falling off his vehicle. A violet-colored light beam shone from the weapon and the animal disintegrated in flames. This weapon had the power to paralyze or disintegrate the victim depending on how long the trigger was pressed. Atalanta quickly regained consciousness and said:

"Thank you Marzo, we will have to land a little further away from this big plateau, I am still very shaken by this experience. I owe you my life thanks to your rapid reflexes."

Nearby was a large clearing. They set the platforms down there and ventured towards the forest. There, among the giant trees there were also huge thickets. Zorga, one of the men, approached a wide open space between two immense leaves. When Atalanta saw him, he shouted: "Get back! Get back quickly!" It was good that he did so by instinctively throwing himself backwards as the huge mouth of a snake snapped shut. This time it was Atalanta who used his indigo ray which instantly paralyzed the monster. The head of the snake must have been at least one meter wide and its body about ten meters long, measuring one meter in circumference. A man two meters high would not even have made a mouthful for this creature. A little further off a huge animal was in process of being devoured by a horde of saurians which had their mouths full of blood and were so occupied with eating that they did not notice the presence of the small expedition.

"See my brothers," said Atalanta, "what things are threatening us here. Fortunate it is that Lemoria brought us to land on the high plateau where these monsters can't reach us. I think that it is much wiser for the moment that we fly over this place rather than crossing it on foot."

That said, they all embarked again on their handy platforms. In flying over the forest, they saw from a distance a large number of dinosaurs, those giant reptiles of all sizes. The great majority were herbivores. Around them a couple of pterosaurs were gliding looking for food. Finally, there were some of those giant bats which had attacked Atalanta, but in seeing them approach they didn't attack the small group. They were probably around to see how men defended themselves in killing one of their own. They cried their mournful cries and flew away.

The V group flew over the great waterfall and arrived near an immense lake where a giant dinosaur was grazing which must have weighed more than 70 tons. At the end of the long neck of this giant creature was its head which must have been almost six meters in circumference. It stared at the flying group with enormous eyes filled with astonishment, observing these humans which circled around him like dragonflies but didn't seem to want to attack. This animal was not aggressive. Marzo came very close to his head to film his movements and the whole scene was now recorded in the control room of the *Gyrosphere* and then sent to Mara.

In the laboratories of the *Gyrosphere* the course of events of the expedition were being examined. After some hours of flight, where still other types of animals and creatures presented themselves, they finally returned to the city of peace where everyone was waiting.

"We could see that your first expedition into nature was full of unexpected things," said Adamos, smiling, "you must have burnt up a lot of energy. Go now and recharge your weapons from the energy source of the *Gyrosphere*. In the future, let us try not to destroy the entities on this planet with the violet ray or the negative green one. I believe that paralyzing them with the indigo ray is sufficient; we have to try not to impose ourselves too much on the terrestrial karma of Alma. But it's fortunate that we have these weapons, without them our survival would be nearly impossible."

"They have a level of consciousness which is wide awake and a rapid means of communication," said Atalanta, "because when Marzo disintegrated the flying monster the others of its species reacted quickly and wouldn't attack us again."

"Yes," said Azor. "I think that should be the same with other species which exist strongly at an intuitive level. You did well to aim at the brain of the serpent with the paralyzing ray, just look at the size of these monsters compared to our own size; we don't have any other means of defense. The paralyzing energy is the most rapid and also the most effective when directed at the brain. Our adjustment to their size can only take place over the course of several years and thus we will be following the evolution of the planet. The disappearance of the dinosaurs is only a matter of time. Our organism must adjust to the environment above all during the nocturnal period when the time of rest is longer. Actually we are really experiencing a terrestrial incubation period and we are undergoing changes in our own bodies at every instant."

"But when is this shock of adaptation going to finish?"

"It is a question of time. The environment being new, the shock is stronger, but when we eat the produce of the planet Alma, that will help our progress and our adaptation. There are new vibrations of greater vitality which enliven us, the general adaptation is followed from one species to another continually, as well as from one life to another."

"Here there are carnivorous animals and vegetarian ones which are devoured by them in a way that is frightening to see."

"That is true. The skin of the vegetarians should be thicker and resistant against the sharp saw-like teeth of the carnivores. Some of them even have horns to defend themselves, others weigh tons and carry enormous mass when they move."

"Do you think there are humans like us or humanoid types of creatures living here?"

"Yes! Lemoria has spoken about them. They are living in our region. We are certainly going to meet them. He says they are under the psychic control of the Luciferians who are like the bestial aspect of the human type so they can maintain control over them. It is the state which the Luciferians want and in with they are comfortable."

"To summarize, we don't need to mix with the dinosaurs since we can live for a long time separated from them. At the top of the plateau where we are, they cannot reach us."

"That is certainly true, Azor, but we have tasks to finish one of which is making life more agreeable on Alma. That is part of the evolution of the planet and we are instruments of it. That has been foreseen like the giant asteroid which will crash into Alma changing its time of axial rotation and from now until then there are only some thousands of orbits of Alma to complete, and our survival here is also part of the plan of human evolution on Alma. It is just the same as our arrival on Mara a long time before. In our solar system, it is we who are going to live through the strategic moments which are going to mark the future direction of Man in these places."

"That is true Atalanta, the future of the men and women of tomorrow is in our hands. We must keep our hopes up in divine protection."

"Do you see, Azor, the worst that can happen to men and their divine nature is to be constrained to make war on other men for the purpose of conquering them. The meaning of conquering is simply stealing by using force. It is true that there are circumstances which force us to face the men who are provoking us and our family and are capable of harming or killing us. We have to defend ourselves if we can; we have to avoid being killed. In all cases to build friendship is the best solution and it is flexibility which makes all the difference. Even in certain cases, one should know how to take aggression without giving a response in order to calm the situation. What is called saving one's honour only makes our pride more conceited at the price of one life or another, it is by paying the price of suffering that we learn the extent of our errors; everything is learnt in the game of life. And that is important because the Luciferian spirits threaten us through our smallest weaknesses in order to test us and mock us with delight when they see how fast we fall into their trap."

"You mean that the final lesson of each test in life should lead us towards wisdom?"

"Yes, the ancients warned us: we have to develop the capability of discernment; it is the only means to open oneself to the truth because it is by truth that we acquire wisdom."

"Therefore in all circumstances we have to keep in view our attachment to God, with an open mind, then to see in everything the signature of God."

"That is correct. We must understand that all is God even that which plays the role of being our enemy and if we can give him love; we have to do that by all possible means. Often, that may appear impossible, but we keep the good intention because it is this final principle which must live in us for the power of expressing itself in all our thoughts and actions."

"But that seems paradoxical," said someone.

"Yes, I agree, but I believe that Azor has understood me. That could appear paradoxical but only in the world of duality which is the physical manifestation. On the other side in the astral world, where there is total truth, that is no longer the case."

"Ah yes! Because only the form changes and could even be destroyed, while the truth which is in the soul and is divine is indestructible."

"That is so brother Mikalien. And in this world which could be Mara. Alma or anywhere, the principle remains the same. We are all born of the divine by our soul which expresses itself in the world where duality is reigning and in our body which is only a deceitful appearance having a cycle of birth and death, when even the life of the body is prolonged right up to its limits and in diverse circumstances everything is only illusory. Only the soul which is God is real and the only true value. The ego and its personality are only limited accessories which are destructible."

"So we shouldn't take too seriously what happens to us, whether justified or not."

"Where what happens to us is justified it is then that there is a lesson to be learnt, that our personal ego should know to accept. Because that is karma, the law of change based on cause and effect of acts or thoughts committed in the past."

"And when it isn't justified?"

"It is our soul who has decided either to provide a lesson or for the purpose of giving aid to other people. Then it is a form of sacrifice, a positive Karma. Sometimes, without being aware of it, we serve as an example to others or make payment on their behalf. Such acts always wipe out the bad karma from the past, so it is therefore an opportunity which is given to us for our spiritual advancement."

"Then should we the take the effects of life so seriously?"

"Yes, but only in the degree where we understand the sense. Whether it is a case of a game or of spiritual advancement, everything happens at different levels of consciousness, levels which we are not even aware of due to our lack of alertness. When we arrive through meditation at the level of God consciousness then the illusion fades."

"So the cause of everything is in us?"

"Definitely it is within us. The difference is found in the interpretation taken by our level of consciousness. We are the cause and effect and we are God, ignorant only of our true being. We have already said "I think therefore I am in the present" but we are not our thought, we are above our thought. So much as our thoughts dominate us we remain the victim. Above our thoughts there is the supreme self which does not need thoughts for its being. Lemoria, our avatar and spiritual guide, has made us understand that many times but that has to mature inside the base of our spirit in order to reach the pure consciousness which is reality."

"Then can we become a sublime being like Lemoria is?"

"Yes, because that goal remains carved in the seeds of our lives, the divine spark which animates us from one life to another. However, to reach an end in this world, the advance takes place at all the levels of consciousness. Contact with an avatar of divine origin can help us along by spiritual osmosis. Then the energy centers of the different levels of consciousness can be opened and we advance progressively towards the light. Each being advances at its own rhythm and follows its own path. We are all at a different level; the personal landmarks make all the difference. The factors which influence advancement are, at the same time, both internal and external."

"But this surely requires the opening of the interior spiritual eye to realize this divinity which is inside us, isn't that so?"

"Absolutely, the variations in the state of a man's consciousness approach infinity. From the commencement of his individual evolution he is still ignorant and wakes up slowly into the first form of consciousness when entering the world of matter. So he transforms himself from one life to another, from one experience to another, from one race to another or one sex to another. It happens that this envelop of physical senses has gradually covered the higher consciousness which remains attached to the soul. Therefore it forces the spirits of men and women to believe that they are only their bodies. When a man becomes aware of his senses as he reincarnates into the material consciousness he compares himself to his surroundings as well as to all the others with their own vision. It is at this crucial moment that he becomes a prisoner in the material world. He then becomes a victim of his own belief."

"So that's what holds his spirit prisoner in the world of illusion. Is that what you mean Atalanta?"

"In this sense, yes, but all this is a necessary process because, gradually, with the help of his experiences with others, he forms an understanding greater than life based above all on the nature of things. This gathering of ideas of being for and against, of doing or not doing, creates some barriers in the individual spirit and serves to reinforce the moral code from one life to the other, in spite of which everything still gets more complicated. Desires multiply even though their accomplishment cancels them out and frustrations are born. To deal with these frustrations the individual breaks the laws and puts himself in error. This is bound to happen because everything is based on the exterior world which we take as being the real one and because of that, we ignore the interior world of our being which is the domain of the soul and which alone is real. The truth is that the soul is immortal imperishable and eternal. Right from the start at the moment of conception and when the embryo is formed the soul undergoes metamorphosis, splits, and becomes spirit. The supreme intelligence is crystallized into the flesh and so loses a great part of its divine awareness during this materialization. In spite of this, the soul does not lose an iota of its energy nor of its own divinity during the procedure, because it takes its place and locates itself in the head and in the heart, remaining always in eternal contact with the Greatest of All which is present in all places and at all times. The spirit in contrast, being separated and divided, takes its place in the feet in contact with the ground, the place of its birth and its preferences. There, it becomes the ego. Its kingdom by contrast, is at the center of the body at the level of the solar plexus. So man is half animal and half god. When the soul and the spirit meet each other at the heart chakra, great stability comes into operation and man enters the divine status, because at the heart chakra is the seat of love. So it is that the intellect guided by the intelligence coming from the head with the help of its instinct and guided by the need to survive in the material world balances itself. It combines also with the energy from the sacred center which is the chakra at the base of the spinal column where it meets love then the man becomes newly reborn and progressively becomes God-realized."

"Thank you, dear Atalanta, for sharing with me this beautiful concept of human evolution," said Azor with respect.

"Very well, go and tell the others that we are going to meet in the laboratory to examine the film that was made during our flight in order to draw some conclusions, for yet another team is going to continue the expedition. We are going to have a period of rest. We will advance in stages."

The team that was dealing with agricultural matters had already prepared the soil of a large garden and was anxious to plant some special seeds from Mara there. Since the temperature was always warm and humid at that time there wasn't any difficulty in achieving germination and growth without which they would not recover from the periodic sunshine and watering. The spring water came from the mountain. It was warm and saturated with minerals.

One of these plants called "saporot" was a complete protein. Alma Gaya, this new earth, also promised abundant nourishment from vegetable sources. Several plants of the legume variety had already been classified as edible and the "saporot" had immense fruits of which one that resembled a huge heart was later named "corosol", and its flesh and juice were delicious. Another plant, a type of cabbage called "lampion" was six feet in diameter. At its heart were fruits the size of a fist growing out in a spiral. There were potatoes from Mara the size of a big watermelon, which grew underground, tangled up with the bushy roots of a giant palm; a yellow flower filled with a sweet nectar having a circumference of six feet, surrounded by a green crown of immense barbed leaves the sap of which was sweet and smelled of vanilla. Another climbing plant attaching itself to the trunk of a large tree had grapes of about ten round fruits, each the size of a grapefruit, that were vermilion red in color and tasted slightly more sour than an apple but which made good eating. A date palm fifty feet high, had a trunk with a circumference of eight feet and produced dates as big as a hand. Another palm produced types of bananas of which the fruit was two feet long. This was an experience of gigantism for the emigrants from Mara who were used to nourish and sustain themselves with such tiny fruits and vegetables due to the reduced amount of sunlight received by their planet. It was fortunate that at that time, they knew how to compensate for this with the radiations of the healing pale green ray on their skins which covered the body and penetrated their blood in distributing chlorophyll uniformly. Now on Alma Gaya people ate much bigger portions to enlarge their stomachs and their intestines, a new procedure which needed a great number of enzymes for digestion, which happened gradually and took time.

At the research laboratory professor Zanga, his spouse and the team continued their tests with the very sophisticated equipment to analyze the quality and digestibility of the food supplies. Certain items had to be cooked out of necessity but the majority could be eaten raw or in liquid form. Each vegetable needed to be examined carefully in case of any toxicity it might contain. The green ray could act on a great number of plants to neutralize the poison as well as that in a great number of animals and insects. Certain of them could be up to six fingers in length. All of them could not be touched because of the poison secreted in their skin or their mandibles.

One of the members of his Zanga's laboratory team, Meril, was trapped by creepers during a research outing. These creepers, which were extremely mobile and sticky, came from a tree with branches like corkscrews. He was seriously burnt by the acid which came out from one of these creepers. Then he struggled against those which dragged him towards the centre of the tree situated between its immense trunks where he could be digested in a bath of acid. Warned of his danger by a signal, Zanga ran towards him and directed his weapon with the indigo ray towards the creeper which was literally carved up making it possible to release the unfortunate worker. In order to get him out of there, he had to defend himself against the assault of other creepers which moved themselves around the tree in a quest for food. Later, after a period of rest when the injured man was able to recover thanks to the neutro-cellular rays which recomposed the burnt tissues of the skin, the group went out again with much vigilance and with great caution to search the surroundings.

It was noticed at times when nothing moved and there was total silence then suddenly, when we approached a corpse or a tree, danger announced itself very quickly. No one was surprised when, approaching another group of trees with trunks covered with spines like conic-shaped needles as long as twenty cm and pointed, a great number of these needles were fired like arrows against the group in an attack. The couple which was in front was pierced by them and some of these long needles were stuck in their skin to a depth of three to five cm. Luckily, they were not hit in their faces or in any vital organ. The effect of the caustic substance injected by these stings forced them into a deep sleep almost immediately. They had to protect themselves quickly using anti-missile shields and it was not easy to lift up these frozen bodies lying on the ground without being attacked. It seemed that the tree having paralyzed its victims, sucked away the nutritious substance of the bodies once they had fallen and then decomposed them by certain specialized roots near the surface. The same procedure existed for other carnivorous trees. Again, it was another dangerous experience which they had to avoid. A little further out a small dinosaur could be seen lying on the ground, having collapsed there, in the process of decomposing and there were a great number of bones spread around it. It proved possible that these carnivorous trees drew in by suction the liquids left by these bodies.

On returning to the laboratory, avatar Lemoria was present to greet them. He called together all the groups, and going into the great hall approached the lingam chanting the solar mantra. The lingam lit up and shone like the sun. Lemoria addressed the gathering with great energy. *"You have recently disintegrated a gigantic Devonian when you had to defend yourself from its attack, I am going to make contact with its spirit. It will be able to reintegrate a new body and thus will be at your service. Even later, its descendants will be to some degree able to serve as messengers between the clans of Zanga, of Afrika, of Adamos and of Atalanta on the occasion of your next exodus to the four corners of Alma Gaya. We need friends among the demoniac entities who people this planet. I know their vital number and they are afraid because if they rebel they could be annihilated forever."*

Then, after reciting a special mantra of the life-number of the Devonian, he threw a special feather in the air and just afterwards, an explosion rang out followed by a luminous glow. Then in a huge grey cloud, the form of an immense dragon manifested, its flaming red eyes beaming lights all around him and focusing on the avatar. Lemoria shouted: *"I call you from the deep shadows Sator, we need your services, you will be in the future the friend of men, you and your descendents must obey our call, your assistance will help your evolution towards the light."* The immense dragon bird lowered its head in sign of submission to receive his blessing. *"You can nest up there at the top of the White Tower, continued Lemoria. I have prepared a room where you and your progenitors can stay without danger. You cannot join your clan any more except to go and find she who will permit you to found a nesting site within a decade. She will recognize you, the others will shun you but they will not be able to attack you. You will be under the seal of my protection."*

With a flap of its immense black wings like those of a gigantic crow, Sator flew right up to the top of the White Tower. From high up there, he had a superb view of the whole area of the palace. He could see the people, hear their voices and read their thoughts. He was now in the service of men: he had become their helper.

"*See my brothers and sisters*", *said Lemoria, "we have with us the help of invisible entities from the astral and now, as well, those who are visible. In the future, we will have to domesticate others of these monsters. I perceive in the near future there will be disputes with the humanoids of Alma who use these devonians as instruments of war and we will have to defend ourselves against them.*"

"Tell us, Lemoria, can you also protect us against carnivorous trees or other types of dangerous monster?" asked a woman.

"*Yes, I have thought of it, but not against all of them. Our personal and group karma will not permit me to do it. Without that, I would constantly be going against my own orders. However, I am going to make a solar and lunar talisman for each of you which will last for the length of your lives or longer, depending on the karma which you create.*"

And with a twist of his right hand, he created from the void for each of them a bracelet half of gold and half of silver. These he gave to each one of them when each in turn approached him. That done, with a gesture of his hand, he extinguished the light of the sacred lingam. On the bracelet was inscribed the letter which described the sound OM. This was between the junction of the two metals. OM balances the positive and negative forces. In wearing this talisman, they were living in direct contact with the avatar Lemoria.

Chapter V

A great lesson of life

One day on Alma was almost a week compared to time on the planet Mara and one night was the same because of the slow rotation of the planet, but this was already better than the case had been 500 000 years before when the rotational period could last almost a year. The difficulty was that at nights, the temperature could get down to nearly -40 °C while in the daytime reaching nearly +40 °C. The fact that Lemoria had chosen a high mountain which had recently formed due to the folding of the earth's crust, gave rise to cooler temperatures, these were as cold as on the plain but lacking the humidity existing there. At night, everyone had to wear warm garments.

Lemoria, with the help of Atalanta, had organized the construction of a heating system in the palace of Shangi Râ based on a supply of hot water available from the centre of the mountain which was connected to a subterranean volcano. Thanks to Lemoria's special power, the materials, special metal tubing and other things, had been made to appear and all that was needed was to assemble the various components.

Atalanta's men, the best technicians from Mara, had brought with them a complete machine shop containing all the tools necessary for plumbing and electricity. The energy was supplied by the magnetic currents of the earth and could be stored in a power plant. The light was supplied by these same waves varying in intensity, even during Alma's long nights. These lights were present in every place and could be called upon. They obeyed a mantra composed of OM, the mantra of all creation. With all these installations, the supply of collected energy was moved away from the *Gyrosphere* thereby becoming independent of it. As a result, they were better prepared for exploring their surroundings. From the *Gyrosphere*, satellites were regularly sent out to get visual images of the planet's geography. Everything viewed was coded as waves of different frequencies and recorded on lined parchment. One could review at will the images in a crystal sphere where each one was kept as a pattern of microscopic particles. This way, it was learned of the existence of humanoid beings of a kind that Lemoria had already described, living fairly far from the sanctuary, the palace of light.

These beings were hairy and resembled anthropoids that is to say half-man half beast. They used traps to catch the animals whose flesh they ate. Another method they used was to cut the knee joints and tendons of the antediluvian monsters, attack them and drink their blood. These anthropoid beings were under the sign of the beast, which is to say the Luciferian influence. Their evolution was still purely on the animal level; their spirit was moving out of the animal and into the semi-human state of consciousness. They lived in packs, making war with each other and practiced cannibalism. Their law was simply the survival of the fittest.

In other places, some female tribes which had formed groups made war on the males and only came together with them at the time of the mating season, and these resembled more a fight than a loving sexual embrace. Any of their children that were retarded were eaten. Compared to this, the human evolution on Mara was more advanced and could serve as an example for these humanoids.

Prince Adamos, captain of the army of Mara, a good fighter, was disgusted at the thought of fighting against these humanoids and he shared his thoughts with his team.

"Dear brothers and sisters, in seeing these pictures, I have been moved to know that a human race is in the process of forming itself here, but I am also not much in favour of getting into a fight against them. They are superior in numbers but inferior in armaments. All the same, we have to defend ourselves if we are attacked."

"Adamos, shouldn't we show ourselves to them and try to gain their friendship?" suggested Andromas.

"That is true and I believe that such is the will within our company. Only the future will teach us how best to proceed. We could try, when the right moment arrives, to offer them our friendship, but their blood is contaminated by the Luciferians. They are carnivores, and that is a condition which keeps their spirit at the lowest vibratory level and only the constant threat of force holds their respect. They don't understand gentleness, understanding or idealism neither do they understand love. They can only reason at a primitive level "an eye for an eye, a tooth for a tooth". We will have to act with extreme caution."

"Adamos, do you think it would be better to wait for the return of avatar Lemoria before trying out whatever is needed?"

"Perhaps that would be the wisest course, Andromas, but do you remember what he said? *"Even if I am absent and you don't see me, I am still with you. If you call me at the most critical moment I will be there for you. Your path through life and its pitfalls must be a spiritual one. Yes, you have to struggle for the survival of your body but you have to struggle even more to regain your divine spiritual state. It is at the height of your struggles in this imaginary world of matter that you can transform yourself and regain the kingdom which is the dwelling place of the soul."*

"So, it's better to let things happen and let them come to us rather than to go looking for them."

"That's right my brothers and sisters. It is already advantageous to be able to avoid danger and not to be taken by surprise. Our task on this new earth is to bring hope, love and comprehension between beings. The worst would be to fail in our enterprise but as Lemoria has explained to us we are in a world in which duality is dominant: at one moment it is beautiful and another time it is ugly. We waver between the good and the bad. It is difficult to keep a balance because our soul wants us to face certain tests. Our ego which is pushing us towards survival by domination, blinds us by its four desires: for power, domination, egotism and greed."

Then, seen through the crystal sphere, the film on the formation of the planet Alma now continued. The stretching of the earth's crust formed cracks which became canyons, and continents were formed separating the seas. Towards the west a huge stretch of land spread out from the sacred Mount Machu and connected it to another immense mountain which Adamos named Mount Shva and he pointed to this stretch of land.

"It is there that we are going to found our civilization. We will call it the land of Lemuria and the other stretch of land extending towards the east, I entrust to Atalanta and I will call it Atlantis. Looking now at the great mountain of this other great continent which seems detached from Atlantis that I will call Mount Kiliman. It is planned that the territory where it sits will belong to Afrika and he will be its king. Over there, further away to the east, those lands still forming which are adjacent to Mount Shva, I entrust to Zanga and his team. This mountain, we can see, is the highest in the world. Whenever our residence here is finished, we will initiate a new exodus and our mission on Alma will be one of love. When the time arrives, I will lead you to your respective territories for we have only one *Gyrosphere* and it will take many long years of work to build another one, that is if we ever will be able to build one. I think only Lemoria is capable of reproducing it!"

"Adamos," asked Andromas, "can you tell us what direction our thoughts should take to maintain harmony on the planet Alma?"

"Well, that calls for a long and complicated answer. One could say that what existed before consciousness is eternal and always stays constant and unchanging. Compare that to human thoughts which are always variable, inconsistent and subject to change. In other words, what existed before is pure truth. It is only when human beings become uniformly conscious of the law of life that all traces of human errors are erased. For the present, it is time which erases errors. To the degree which it flows, the passage of centuries clears the fog of matter by the evolution of intelligence. This is what brings new ideas into the daylight of the human spirit and pushes it towards the truth of the universal cosmic source.

Look, why is it that the ideas which replace past memories face up to the facts of the present and can only be transformed before prophecies of the future. People change under the effects of action and reaction which pulls them back each time they go too far in their personal creations. It is thus that the law of karma exists; it is not for the punishment of human beings but only to maintain the integrity of truth in existence which was and which will continue to be throughout the whole of creation. See why it is that humans pay their debts, what is false must be replaced by what is just, that is the law."

"It means that everyone who acts badly must learn to act well. Otherwise they will always be repeating their errors and be pulled backwards."

"Very well said! The great cosmic law which is always polarized in the sense of equalization, balance and harmony never permits life to go astray. It keeps it on course just like it does with the planets after their expulsion into their orbits and continues for ever despite the contrary views of unbelievers, idolaters and dogmatists. It is only when this law of absolute truth and of love for the next being will be universally followed at the greatest depth of human consciousness that the falsehood, the lie, which is not in accord with perfect unity and cosmic truth will disappear."

"Thus it is that our thoughts followed by our actions should follow this course of truth."

"Yes, for it appears as if the thoughts of humanity having become imperfect, being born of half-truths and falsehoods, were abandoned as soon as the truth became manifest, because the cosmic law which seeks out the absolute must be fulfilled in one way or another. See why people of little scruple will have to be called to account. The laws of harmony cannot be disturbed without there being some effect. The ditch into which all the blind that follow the blind fall into, is a stinking bog of false ideas, hypocrisy and lies stuffed with superstition and ignorance, created by personal thoughts. The law also stipulates that all living beings must participate in the movement of the expansion of the universe. That means that all humanity must firmly clear itself from its false beliefs. It happens often that in basing itself on false religious beliefs, the race must suffer or make others suffer before finally realizing that it was following the wrong path. It does happen that human thoughts create in the thoughts of races and nations a spiritual state which does not conform to pure reality. If that remains unchanged the law will interfere with the progress of that race. This will cause a projection in the karmic mirror the appearance of which reflects the error and the false vibration that will accumulate into internal conflicts or calamities. Such things can surge in on every side and cause the race to be wiped off the planet by wars. The race will thus be recharged by currents of pure essence revitalizing their descendents. Do you see my brothers and sisters, this message is very important for our future on this planet, the truth cannot be degraded. An accounting has to take place."

"That means that our future as the human race depends on the code of life which each must follow."

"This code really exists in each of us. Every time that a people think of God as being the source of absolute life, such people recognize themselves as being Gods, for the idea of being God is manifest in oneself during the whole time that human beings love that powerful idea with their whole hearts. They are going to reverence Him and become like Him. By this fact, a person inherits everything to which he has the right and life becomes a beautiful experience. That is how great waves of happiness and wisdom are going to spread out on the earth. All those whose breasts are beating with their thoughts and their love become the heart of a new race forming the crest of these waves; the higher consciousness of this people unites itself with that of God. Thus it is that the emaciated ghost formed by human ignorance which has blinded human beings in their egotism gives up its place to pure love and to peace. These human beings will discover that after having removed all their limitations thanks to the profound knowledge of the self, they will be able to raise themselves from the human state to that of god-man."

"In this state, Adamos, can we attain that of avatar Lemoria?"

"Not completely, but in arriving at this ideal unity there are created inaudible vibrations of peace and harmony caused by internal joy. This leads to the infusion of thousands of things necessary through which the evolution of the human race can take place, for when the right vibrations are put in motion, effects are going to follow and all the perfect desires that humanity needs become condensed and appear as reality. The vast ocean of the creative space of God is as transparent as a crystal and full of energy. All the elements are dissolved in it, obeying the forces of vibration which put them into action and permit them to condense themselves into material forms. See why the advanced being who knows the laws and the only truth can put in movement, by his own thoughts, the creative vibratory influences. So then, the component elements do not have any other purpose, they hasten to fill the world formed by the desire of accomplishment."

"So all thoughts are vibrations?"

"Yes they are. All transmitted vibrations don't stop their actions when leaving the physical perception. At the moment when they lose control, the spirit takes them and spreads them over a wider range which reacts best to the vibratory influences of the thought. The spirit has the capacity to penetrate all the cells by interpenetrating all the smallest particles of matter whether solid, liquid or gas, like a force in action building the mold with its different forms. The evolved person can be the projector and even the coordinator filling the different molds with material substance. Our sun and our universe were created in the same way for that which is lower is like that which is higher. The infinitely small is a reproduction of the infinitely large. Remember my speech on waves and vibration."

"Yes we do. Adamos, where did you acquire this knowledge?"

"For the most part from my father, it was what he taught me during my youth. I also have knowledge from my experiences in thousands of previous lives. As for the rest I still converse with my father and other spirits who have passed over."

"Our mother the sun is a living entity having a spirit and an intelligence which is in close contact with us and I think that she must communicate with the mother sun of the universe."

"You are exactly right. What we call our universe which turns around this sun is only one of 91 similar universes which turn around the great central sun. The mass of this sun is 91 000 times the combined mass of all the 91 universes together. In fact, it is so colossal that each of the 91 universes which turn around it in a measured order is as small as the most infinitesimal particles of an atom. Our universe takes more than 26 800 years to travel only once around its orbit of the great central sun. At the centre of this mother sun, the core, the white globe, has a red mark in the centre from which bursts out a brilliant beam of pure light, the spark of all life which includes the three marginal rays. Throughout the millennia of millennia, the great central sun of the centre of the universe, the creator, has attracted to itself the harmonious pulsations of all the energy emanations which are given off either through radiation or explosion. That's what the ancients called the left eye of God. It is the total manifestation of its will of being, and matter obeys. Now the same thing is reflected in our own sun and its planets.

Let's take Neptuna for example, at its birth it was only a great conglomeration of microcosmic particles ejected with powerful force from the solar generator. The white mark which appears with its expulsion and which interpenetrates the particles of the planet is itself a small solo centre which possesses in its turn the power to attract the most infinitesimal particles necessary for its survival in order to maintain cohesion. It is not an accidental explosion but a foreseen birth, that is part of evolution and it is because of this intelligent law that the gases keep their cohesion and take a spherical form. We can call this spark coming from the centre penetrating the core giving it life just what it is. It is the cosmic Christ around which turns all humanity. He is the force of the creating spirit whose law prevails over all human individuals.

This spark which penetrated the first cell to give it its life grows and divides itself infinitely, communicating its light to all other cells. Born out of this division, these remain attached from the start by the forces of cohesion, that is what we call love. In all births, nourishment and cohesion of the component parts are already assured just as a baby is nourished by its mother. The planet becomes a child of its sun which itself carries within itself part of the core of the central sun. Further, this core is in the image of and resembles the parent which gave birth to it. It possesses the same powers as its original to attract, consolidate and maintain the vibrations of the energies which surround it. These are necessary for its life and growth, and then, finally, its strengthening into maturity. When the planet is still close to its sun, it can pull out the maximum amount of vital substance, then, on moving out, it gains strength. From the mass of gaseous and cloudy vapor, the elements start to separate themselves, to condense and combine chemically. The pressure intensifies in the interior, while the exterior hardens all the soft substances producing a crust which is hard, heavy and dense. This crust assimilates more of the external particles as it undergoes cooling and when it is solid enough can support a rotating mass. This rotation is faster so that the primitive rocks can take their shapes."

"Adamos, was the first human race closer to the light at the beginning of time?"

"Yes! The first humans of the first planet were superior beings of the race coming from the human amoeba and not from animals, for the human amoeba were conformed to the human spirit. At that time, there was no inferior organism of the animal type because the planet Lucifer was a planet of light entirely dedicated to the evolution of man. Those beings possessed the human structure resembling a little that of our times, but they received their subsistence directly from the cosmic ether. The hunger for food like that which now keeps us eating the fruits of the earth did not exist then. The digestive system had not developed like today. They drank more water purified by the sun and the juice of fruits produced by trees. The first race was filled with beauty and perfection; they knew how to maintain mastery over the elements. When a being expressed a desire, that was immediately accomplished by his creative thought. It was only because of egotism and the desire to possess with covetousness the property of others that divisions appeared and the spirit of wastefulness inflamed their hearts. This meant that instead of wanting to create in harmony with the Creator, each of them wanted to surround themselves with needs and personal pleasures in greater and greater self-indulgence. Then the very opposite of divine beauty, such as ugliness and shallow personality replaced true individuality. Creations became objects of vanity and the egotism that was rampant. There were fights which developed into wars. Different groups became separated. They accepted the fact that evil could exist. The good ones separated themselves from the wicked ones because they could no longer live together. The more the planet approached the black sun, the more the negative aspect became pronounced. Love turned to hatred under its influence."

"Were the first humans able to change and become faithful to the Creator?"

"Oh, definitely, all men would have needed to attach themselves to the light in order to follow the perfect model of divinity, that would have permitted them to construct a physical world more divine and harmonious, but under the influence of the black sun, those who accepted the evil side effectively increased its qualities and got more from it and more of the hidden powers of creation. It happened that their wicked thoughts poisoned the whole atmosphere so much so that the mother sun sent them a series of cataclysms to maintain equilibrium, thus the evil started by their thoughts of evil had evil results, causing the generation of negative karma that was hell. Whatever we do not learn by the good, we are forced to learn it by the bad. The small number of those who kept in contact with divinity not having wished to abandon their divine heritage were constituted into angelic bodies capable of traveling in the spiritual planes which surround and interpenetrate the 91 existing universes. In this new form which God gave them, they were able to preserve their knowledge and pass it on to dawning humanity, but now transformed by the experience of evil. It was on account of their highly placed ideals and their divine will that we were able to be saved. The good Luciferians guide those who fight on the side of good and the bad Luciferians direct those who take up the path of evil. We are their direct descendents and they form the roots of humanity except that those on the side of good preserve the ideas which God has created for man and his evolution, that is free will and it becomes the sword that cuts the choice of the right path to take."

"Each of us, in this case, is a divine being."

"Quite true. Before taking a personal name, we have to know that we are God. The word divinity is given to distinguish the central coordinator who organizes all the movements in creation. The beatings of the human heart resemble in miniature those colossal pulsations of the cosmic heart. In lifting our gaze towards the sun, we should think: "I come from the supreme intelligence which commands all forms of life in which is the cosmic protoplasm, I draw my energy from the same substance as the grand central sun, the mother of mother-suns. In this way, I am a unit of humanity organized like a divine universe. However, like the cosmos, we assume charge of the responsibility of being a unit of the divine which must fill an indispensable role in the world of creation. For that, we have to try to understand our universe and its divine plan. A single human being possesses the original intelligence which interpenetrates everything which exists and which was given out from the primordial substance that impregnates the simplest physical forms. Here is a grandiose example: if for example all the universes were destroyed, a single human being in cooperation with the original intelligence could reconstruct them starting from the existing light-emanations. The human being would become the power and the force finding its resolution in universal intelligence where no destruction exists. Once a man has reached the realm of his own divinity, he is part of the infinite and time has no more effect on him, he has become time itself. He still conserves the consciousness of his life's experience. Further, due to the perfection of his spirit, failure no longer has a place in his consciousness and it is there that the microcosm rejoins the macrocosm. The infinitesimal becomes the infinite, master of all forms. Everything such as the cells of the body contains the germ of the personality. Wisdom being itself raised up from the shadows of ignorance into its light can say "I am the transcendental light, nothing exists outside of me, I am He and He is in me."

"We thank you Adamos for sharing with us your concept of life and in making us face up to the difficulties of our adaptation here on this planet now in transformation. We need courage and confidence in ourselves and you have given them to us."

Evena closed the talk by Adamos with some words of her own: "We need courage, it's true, but as Adamos has said, we must enter more deeply into ourselves through meditation in order to meet with God. Matter is not the basis of all neither is it the whole of existence, it is only an aspect of force, even as life and thought. The problem can only be resolved when men and women will have returned their thoughts to God. In facing up to the forces of nature, a man is not slow to realize his powerlessness. So in this contest of forces is born the idea of God; however study of the mechanisms of thought teaches us that man is incapable of visualizing the unknown other than remembering whatever is known. The idea of God will always depend on phenomena to which men attach the actions of God and it will evolve along with the development of thought."

Chapter VI

Amos transforms Mara

On Earth, the story of planet Mara intimately linked to the planet Alma became a matter of sensation. Everybody wanted to know what had happened, how it had happened and the news traveled so fast that the President of the United States, himself very interested, perhaps because of a very ancient link through one of his incarnations, wanted to know more about this extraordinary being Adamos. Adamos himself was as special as the avatar, the same one that we also call Professor Lemoria. His question was addressed to Evena, the companion of Adamos.

"We know now that via the crystal sphere which originates all these pictures, we can correspond with our ancient ancestors, parents of the human race."

His message was as follows: "We are interested on Earth to know more about the origins of Captain Adamos. Who established civilization on our planet? Can Evena, his companion, perhaps inform us about this?"

Evena appeared on the screen. "You have called me in order to ask me a question and I have the right to respond. For that purpose, I am going to go back to the epoch of his life in the form of prince Amos, governor of the *Eïz* triad grounded on the planet Mara which you call Mars. I am going to concentrate on the screen images received through the akashic mirror of Mara. We are going to travel back to the past when the planet Mars was in the place Alma was many thousands of years ago." Thus appeared on the screen older pictures, when prince Amos was at his control panel, made of pure gold, situated in the centre of a great pyramid amidst its satellite space craft. There could be heard his melodious voice with its magnetic power gliding over the turquoise colored water around the golden command table that contained the cosmic lingam that had the great power of the universe. His voice like a sacred mantra penetrated the core of the lingam as would do a laser beam. He said: "O divine power of the universe, spirit of the magnetic principles of the forces, listen, I am Amos, prince of Amora gracious city of Sandoma, son of king Amon and governor of the triad *Eïz*. We are in sight of the planet in the solar system called Mara. Place us in an effective orbital path and prepare for us a good landing site on Mara."

It is thus that Mara felt the coming on to its soil the space vessel *Eïz*, commanded by captain Amos, son of the ruler of Amon, situated in the Andromeda galaxy. The welcome from the planet was not reassuring: spouts of steaming water shot up into the air with much bubbling and a terrible roaring. The condensation of water on the planet was not like it was before, there were no deep cavities to form seas, lakes or oceans. There were layers of subterranean water which were exploding at every moment projecting earth, clay and soft rock in whirlpools of steam like the output of a gigantic kettle. *Eïz*, with an immense blast of air landed noisily crushing a quantity of marine vegetation in sinking about a third of its depth in a deep marsh before coming to rest.

Amos came out of his command pyramid, and at a brisk pace, walked towards an octagonal multicolored building having staircases of emerald green. With a signal of his hand, a huge panel opened followed by another offering him a passageway where the panels closed silently behind him. In the corridor, Amos met Seigia and her husband Okros, walking hand-in-hand. These two were of the black race. Amos took them on board with him when he was passing by the planet Neptuna. Another couple with bronze-colored skin approached. These were Antina and her husband Nacro coming from the planet Satur, with another couple Ho and her husband Fri who had golden yellow skins from the planet Jupita. Behind them, a beautiful lady having white skin like Amos, golden eyes and long auburn hair advanced towards him. Amos with a smile made an announcement. "We are on the planet Mara, dear brothers and sisters."

The beautiful lady was called Aïn Androgyna. She was the princess whom Amos came to save from harm at the time of a bloody revolution, which had happened a short time before on the planet Satur. This was when an undisciplined mob was rushing to where the princess was in order to take her prisoner. Thus it was that Amos turned on her his disintegrator ray from the centre of his pyramid to reintegrate her immediately on *Eïz*. Turning her face to the prince of Amora, she collapsed into his arms, unconscious. At this memory, Amos could not repress a smile. Androgyna in a brown transparent robe exhibited the Saturian human body in its most beautiful form, being stretched out over a long sofa covered with a material resembling green foam. Very close was a spring of water cascading into a natural coral-colored pool. All of that had been materialized by Amos to recreate an environment similar to that of Satur. Amos approached her and held her for several moments.

"We are going to get ready for the descent to Mara. You aren't afraid?" he asked.

"Oh no! with you I don't fear anything."

"In a few minutes, we are going to have lunch. We'll wait for you in the dining room."

"In that case, I'll see you very soon, she said stretching herself in a very relaxed way."

In the dining room, a large table of yellow crystal was prepared. There were different fruits on it, various chopped vegetables and nuts. Everybody came to the table and served themselves with something to eat.

"This will be our basic diet, said Amos because we don't know this planet and the kinds of fruit which are found there."

"Great master Amos," added Okros, "tell us this once, who prepares this table with all this food coming from several planets? We haven't seen any servant here and you are alone on *Eïz*, your traveling satellite."

"See now, dear brother Okros, I understand your astonishment. I have surrounded myself with beings invisible to your eyes who love to serve me. Perhaps you are also asking yourself why I am not eating the meal with you. I really want to answer your questions. The fact is, that not possessing a physical body like yours, I don't therefore have the absolute necessity of eating like you do. Think, a few minutes ago, I was communicating with the powerful spirit of light in order to guide our satellite *Eïz* on to Mara, and as you must have noticed, everything went without a sound and without a hitch. In the same manner, light which is the source of all life has fed my etheric body for a long time, just as your body must be nourished by forces ingested by plants or, as in the case of the Luciferians, by the blood of animals."

Nacro, the husband of Antina, then asked: "You were just referring to the Luciferians who enslave our planets and the humans on them, how can you seize them and destroy them?"

"See now, I haven't spoken of all those matters up to now but tomorrow at sunrise we will have to face our enemies, the Luciferians, who have also invaded this planet. Recently, when I entered your solar system, I saw through the translucent sphere many pictures which showed life on all your planets. Only the planets Mara and Satur revealed the existence of human beings with a stature like yours. You yourselves originated from an ancient expedition to your solar system by men of my race, our forefathers of Andromeda. The famous pyramidal glass mountain on your planet Satur was our means of communication with you. Thanks to it, evolution was able to go on but all those events happened such a long time ago that nobody among you remembers them. The means which I have mentioned allowed us to learn about the invasion of your solar system by the Luciferians. I was told that the battle will be fierce and that I would have to use all the best means put at my disposal by the solar avatar. You must have figured it out since you are all that is left of the few remaining survivors."

"You mean to say," asked Antina "that Mount Isux, that mountain of opalin crystal, an unknown and mysterious vestige of the past of our planet Satur, a mountain which has even caused wars between two races (Ho and Fri can remember it) was actually an ancient pyramid constructed by the Andromedians and serves thus as a huge videotransmitter unceasingly transmitting information on our civilization to them beyond the solar system."

"Quite so. It is thanks to this device that my father knew about the infernal spirits attacking your planet how they aroused intrigues and hostilities between you. When the Luciferians saw you feeble and disorganized, they sent you agents of weakness and confusion. Since the Luciferians are cruel and depraved beings they used force and malice to subjugate you."

Listening to that, Ho spoke up. "We remember it," he said. "We were taken by force. Those amongst us who were saved from it turned against their brothers, then everything was ruled by doubt and hypocrisy. Wickedness was established between each and every one of us but nobody was aware of the strategy. Everything was achieved with perfect cunning. The enemy infiltrated themselves among us like innocent sheep. Unfortunately, these were black sheep sowing the seeds of discord. Our whole race, buried under a pile of egotism foul and stagnant, slowly but surely fell apart. All those who in the past were united by the joy of common endeavor were now delivered into indescribable chaos. It was a fierce battle to which hatred had led them through the power of jealousy. So it was that this nation, proud of its union built on fraternal love moved to the opposite extreme. It was through the penetrating will of the demonic forces and the seeds of their destructive power that our ways turned to suicidal fratricide. It was awful, really frightful."

"Oh! How well I understand you, brother Ho. It was with great agony that I was obliged to destroy your dwellings on Satur but often one has to destroy something in order to save a world because in an extreme situation one cannot separate the grain from the chaff. On other planets in other times, where the diabolic power is not so strong then peace can be achieved without great trouble. With time and experience, however, the powers of evil can organize themselves and gain a lot of ground. Now, at last you are here on Mara capable of carrying on your race while still safe and sound. This world has already known war and the men who inhabit it have perpetuated their race and are ready to accept you. You represent mankind in your solar system and your task will be to represent the creator in your evolutionary form up to the moment of your deliverance from matter."

"O Amos, our brother from space, if you will permit me to call you that," said the giant Okros, who with the agreement of Amos continued. "We must thank you for the profound love which you are showing us. We are not perfect because the unwholesome spirits are still working through us, and we can well appreciate that you are different from us in all aspects. You saved us from the clutches of the Luciferians, you have modified us for life in peace on this new planet. How then can you put all your confidence on beings such as ourselves who, for you, are unknown?"

"You need to see Okros, it isn't in my power to discuss the instructions of my father neither to criticize God's work, work to which my father dedicated his every heartbeat. It is only in the future that I can teach you things which you still do not know right now and after that my task will be finished. You alone remain the free agents of your destiny. Your life in some sense belongs to you. The knowledge which I received from our fathers must be transmitted through the love which I have for you. So, in truth, we are all brothers in space and we all have to learn to love one another. The good is latent in each of us and will have to triumph over the evil. You will then be capable of mastering your destiny. Order will be re-established in yourselves and also around you at the same time."

"Explain to us O Amos, how you made the planet Lucifer disintegrate," spoke up the princess Androgyna, while serving fruits, which miraculously appeared, to everybody who was seated around the table of golden crystal.

"Well, it is too long a story and I would not wish to go into details right now, dear friend. However, I can project for you some images which have been preserved in the akashic records of your solar system. It was already a long time ago at the earliest period of your solar system when Lucifer, the planet of pure light had rebelled against its radiant God. I was there. That was the first time that my father sent me on a mission from Andromeda."

At that, Adamos pointed the middle finger of his right hand which carried a ring with a mysterious double pyramid carved in an emerald on its face and after a moment of concentration said: "Please turn and look at the wall on your left. There you are going to see what none of you have seen previously concerning the past of your solar system."

The immense wall of crystal became almost milky, of an opal color, as if an unknown substance was flowing between its molecules and, suddenly, pictures formed, filling up the wall. A huge glittering sphere could be seen. It was reddish in color and encircled by three other spheres very much smaller like moons. This was the planet Lucifer, seen amidst its satellites *Boz* and *Az*, directed by *Eïz*. Then came an impressive picture of a shaggy people like anthropoids who were running in all directions in a distracted fashion. Their cities were built underground in caves. They were troglodytes. That is how they had to survive since their separation from the sun. Their most evolved individuals were able and possessed the capacity to disintegrate themselves and reintegrate in space but very few amongst them had received this power. They transferred it under strange circumstances. Lucifer, the creator of evil, with his occult power had given this subtle initiation to three of the last of them before leaving the planet to continue his infernal tasks. In his own universe the three biggest principles of contamination of the spirit namely pride, vanity and envy were being dispatched. These were capable of degrading human beings, even the most intelligent, and reducing them to the lowest level of bestiality due to the capture of their sense and instinct. Satanas, one of the demonic forces has a fine appearance like Demos. Beelzebub, who has a frightful bestial appearance, and the Gorgons are all with him. At this moment, the thought forms of Satanas were held captive on *Eïz*, he was sending out appeals for help in order to attract the demonic forces to come and rescue him. Then could be seen prince Amos in a state of extreme concentration, his thoughts were resisting the ceaseless calls that the demons were sending out as they continually changed between dreadful menaces and pleadings for pity, weeping and showing distress. In all this, the thought of Amos remained implacable, strengthened by the extremely powerful concept of justice, which was driven by the firm decision to faithfully follow the divine plan. All of this was fused and consolidated in the heart-centre of the pyramid holding the lingam of all creation.

One could see literally spreading out from the pyramid's apex, blue flames taking shape and becoming solid to change into destructive entities. There were now thousands of beings conceived in Amos's image appearing on Lucifer to face up to its inhabitants who had become like demons. Each of them aimed their index finger to their forehead and with the left hand open facing the enemy caused them to disintegrate. Only the powerful demons initiated into the power of evil were resisting. So Satanas the proud encircled himself with a thousand of his faithful ones like a bat with its wings, and inside a blazing cloak, he defied the thought of Amos in opposing him directly with his force.

"Ah, if Lucifer were here, we would know how to defend ourselves! We must attack," he said suddenly, his look becoming savage. "We can destroy Amos's magnetic force and turn it against him." He moved impetuously towards an immense parabolic mirror and with his acolytes began a Luciferian ritual.

It was with bewilderment that the spectators of this drama saw displayed on the wall blinding images of powerful light leaping up like flames from the world, even the planet Lucifer, to throw themselves against the satellite *Eïz*. They transformed themselves into burning balls like lava, becoming suffocating and smoky, destroying everything in their path and breaking up the soldiers of Amos.

Seeing this, Amos straightened himself up, got up from his chair in order to approach the golden altar from which emanated the power of the three lingams blazing with light. He knelt humbly and in a state of devotion, raising his hand to heaven, he evoked the divine spirit: "O Eternal Lord of creating light, all-powerful supplier of life of whom I am only the humble servant, I pray you, isolate the satanic forces of this planet so as to rebalance the vital forces of evolution. May your will always be respected, because it is only you who knows all things, so may my faithful heart be emptied of errors".

At that instant, a dazzling light rose suddenly from the centre of the altar. The force was such that Amos was thrown to the floor, panting. The light spread through the sacred pyramid filling every corner and *Eïz* was surrounded by a concentric ring of light. This light, like a powerful laser, focused itself on to the planet Lucifer for at least one hour. The whole planet shook and its internal pressure increased so much that it inflated like a balloon and exploded into pieces blown out in the six dimensions of space and all around the triad of *Eïz* which itself was not affected. All at once, Amos heard the feeble voice of Satanas rising from the infernal ruins of the planet's disintegration.

"Amos, damned prince, you have forced us out of our home but you cannot destroy our existence, you can only slow down our activity, our spirit is immortal and we live in the astral world. Look out, if you weaken some day, I will find you and get my revenge." Then the speech ended with a sardonic laugh in the dark night of time.

"Now you have the story of what took place on the planet Lucifer," said Amos as the images became more blurred and gradually disappeared. "As you have been able to see, the demons, freed from their bodies always remain active in the lower astral. However, physically, they were banished for 108 generations after which they reincarnated and become active once again in the solar system."

"Prince Amos," said Okros uneasily, "there is still the demon Beelzebub in our solar system - is he more powerful to fight against than the other two?"

"No, not necessarily but he can communicate telepathically with his acolytes which makes him difficult to oppose. Believe me though; the forces of heaven are invincible when they are put into action. Tomorrow we are going to set our feet on the ground so it is advisable that you rest comfortably tonight in preparation for that event."

"How about you Amos," said Androgyna, "you never rest and I never saw you sleep."

"Sleep, Androgyna, is not really necessary because my body is not like yours, it is more fluidic but to your senses it appears the same as yours whenever you see or touch it. The reason is that before meeting you, I had to reduce the vibratory level of my etheric body and bring it down to your level so that I could communicate with you and be visible and audible to you because you are living in an astral dimension different from mine. Although in the past I have already had a form like yours before our absolute evolution beyond the physical and before we had reintegrated into our unique etheric form. One day, I will speak to you again on this subject, so sleep well for now."

The couples went out to their respective rooms still puzzled by the events at which they had been present. It was not easy for them to understand how it had all happened. In the images which Amos had made appear to them, there were omissions in a large number of details of these events and the reasons for them. However, for all those present on the Earth of today, the showing of the immense puzzle in the history of the solar system, the same conclusion was reached. Everything repeats itself in time and space, the story of suns and their planets, then of life on Earth, of the evolution of forms and species, then that of the human races. Everything that happens in the past returns in the present and repeats itself in the future.

Chapter VII

How Amos prepared life for evolution on Mara

That morning, a thick warm fog invaded all parts of *Eïz*. The small expedition prepared to descend to the soil of Mara. On leaving the temple, an infernal noise attracted their attention. Above them, gigantic and monstrous birds were gliding and squawking and at times giving out a roar like a wild animal. One of them rushed at the group. Each member fled in a different direction. Amos, seeing that, extended his hand and commanded that the magnetic flux become stationary and at the same instant, the monsters appeared suspended in the air. A flaming aura then surrounded them and made their gigantic bodies vanish instantly. The heat rose very quickly and the air became suffocating as they descended to the ground, oxygen became thin. Amos took note of it when he saw his companions succumb. Androgyna quickly collapsed unconscious. Then Amos concentrated his attention on a small blue stone in his ring. It was a symbol of power over minerals and gases. Right away the air around them was purified little by little and became more breathable. They continued on their way and reached the boundary of *Eïz*. A large gate opened sliding on its hinges and they made their first steps on the soil of Mara. Around them greenish sulphurous lava flowed up like volcanic effluent, other creations could be heard as a raucous muffled cry and a murmuring followed by shaking of the earth and splashing noises.

"Hold it, said Amos, extending his arm. There exist here apart from the winged monsters, other huge animals which have come into the service of the Luciferians. I saw them on my crystal screen. The Luciferians devour their flesh. It could be that one of these monsters will pick up our trail."

At that very moment, a disturbing clamour followed by a shaking of the ground could be heard all around them, then, coming out of the thick mist which extended in front of them appeared a monstrous head. It was the swaying head of a huge reptile which possessed a jawbone like a crocodile equipped with pointed teeth, ready to open. At the sight of this, everyone fled, shrieking. Amos, straightening himself telepathically ordered the big lizard to go away. By way of a reply, it gave a frightful roar, advanced a step, defying Amos and opened its mouth displaying a large blackish tongue. Its gigantic stature was better viewed now that it emerged from between the huge plants which were growing in the misty marshes. Then, when the large reptile was going to make a big mouthful of Amos, he lifted his hand and there could be seen coming from his ring a dazzling blue light which reduced the monster to a formless mush resembling the ones made of the other flying creatures.

Then, a hairy being the size of Amos bounded into the middle of the group. He had green eyes which shone with the flames of hatred. He made guttural shouts that he addressed to Amos. His shaggy anthropoid head was shaking with rage. Here, no doubt, was one of the leaders possessed by the Luciferians. He brandished a weapon made of wood resembling a lance which he threw at Amos piercing his chest. At the sight of this, Androgyna fell in a faint. The lance went right through Amos's body and impaled itself on a tree trunk. The gaping hole left by the lance closed up at once without leaving a trace, as if the lance had gone through a body full of air which would close up after its entry.

All of them were stunned by this morbid spectacle. Amos lifted up his right hand once more and the magical ring burnt up the hairy man who had become hypnotized by fear. Amos, with the help of Okros, lifted up the princess. She, with a big sigh, turned towards Amos and opening her big eyes all wide, looked at him with great surprise.

"How come you aren't dead?" she babbled.

"No indeed princess," replied Amos smiling. "I possess at this time a fluidic body of a different type from yours that I can solidify at will, if you prefer, making it hard and mortal like yours. Your body, imprisoned in solid matter is subject to the laws which rule and limit its action. In the remote past, my body also was subject to the same laws."

Once again, he was interrupted by terrifying roars and whistles which were coming nearer and there were also the muffled noises of breaking branches and plants being crushed. Everything, again, started shaking.

"Master Amos," said Seigia, "I am afraid for all of us. These monsters, even if they don't affect you, put our lives in danger all the same. See now there are others approaching. What can we do?"

Amos said simply "come along, follow me." Then he set out towards a hillock which was fairly high. They all forced themselves desperately to run after him. They had reached the summit when around them gathered a crowd of threatening beings mounted on antediluvian reptiles having menacing fangs drooling foully. They were ready to leap forward and tear the group in pieces. Another hairy demon, the biggest of all, with a horn on his forehead and wing-like forms folded on his back, jumped on to the burning ground and advanced, fiercely, holding a lance in one hand and in the other, a rope with a grapple of five balls which he threw deliberately at Amos who had now risen to his full stature, defiant and smiling. The grapple wrapped itself round Amos's neck and without taking hold fell into the burning swamp. Then his soft voice rose powerfully above the silence which followed. The rash confidence of the winged anthropoid being ended at once and all the other monsters seemed terrified. They had never seen beings like this, holding their heads up towards them in this fashion.

"Beelzebub, we have come to announce the end of your reign as colonizer of the planet Mara. This world is required to be a nurturer of mankind, those who must evolve between the good and the evil, between the spirits of earth, air, water and fire. Leave this world together with your followers and the herd of monsters. I direct you in the name of the eternal one of three faces."

At that, Amos traced a sign with three fingers of his right hand to each of the four cardinal points. The demon started to advance with a roar of anger and bounded in front with a beat of his wings. The circle closed in on the little group with hundreds of threatening and drooling mouths which opened ready to crush their bodies. Amos stood up straight and addressed his friends. "Make a chain holding hands around me. Fix your gaze on me and don't turn round!" Beelzebub gave a loud sneer. "You won't escape me, we are stronger than you would believe." And he shouted to his monsters, "kill them, kill them."

The ground started shaking around the circle of our friends when the vile spirits and their monsters advanced to crush them. Amos lifted his arms towards heaven and prayed fervently: "O supreme powers of the three creative forces of the universe, protect us as much as we follow by our just action your supreme will in this world. May your all-powerful glory manifest in this place."

At these words, a blinding light descended from heaven and connected with the surface of Mara, covering the hillock and the whole planet. A searing and suffocating heat filled the atmosphere around the circle formed by Amos. The saving fire from the celestial powers created a destructive effect like a powerful atomic bomb. The huge bodies of the reptilian monsters and the hairy bodies of the anthropoids twisted frightfully in agony for several minutes. Their heads could be seen smoking and grimacing separated from their shredded bodies, disintegrated and burnt, strewn over the ground in all directions. The light went completely round the world, destroying all the wicked beings who were faithful to their master. Those that remained were the ones who avoided the hypnotic call of Beelzebub who, for his part, having been thrown out of his body, had all contact with his people cut off. The perverse spirits no longer had any hold over them.

On the advice of Amos, the friends broke their chain of unity and returned to *Eïz*. The ground was covered with shattered and smoking skeletons; all the reptilian monsters were spread on the earth in a mass of sludge.

"What happens to the discarnate spirits of these monsters and these half-human beings?" enquired Okros.

"By the grace of the most powerful universal trinity, the spirit of these beings who were enslaved by those demons will be free and will enter our next planetary existences, by successive periods of reincarnations. They will become part of your families. As for the demons who were very advanced in evil, those who were initiated into the occult forces of the black sun, will have to remain disincarnate for 108 cycles of the evolution of Mara. However, they will have the power to influence the thoughts of humans periodically after following Marian lunar cycles. They will also be able to inhabit the bodies of those who will accept them as guides in the form of possessions or of mental illnesses. The anthropoid beings will degenerate into monkeys so that at least you may pity them and your love may conserve them again in the course of time and help them to evolve. That is all I can tell you at this moment."

"Are you going to leave us alone now on this planet?" asked Androgyna anxiously.

"Most definitively, first however, it will be necessary for us to tilt the planet's axis so that the cold hardens the crust to make it more habitable. It is already far out from the sun. Now, follow me dear friend."

Walking steadily, Androgyna came towards him.

"You know, Amos, the power that you possess over matter and the elements is tremendous, it gives me the shivers. How can it be that you have everything united in you? Does everybody on Andromeda possess this power?"

"Princess Androgyna, I believe I told you that I don't possess anything. It is all the power of heaven, without which one would call in vain. It is thus that we use the latent forces which are active in the different cosmic rays. So, for example, our ultra-solar pyramid unites the magnetic vibratory powers of several suns which can be concentrated by thought into the stone which I am carrying on my finger enormously amplified. That allows the transmutation of matter to take place but these forces cannot be made available to everyone. Each access to the supreme power requires a mind of matching wisdom accompanied by great vigilance. On Andromeda, several thousands of earth years are allowed to men to acquire these essential qualities. There has to be the union of thousands of souls into one and such is my situation. It needed the reduction in the quantity of existences lived, of souls on different planes to obtain the divine quality in one being alone. For that reason there are only hundred eight brothers living in our family on our sun. In each of our planetary systems, the evolved souls are reduced in number in accomplishing the divine quality on their own sun, and there they live as beings of light who are free to belong to their galaxy and stay within it or to go anywhere in the universe to bring aid and service to mankind. So it is that our brothers and fathers separated themselves from the occult negative powers in our galaxy to attain peace. However, peace can only be maintained by gratification in the fight for good. That is why we voyage through space to struggle against evil and stabilize the good."

"It is a noble task but isn't there peril in the fact that you forget yourself as being alive? You don't have an ego any more."

"The scale of value in my life is not limited by a number of years but the ideal which governs my behavior. The universal trinity has permitted the awakening of senses inaccessible to the physical perception. For example, the spiritual vision which includes hearing, the senses of smell, touch and taste has been allowed for a long time. The biggest manifestation of deliverance in man is in leaving his state of slavery to matter up to the final metamorphosis into the infinite, and there, the inferior self is completely forgotten in the abandonment to the higher self. One obtains the infinite consciousness of being awe-inspiring in the limitless unity. That is also the goal of existence of everyone in all the planets and galaxies. The kingdom of life enfolds and also the kingdom of death. As for my ego, it has divided itself and gives service in thousands of existences."

"Oh! How your words seem to be different from those I heard when I was small and subject to the knowledge of my tutor, where the nature of love meant no more than the sensual enrobing of physical beauty, where each caressing glance became the subject for a poem and where romanticism took on a riotous allure. I see the difference in this moment in the level of what I have heard. It is an insignificant coronation beside the ideal of stripped-down egotism and the astonishing power which results. O how I admire you."

"Allow me to tell you that your admiration, dear friend, is in fact the reflection of an inspiration flowing into the depths of your soul which reveals to you the existence of another world where there are other levels of knowledge and other levels of understanding that you will one day attain."

"Yes, you are right; I will have to learn to know myself better."

"Now we have arrived," said Amos walking towards the group. "Dear friends, please return to your apartments, we are going to leave Mara in a short time to go up into space."

While the space brothers of Amos were taking their bath in the natural swimming pool of *Eïz* where a waterfall from an underground spring heated the water, Amos piloted his satellites in the shape of a triangle with his negative energy satellite *Boz* on the left and his positive satellite *Az* on the right. In putting his magnetic control device in maximum oscillation over the north pole of Mara, the planet suddenly started to wobble and to rotate about its equator. Mara gradually moved into a more inclined orbit. In its oscillation, it retreated some distance from the sun like an ocean liner guided by tugboats into a major seaport.

Amos's plan was very simple. Mara had to be established on the physical plane, in a new orbit suitable for all the levels of life to be in harmony; the animal, the vegetable and the mineral. This was so that it could contribute to the evolution of the human species, a kind of compensation for its limitless nature, from the fact that nature, like spirit, is imbued by the eternal law with an existence lacking either beginning or end. Mara could now achieve a balanced environment to maintain homogeneity. Thus it was done when Mara stopped its stellar journey to remain in rotation in its orbit. The vital positive power of cosmic space entered in a spiral form by the mouth of Mara which was located in the great desert of Bori crossing the central axis from East to West and the sun from its zenith to the nadir to exit in the region of the island of Para from where came out the spiral of negative energy. Thus Amos invoked the divine trinity to establish *Eïz* in the "navel" of this new world. So it was that the vapor overpowering Mara became solid and condensed into a liquid, the crust solidified and the mountains formed forcing out the fire in expelling a multitude of rocks of all sizes from the planet's interior. Lakes were created and the marshes disappeared following the onset of deluges of rain. The two satellites *Boz* and *Az* orbited the world of Mara sending transmissions of peace for generations to come. These were derived from their inner vibrations and that was because Amos gave them the order to stay in their respective orbits.

Prince Amos approached Androgyna who was warming herself in the sun and asked: "Tell me princess of Satur, would you like to see flying animals more beautiful than those which attacked us when we arrived?"

"O most certainly," she said getting up. "On Satur, they were really much more beautiful, we called them birds."

"Quite so Androgyna. Your love on your planet is like what there is in all the solar system. That is why I asked you. Would you like to see on this world some of these beautiful creatures?"

"It is my dearest wish, prince Amos."

"Very well, in that case, follow me."

Then he walked away, followed by the beautiful Saturian, in the direction of the temple of knowledge. It was the first time that she had entered this mysterious palace which was the temple of the sacred trinity. The outside was of transparent crystal and the outside light powerfully concentrated within. At its centre stood the square golden cube, it was a huge block of pure gold. Three light beams coming from clear faces formed a triangle from which shone the heart of the pyramid. Amos put his attention on the centre of the altar and they approached it respectfully.

Amos said: "Princess Androgyna, move your hands towards the top of this ball of red crystal." Androgyna moved her hands forward towards the sphere. The beams of light came out of it and she felt herself trembling, shaking throughout her whole body, an indescribable warmth infused everything.

"Now, visualize the sphere and concentrate your thought on each one of the birds that you know: see their form, their color, see them alive, each one in particular with all the details and do the same thing for all the types you want. When the work is finished, pronounce the following words OM TAT SAT so that the task will be achieved at all the cardinal points in the skies of this world."

"Prince Amos, can I see them in the Saturian trees and also surrounded by various flowers?"

"As you say, whatever you see will be reproduced in the field of creation on this world by the divine trinity, always present, don't however think about harmful, monstrous or destructive creatures, because they are the work of demons. They are implanted in the spirits of wicked beings and will take form sooner or later. Rather think of whatever opposes evil and that is beauty."

Androgyna took with good grace what the mysterious Andromedian asked of her and instantly in several places in the world living seeds came into existence from her thoughts now at the point of hatching.

"Avoid imagining any person," he pointed out to Androgyna, "I beg you, because the creation of human beings is a task which can only be carried out by a master of light and people like us cannot conceive them without making errors. God alone as trinity can create souls which are sufficiently evolved. For if it was otherwise, speaking for myself, I would only have imagined you and nurtured you in my thought at the place I want to find you instead from so far away."

"So you desired me in the depths of your being? It was not just by chance?"

"Very much so, this desire led me to find you in this world."

"What about animals?" she asked with some scepticism. "Do you mean that the vegetable and animal kingdoms have no souls?"

"Their soul is collective and not individual but it will be transmuted by the grace they will receive after living through experience as humans, that is the law of evolution. Don't forget that you are made from matter, so all the elements are present in your physical body and your spirit which is normally free finds itself imprisoned in matter. At first, it floats above the body but the more it limits itself by thinking no further than the physical senses, the more it is trapped. And so much longer will be the wait before it returns to the original spiritual state."

"How about you Amos, you are different from me."

"Yes, in a sense, because my spirit is really floating over my body. It is not held to my body in any defined manner. This is why I have the ability to dematerialize or rematerialize myself as necessary. The art of thinking in a human should become the art of living. Your thought becomes amplified thousands of times in importance when it is placed in the creative fire of God. It's a bit like when you see a grain of sand through a microscope, it can look like a mountain. Everything becomes possible in the sight of God. You must understand that it is necessary for you to see with the eyes of the spirit when the object is at the point of being created. You have such a habit of living in the created world and its manifestation as matter that the object which is the divine power in matter seems for you not to be a reality which, in fact, it is!"

"That means, then, that I would possess a power similar to yours prince Amos."

"I believe it Androgyna, only ignorance and the loss of former faculties together with the doubt which resides in your thoughts have effectively eliminated faith in this same power. Instead of starting on the spiritual path, which has nothing to do with any religion, your parents, themselves having lost this knowledge in accepting bad habits typical of their times, couldn't give you what they didn't know. However, at your deepest level of consciousness, you possess the knowledge which is the seed of all the powers with their expressions. Even if you don't let it grow, it is there and awaits the time of sprouting. Faith in the divine spirit is its yeast.

For millennia, our scientific spirit on Andromeda was trying to isolate the divine substance taking an error-strewn road, then truth rose up and finally materialized it for what it is: very simply a mediator through which the divine essence expresses itself."

"So you use the power of crystals to transport your thoughts?"

"That is partly true, except that the spirits of the crystals are sublime beings completely frozen in their mode of expression. They are living to work for their salvation through the subtle will of the creative thoughts which use them as channels. This is still an act permitted by divine law in order to allow them a rapid evolution."

"When you talk about evolution, do you mean to grow spiritually?"

"The eternal living spirit, having come to be incarnated into a state of temporary separation from the divine source, must learn the journey through life and death as well as the good and the evil, to be aware of God and to be able to adore Him. Its return from an existence limited by the power of time and space give it a foretaste of its opposite mirror image which is unlimited, knowing neither time nor space. That is one of the forms evolution takes because evolution operates in a cycle in both senses. However, evolution is a matter of consciousness."

"Then it is as if the soul makes a return journey in a different dimension?"

"Yes indeed, the dead live in the same sphere but because their vital vibration is higher, they can move around you while staying invisible to you. Their creative thoughts do not possess any more of the same power than in the physical state. They cannot create anything for the living but only for other dead beings like themselves. They are at the time unaware of the world of the living in the same way that the living are unaware of the world of the dead. The only difference is that in the active domain of matter, the thought can mold the individuality by means of willpower. That is something which no longer exists in the hyperphysical domain, where ego is not present. All changes concerning the character of the personality must be made during the time of an incarnation. I know what should be your intermediary task. Tomorrow, I suggest, that you think of populating the waters of this planet with beings that you know and in the following days, this world will be enchanted to become host to some other species known to you. In the future, other species will copy those which you have called, who are going to adapt and perpetuate themselves to the end of time in accordance with the divine laws. Now, I leave you Androgyna. Continue this work with the flowers and we'll see each other at dinner."

Amos went away with a light step and left the palace of knowledge to return to the command of the control pyramid of *Eïz*.

A short time later, the new friends of the world of Mara saw alarming lights appear between the ground and the sky. Threatening storms with thousands of lightning strokes furrowed the sky and a deluge of rain started falling. Amos commanded the satellite *Boz* to travel more rapidly in an orbit closer to the Marian surface to assist the winds and the tellurian currents to stabilize the climate. Harmony between the elements had to be established in order to create a livable atmosphere on the planet because Mara also needed to pass through an infancy in order to reach maturity.

Chapter VIII

The flight of the Luciferians from Mara and their extermination

At the precise moment when Beelzebub and his lieutenants disintegrated on contact with the higher astral light which swept Mara in its parabolic field of action, a group of beings consisting of about a dozen slaves, men and women together with some children and their Luciferian guards climbed up to the surface of the world from the caves where they had been forced to work. These were the royal family who had been taken from the Iona region at the time of the last infernal raid by the Luciferians. They were the sole survivors of that large island where thousands of people were massacred and given as food to dinosaurian monsters thirsty for blood.

On seeing all the burnt-up corpses spread over the ground all round them, they started to run frantically in all directions, then finally calmed down and come together. They set out to walk up to a hill where the ground was rocky and arid covered with shining debris and then getting nearer, they saw that the sharp rocks were precious stones and crystals. There were emeralds, amethysts, sapphires and rubies of enormous size. Right close by, one of the rotting monsters was being devoured by four Luciferian anthropoids who had thrown themselves upon the smoking meat. It was then that an unexpected thing happened: the earth under their feet cracked open and the marsh drained away as if it was siphoned with an infernal suction noise; the monsters were buried and very high in the sky, *Eïz* flew away, leaving around it a gaping hole.

A short time later, the King Eon and his wife Eona saw with pleasure that the hairs which had been starting to cover their bodies and which made them resemble the Luciferians, were beginning to disappear. "My wife, said the King, my skin is becoming again soft and sensitive like it was before. Could that be the new vibrations that our world is receiving is purifying it of the negativity left by the Luciferians?"

"I believe it my husband," she said, "my skin is also clear and see our children. One could say that they are more beautiful now."

"You know, I have bitterness and hate in my heart. I believe that I will never again be the King Eon like I was before."

"You remember our two Luciferian guards? They were children of our own people and after becoming prisoners, they were subjected to the yoke which filled them totally with evil influences, so that their bodies and their spirits changed. That was what began to affect us also. Something strange must have happened here. It looks as if all the abominable Luciferians have disappeared."

The King and his family started to walk towards another hill.

"Look," shouted the King, "there are trees here bearing fruits."

"Oh! Yes, splendid fruit," she said picking some. "It's so long since we ate such a thing. Since we were prisoners, they forced us to eat that horrible flesh."

"Look at our children's faces, they are still young and don't have the memory of good fruit. Here Soph, taste this apple."

"My spouse, a voice inside me is telling me that this place is now inhabited by other creatures. Perhaps those which planted the trees."

"Quite possibly," she said, "and if they eat fruit they must be different from the Luciferians. Could it be that they are not savage?"

"It would be lucky for us, we have just come out of slavery where we were forced to work in the depths of this mine underground. It would be a pity to be taken by other perverse entities just as bad."

"Yes you are right. They must be powerful to have destroyed the Luciferians and their monstrous creatures and, since they kill, they must be savage."

"They could mistake us for Luciferians since our bodies resemble theirs and we could be confused with them. How are we going to explain ourselves to them? Surely they won't speak our language."

"Let's be patient and wait, meanwhile, this fruit is delicious."

They returned eagerly, their arms full of fruit, over hills and valleys on the way to their camp of fortune. There was a big lake to cross which was a little deep. It was this lake and its water courses which formed a natural basin. In crossing it, they didn't doubt that at the other end, they could meet the best friends of the world of Mara, the brothers from space.

All of those who had stayed in the encampment, some women and children, welcomed them joyfully. They had been anxious to know what had happened to the Luciferians. They had been left alone when their guards rejoined Beelzebub's army. The children rushed upon the fruit which was brought to them. King Eon started to explain to them about the disappearance of the Luciferians and mentioned the coming of strangers who might not be trusted but who had made the trees grow and bear fruit and who are perhaps vegetarians. "How then, he pointed out, were they saved from the cataclysm?"

One woman said: "if they eat fruits, vegetables and no meat, perhaps they are peaceful!"

Another woman shouted: "We have to protect our children. If they killed the Luciferians, perhaps they are going to kill us too!"

At that very same moment, the ground shook and a wave of heat encircled them.

"Look at that!" cried a man in horror pointing upwards, a huge ball was climbing up to the sky.

Strong gusts of wind began accompanied by heavy squalls. Everyone was pinned to the ground, panting, petrified with fear and several of them fainted. The air was stifling, then an immense rainbow covered the planet from East to West. This was the moment when Amos in his central pyramid placed his satellites in magnetic formation to guide Mara into its new path.

Several days passed where stiflingly hot and humid days and freezing cold nights succeeded one another. Planet Mara lived through the same vicissitudes that Alma was to experience in the future. Cold, the master of contractions, made appear on the world a crust that broke up and formed into crevasses, rocks fused together which, after being cooled down caused erosion. Mara suffered. She nurtured in violent toils like as if in labor a surface which would support the life of hard-working and happy children, recognizing the efforts and sacrifices that this mother world offered them in filling them with blessings.

So, time passed. Amos, son of the gods, had taken Mara to a good haven, she felt more assured now that the satellite *Eïz* was at her side capturing all the vital currents from the spiral of cosmic energy. King Eon and his small family had decided to return to their own land, an island where they could plant the grains and seeds which they carried with them. That took them a march of six weeks over rocky terrain. The days and nights were now shorter; nature seemed to slow down its evolution; the minerals changed their state of being – slowing down their lives by increasing their period of radioactivity. The cold acted as a powerful brake, reducing rapid growth rates and the effects of heat on gases.

The perverted discarnate and restless spirits attacked every living being that possessed the light but whose faith was wavering. Those with strong spirits defended themselves against these attacks on their minds and rejected evil thoughts. Some of the terrifying animals had been able to resist the massive disintegrating force which was unleashed by Amos. The evil spirits were strongly occupied with reanimating these creatures and working hard in transforming their modified but still hideous forms also capable of adapting themselves to the newly created environment. Above all, it was in the domain of reptiles that the hostile forces had the most scope. Their thoughts were attaching themselves to the innumerable eggs floating with the currents of the rivers, penetrating the DNA of the mother-cells. There appeared among the aquatic and semi-aquatic beings serpents with the heads of dragons, winged salamanders and giant crawfish. In the seas thus formed were thrashing around gigantic octopuses the last vestiges of the monsters. Also the unclean spirits now hovering above the earth incarnated themselves in mammals having hooves, contrasting wildly with the birds of multicoloured plumage and the beauty of the butterflies created by Princess Androgyna.

After a considerable amount of traveling, this little handful of men and women together with their children did not recognize their world and its environment any more. "How," they asked themselves, "could it happen in such a short time that the climate, the animals and nature itself had changed so much."

"It is perhaps the other face of the world," said the King thoughtfully, "but why is it now so cold?"

"I think," said one man, "that we are on a mountain and that we climbed up it without knowing. See how there is no longer thick fog around us."

"We aren't breathing the same air any more. Before we found moving painful, we were always tired and now we have more energy."

"Far away, over there, I see a cave. We should be able to shelter in it from the rain and the fire in the sky."

"You are right, Barol," said the King. "Over there to the shelter where the fire from the sky will be easier to keep dry. Let's go."

At these words, a squall of deluging rain beat down on them and the little traveling band started to run with all the strength of their legs towards the cave. As soon as they made it, hailstones the size of oranges began to fall, falling over each other with a terrifying noise on to the ground which, having hardened, offered more resistance.

"It will be difficult to make fire now if we count on lightning to get it started," said the King.

"You are right. Of all these thousands of lightning strokes which furrowed the sky in every direction, none of them hit any dead wood."

A woman shouted for joy: "I found some dry wood in the forest, look here!"

"Well done woman," said her husband, as he prepared the wood.

He started rolling a stick making it rub against some bark. The kindlings ready to be thrown on were there, others prepared torches with grease mixed with pitch from trees. The women and children made a circle round him, preparing themselves for the sacred arrival of the birth of the fire.

"You know woman, it has been several years that we have lived as savages at the same level as the animals under the enslavement of these monsters. I find it hard to believe that this nightmare has ended. I still think about our brothers who, because they didn't participate in their orgies, were thrown as food for their monsters or were devoured by those cannibals."

"I think I can say that we are the only descendents and survivors of our planet on this world," said the King sadly.

"That's so," added another woman at his side, who had fierce eyes and thick hair, "we are only thirteen families with their small children."

"Hooray!" shouted the children suddenly, exulting; "the fire, the fire."

So it was, the destructive element par excellence burst into flame amongst the kindlings of wood. The little group assembled feverishly around the fire which was lighting up the cave and was growing as they watched. The children, excited, danced a joyous saraband.

A good amount of heat radiated from it and a light smoke made its way to the cave's roof. For them it represented the taking up of a formidable force put there for the use of men who could control and use it at will. The force had the power of heating, of expansion, consumption and extraordinary amalgamation, permitting also that man could evolve in the use of materials, thus enabling him to master the material universe.

In the days that followed, hunger stalked them. Animals of all kinds made their appearance round the cave and on the plain, animals which they had never seen previously, hairy and so small, which moved forward rapidly with bounds. A good number of these fed themselves on small cold-blooded reptiles which possessed hypnotic qualities which gave them of a slow and crawling nature. Amongst the men and women, there were those who had tasted the flesh of animals a fairly long time before and rejoiced enthusiastically to see the multiplying of the animals which they were used to thinking of as fit for killing and eating.

These people had muscles which were big and powerful, also with hair long and thick like the Luciferians with sharp and incisive teeth. Instead of being able to evolve towards spirituality, they started to devolve towards bestiality.

The thoughts of men in that time, thanks to the teaching of Amos, had great power over nature and transformation happened more quickly in the world of creation. Men also had at that time a great deal of power over the world of animals and there were also those who liked that and took advantage of it but only the king and queen stayed faithful to their beliefs. The principles with which they had been brought up were founded on their styles of living. They were not often in agreement with the almost savage actions of their contemporaries and they knew that the vestiges of Luciferian thought were still around. The Ionians were not able to purify themselves again. Some of them went back to the rituals of adoring certain animals. The demons liberated in the hyperphysical world threw themselves on living beings by all means available to them in the physical world. They made use of their influence on thoughts acting through the channels of the instinctive desires for survival in the world of flesh, and over the years they succeeded.

There exists an active principle working through pure faith, having latent effects to operate on all levels of the evolution of the spirit in time. The principle is universal love which reunites opposites in an unceasing desire of accomplishment.

"Our task is to awaken anew the spirit of love in our people," the Queen often used to say in the past.

"That is true," the King used to say. "They don't want to listen to reason. However, now they were no longer a small group, the problems had changed. The King and Queen wondered how to separate them from the taste for flesh. They decided to pray that they might receive some help. The law of nature requires that any degradation in evolution needs to be stopped by a reversal in consciousness."

"Yes," said the Queen, "and let us continue to nourish ourselves with fruits, plants and nuts."

Sad to say, these proposals and wise decisions reached the ears of the evil spirits who then decided to make life hard for the survivors. As the days went on, food became scarce and certain plants due to their toxicity caused sickness. The peoples' instincts were undependable due to problems in the past. These strategies worked so well that they felt forced to hunt animals. Their children were bought up carnivores and fresh meat, warm and pulsating had been eaten raw.

These newly arrived people whose destiny it was to plough the soil of Mara had now to prepare themselves for a task which had little appeal, that of survival. The former Ionians had difficulty in adapting themselves physically to the new life. With the passage of time and the changes in their surroundings and being under the constant pressure of the influence of malicious demons, nothing was saved for the royal family. Adaptation to the new environment became a major issue, the era of instinct took precedence over what remained of the Ionian intellect. The perverted spirits understood perfectly that the necessity of staying alive forced human beings to renounce during such a period the world of dreaming where thoughts could evolve. In such a situation, the human being descends into a savage state cut off from the poetic sweetness of love. A kind of hardness and rigidity of the rough and blood-hungry hunter appears where hunger is the master and desire is the guide.

Those spirits which are primitive and combative were progressively swallowing up men's thoughts and that was what the King had foreseen. If he had been younger, he could have fought valiantly against such trends because he possessed that love of his people for which he had been initiated into his role but that was no longer the case.

In a dream, he saw his daughter, princess Asi in the person of a priestess, dressed in a white shining robe and, in the morning, he admired for a long time his daughter resting half-asleep, covered by the skin of an animal, close to the fire at the end of the cave.

"That's the answer," he exclaimed, "she will become a great priestess and we will build a new temple to the sun. That will prevent our people from falling into degradation and debauchery." At least he hoped so, and he meant it well! But time would tell!

Now the satellite *Eïz* incorporated itself with the world of Mara. The intense vibrations which it gave out infused the veins and arteries of the world and went right into its nervous system nourishing its energy currents. The underground pathways precipitated liquid minerals and caused them to crystallize and increase their mass making mountains on the surface and under the seas. The satellites *Boz* and *Az* continued in space, concentrating their interception of energy on to *Eïz*, supplying the world with new solar and celestial energies causing it to become enriched as its plains and valleys flourished with life. Mara resembled a giant spinning top, pivoting on its central axis in 24 hour days, both receiving and giving life. Immense chains of mountains prevented the raging oceans from invading the delightful valleys which were the principal sources of sustenance for the future population, those billions of souls ready to incarnate.

Amos approached the central pyramid. As he ascended the large staircase, crystal clear like glass, he seemed thoughtful. "I believe that my work here is reaching its end and I see appearing in the future the spirit of sacrifice which requires my attention. It seems that I will have to leave aside for a time my purity of spirit in order to support a new involvement in the world of duality by being separated from my full divine nature."

A certain sadness entered his heart when he approached the obelisk of the sacred diamond. And there, in the position of the stars, his head raised up towards the glittering sphere, he remained for a long time in meditation. Suddenly, a soft and melodious voice became audible to his hearing. It was the voice of his father.

"Go ahead, Amos. You have reached a new path in your destiny. Here is what awaits you if you accept this bitter fate. Within a short period of time you will be attached to this world, a new leaf will turn in your book of life and your name will appear on the first page. Married in this world through a loving relationship from your remote past you will teach your son so that future generations will follow in your footsteps and create a perfect evolutionary cycle in order to enter, through you, into the Lord's supreme grace. As you know, the laws are in place and God will not change a single iota, except in certain cases where they can be softened. His justice and mercy are combined with His love for you and you have a vast destiny. Often, it will appear in the form of an avatar to prepare and sweeten your path. You know the law of love and your responsibility in the matter is known also.

However, you will be under the yoke and in due time the enjoyment of good times will give place to the sorrow of bad times up to the end of your mission and the return of your descendents to God our Creator. You will always find me close to Him and I am always at your service."

The voice of his father fell silent and then came a melodious and celestial music. Amos, dumbfounded, crouched on the ground and stretched himself out on his back, his arms extended making the form of a cross.

"I have chosen, Lord, he said, I am your humble servant, I am aware that I must enter this phase of existence to prove my love for you and our universe so as to be able to serve your higher purposes. May your will prevail and may my existence forever be linked to it."

A sudden flash of light darted down from heaven onto Amos, radiating over all of his body resounding like thunder as it penetrated every part of him. The voice said:

"You are the essence of My thought and My eternal love for you, Amos. Your will is my will, even when it is forgotten or should you take the opposite course and act against my will. I accompany you and I will be always at your side. I am in front of you, at the side and behind you, and that is how it will be up to the time of your return to me."

In a sublime moment, the whole of his future was shown to him. So, Amos who was composed of a myriad of souls and spirits, had to return to the low-level existence of the material universe in order to bring back through knowledge other myriads of souls imprisoned in the darkness of time.

Tears of joy now flooded his cheeks. He felt coming into him a Love so great as to be beyond description. It was so sudden and so great that he experienced for a minute the vast eternal love which God has for the universe. This feeling of unity became all at once human, then nothing, and he felt himself separated, expelled, inert and abandoned. He had just received, inevitably, his ego, his double, which invaded his whole being. He woke up anew into his prison of flesh. In getting up, he realized that his limbs had become heavy; he had hereafter become a mortal, except that his vision of the Creator remained immortal and the Lord had left him some gifts. He knew himself to be a mortal who was immortal and the power of the sun was still with him. God had not taken everything from him. All his being seemed to have become, in totality, a dream and forgetfulness overcame him little by little. He fell into a deep sleep and a vision started. He saw himself returning to his birthplace where his father awaited him smiling in a welcome attitude and what a surprise it was to see awaiting him at his father's side a young girl of pale complexion and straight hair.

"We were waiting for you, he said, to celebrate your marriage. It is an important ceremony for all humanity and I received an order to solemnize it on Andromeda. The whole galaxy is going to benefit from this action. In your name, a pact of friendship is going to re-establish the birth of humanity on this world, this blessing is happening by the will of our Lord. Don't forget my son that you are androgynous and in order to live on this world your female part must separate and partly leave you. She will await you close to me on Andromeda. After this ceremony, you will feel yourself disjointed by the break-up and your physical body, henceforth a human one, will have to endure for a time two sexes, except that the erectile masculine principle will alone be active and dominant. That will change your character and will be able to assist you in the future to become a man. Life on the world of Mara in the times to come

will be composed only of beings having opposite sexes, such as the couples that you brought with you and those which you are going to meet here. The directive and creative intelligence in the etheric plane here is given over principally to the male sex and not like in your dwelling place where each one of us possesses the two dominant principles in a harmonious state within the individual making for you and your brothers, at the same time both a father and a mother. During your next active life, you will be subject to low-level tasks where you will have to work with the sweat of your brow. These tasks will be perilous because your whole life will depend on your actions. You are, however, a mortal in the physical universe and you will have to protect your chosen wife and your children. This separation is going to cause in you the birth of passions and instincts where you will constantly find in each woman your female principle Amora and that will be the case even among your descendents. She will always be waiting patiently for you here up to the end of your cycles of service. One day on earth is nothing more than one year in Andromeda. What will be necessary for you and thus be your obligation to exist will be to promote the growth of several bodies which will be following you through many terrestrial incarnations right up to the final reintegration in the same entity as Amos and Amora. Then you will be newly enriched by all the personalities which will be formed and which you will possess in yourself in the name of the Creator and you will be the god of the world you will have created."

The father of Amos thus repeated his speech to his son to all the 54 000 solar years. In times of great changes he warned his son with these words:

"Each time a planet is juxtaposed in its life-supporting ellipse for a physical life in the plane of duality, you will have to reincarnate to guide the new humanity in its earthly adventure, then you will return back here to our celestial Andromeda. You will be the Adam of the earthly paradise and will instruct human beings imprisoned in their bodies how to return to their celestial paradise. As you know, time spent on earth is only an illusion which the soul must experience but without remaining attached. Maya (the material world of illusion) will always be present in the darkness of time and over centuries of centuries.

The solar system is unique in the universe of universes, it is the only place that man can take on the human form and you are the ideal guide. The human family has become your family; you are its descendent just as they have become your descendents. That is how the wheel of destiny turns. Also, half of your spirit will be always on Andromeda; you will return to us between each episode of mortality. You will stay in contact with me by thoughts only or by the channel of the sacred pyramid and the holy lingam of life. You are going to forget starting from now that you have a family over here and you will only be able to ask for things strictly necessary in your earthly existence from the summit of the three control pyramids which are going to fall apart with the passage of time. Eiz will remain attached to Mara and it will be a means of control and communication if such becomes necessary between us and the Earth. You will have to guard the sacred lingam as something very precious between each existence both in the present time and in the future. In any case, infant humanity of whom you are the guide will not be abandoned. The Lord will not permit it. Only the means of communication could differ with time and in space who is our mother. Now my son, let us get ready. The marriage ceremony with Princess Androgyna must commence, because in a short time you will wake up on Mara and time passes more quickly on that planet."

Then, everyone together moved towards the entrance of an immense temple of great beauty dedicated to the eternal God of light. There, everything was filled with light, it had the form of a dodecahedron which would be copied thousands of years later at Muria, in the earthly country of Lemuria on planet Alma when Amos would reincarnate as Adamos.

As soon as the little group entered, a dazzling light illuminated its interior and increased tenfold on the outside. A sweet music with a celestial rhythm filled the air. The divine OM chanted by a choir of women's voices was followed, growing louder, by a choir of men's voices. Forty-seven inhabitants of Andromeda were present, making a total of forty-nine with Amos and his father, each representing several billions of souls living elsewhere in the galaxy. Several of them were already involved with missions in different regions of the universe. At the centre of the building where all the light converged were Amos, Androgyna, the king of the city of Amora and Amos's father. They all placed themselves in a perfect circle while the Andromedians also seated themselves in a circle around them, intoning a mystic chant resembling a sanskrit mantra. The great King approached the crystal altar where sparkled a golden sword with a diamond hilt sticking into the centre of the altar in the form of a cross. He easily removed it from the altar and raising it above his head, twirled it three times in a circle and then in a cross while speaking in an unknown language. Androgyna was awestruck to see with what ease the king of Amora handled that sword which looked to her as if it weighed a ton. Then he made a complete circle around them in the course of proclaiming them united. He proceeded in the same manner towards the pale young woman with the golden hair who had followed them. Androgyna felt at the same moment that an indescribable force enveloped her. For an instant she remained frozen for what seemed like an eternity, believing that her life had been ended and that an electrical current was passing completely through her from head to toe. All at once, she saw the great King move towards Amos and place the blade of the sword on the middle of his head. There was a flash of light and a cry tore through the monotonous chant of the group. At the same moment, an identical double of Amos detached itself from him. This double had a feminine appearance.

"Amora," announced the great King, "remain with us, wait in anticipation for the return of Amos."

At these words, the double of Amos detached itself with jerky movements and left the circle to incorporate itself into Amos's father. At that precise moment, Amos got up from the ground at the foot of the altar where he had fallen asleep and felt the soft hand of the Saturian lady caressing his hair.

"Prince Amos, said Androgyna in an anxious voice, I came to look for you, I just woke up with a start from a strange dream about you. Somebody married you in a great ceremony. I got up to find you stretched out lifeless at the foot of this altar. What happened to you?"

"Do you remember your dream, Androgyna?" said Amos standing up.

"Yes, I dreamt that I was in a fabulous city populated with men, only men. They were men and women in one person, I even dreamt of being married to you in a strange manner, very different than on Satur. It's odd, because you aren't the type of man to marry someone."

"What are you saying Androgyna?" exclaimed Amos in a surprise. "What kind of image do you have of me?"

"It is that I think, or rather that I sense, that you are so strange with all the superhuman powers you possess, you appear to me like a God and, being like that, you couldn't lower yourself to love a simple mortal such as me."

"You are quite right, Androgyna, only the demigods as you call them, are entrusted to fulfill missions, which make them take on life in different forms, more spiritual, purer, and devoid of sexuality. It is thus that lowering themselves, as you say, no longer fits in the same mold. The reasons exist which are known only to God in his creation. You have placed me so high in your estimation that you can only identify me with difficulty but that needs to change now that I am completely at your level."

"You mean," she said perplexed shaking her long ebony-colored hair, "that you desire me but you can love me in spite of your rank?"

"Yes, that is so but the love that you know arises from your sensual pleasure and is different from what I have learnt to understand. In that, I am different from you. Do you see that I cannot belong to you because my conception of existence is different from yours. If I become an object coveted by your desire, my love for you will only be the posthumous exchange of the effects of divine will, permitting me to love you as you are in the present and not what you represent but rather that which you will become."

She approached him, with an air of anger.

"Does that mean," she said, "that you can neither embrace me nor caress me and that you have no feelings for me?"

"It's a bit like that, because my sexual organs are not yet formed. It's a type of platonic love, which is not well interpreted, because that form of love doesn't lead the lover to love in a masochistic or sadistic way. Such would be the case under the bestial influence. It leaves a certain liberty to be desired."

"What you are saying is also bestial; not to show any attachment towards the one which one loves or not to be overcome by love, it's a thing filled with egotism or again, it's a joining of pride with egotism."

"Still, Androgyna, it will depend on what level and in what sense or from which angle one interprets love. It's difficult to judge the emotion which creates love between lovers. The morality of it is often badly interpreted and does only satisfy those who depend on it. Sexual love differs from platonic love by the fact that it blends the bodily sensations in the interplay going from the simplest touches up to orgasm. This form of loving can join lovers who do not know each other nor do they have a lasting relationship. In the other case, the lovers can love each other without sexual desire."

"Sexuality in all its forms can also overcome with love and desire lovers who are learning to know each other and deepen their love," she added.

"Yes, you are right; however it is necessary that there be balance in their interplay. That one who practices by necessity chastity, without love, wants everyone around him to practice it also and has no tolerance towards those who do not follow the same course. He ends up judging them as sinners."

"How can one make love without being in love?" she said with tears in her eyes. "I love you, without looking for all sorts of complicated explanations about loving. Don't you have a simple approach to life?"

"Yes, yes, Androgyna, and it is you who will bring it to me in the future. Do you see that it cannot be said that attachments do not exist in the type of love that I am telling you about, but it isn't of the same nature which affects physical existence. It is more spiritual in its essence, which makes it indestructible, unchanging and powerful. Now listen to me. Your dream is a reality, we have been united this very night on Andromeda by a worldly union and I owe you an explanation at the same time I allow you to share one of my secrets! Come, give me your hand, we are going to walk together to the palace. Then, behold! This night while you were sleeping, your body's etheric double left it and we brought you to Andromeda, the solar planet of our galaxy, to the city called Sandoma and the guides, my brothers, took you to my Father in front of a magnificent temple with white shining walls. Do you remember a little of it?"

"Yes it is so, I remember. Then it was true. I didn't just experience a dream."

"No, it wasn't just a dream. It was completely real. At the time of our marriage ceremony, my Father took away from me all my rights of survival and the malleable freedom which my body possessed so that I would be able to live with you. In this way, I have become mortal and attached to my physical body as you are."

"So, as you say," she interrupted, "you have shed your high spiritual status because of your love for me. Do you really love me that much?"

"Yes, very much but doesn't your love represent the whole of humanity? The universe is in you, because you are part of it. I didn't shed my spiritual status for pleasure. I simply changed my plan of existence in order to serve God's eternal universe. I have entered the realm of the existence of desire where the balance between good and evil must be maintained and suffering is the guide."

"I am trying to understand you, prince Amos, but my dearest desire is to be loved for my own sake, it is a deep feeling, also my second desire is to share my life uniquely with you."

"What you are feeling Androgyna, is part of an egocentric force which was ingrained in you from your birth and will only leave you when you have become the mother to your firstborn. You are thinking at the instinctual level of human creation, which is quite normal. You are guided by the loving instinct which will transform itself into the maternal instinct. I represent in you the symbol of love for the one who is going to be born and with whom you are going to share your life. To become what I have now become in this world, I had to shed from my being the potential arising from some thousands of existences lived in different places in our galaxy. I had become man and woman united in the harmony of just one entity. That enormous potential is now incorporated in my double Amora that is my soul who remains on Andromeda up to the end of my present commitment and that will be perpetuated in our human species and one day will be explained by a mystic being who will be called Adam Kadmon, one who is the macrocosm of the universal divinity."

"Oh Amos, how overwhelmed I am by everything you are telling me. I was never imagining such strange things could exist in life. It was all so simple before, we were only women who lived like amazons, the few men who lived with us were only kept alive for the purpose of reproducing our species. Like on Andromeda you were only men who became androgynous, we only lived amongst women but now I see how vain we have become to live only subject to the dictates of instinct."

"The call of instinct. Ah! Yes! That follows its course during the cycle leading towards the evolution of the spirit. The Luciferian spirits have a certain control over it. In our future, we will have to be vigilant because we will be put to the test. We will have to learn to hold on to each other from one incarnation to the next. That will strengthen our love and help us to bring up our children. It is all very important for human evolution on this planet."

"I'll always stay vigilant by your side to keep our love," she said going within his arms.

"We will see changes on Mara and one day we will have to leave it because wars and cataclysms will arise. I was made to see all the images of the future. We will have to reincarnate many times forgetting our past, except at the crucial moment when the need arises for us to move to another planet."

"I am not afraid Amos, because you are with me."

"Yes, I know, but I am not alone, God is with us! And I have known you for a long time!"

At these final words from the two embracing lovers and their hopes, the images faded and the image of Evena appeared smiling broadly to all the spectators of planet Earth and the story had ended! Then she said: "You have just lived through the transformation of the ancestor of my husband Adamos in one of his past lives and that of his wife Androgyna. The past repeats itself often in similar circumstances from one life to another. All this allows you to understand the present time and the future which depends on it."

Then the image of Evena disappeared from the screens on Earth and everyone on Earth felt as if they were waking from a dream, a kind of daydream. The American president seemed satisfied with Evena's reply but some anthropologists and historians who were present were not in agreement. There seemed to be the discrepancies between the number of years which had passed and which did not correspond with their calculations based on radio carbon dating. The astronomers, for their part, did not accept the idea that a solar system in the Andromeda galaxy was involved in the matter of evolution on the planets Mars and Earth. The problem of confusion amongst the Earth's inhabitants was not new. At the time of Galileo, it was firmly believed that the Earth was flat, so nothing could be done at the time to solve these disagreements. At the present time, the leaders in government and investment are considering the possibility of going to Mars to find things which are not present on Earth. If there is no oil or uranium, there will perhaps be the remains of an ancient past which attract those men who are curious to learn about its origins.

Chapter IX

Meeting with humanoids on Alma

Adamos appeared on the screen and approaching Evena said: "Evena, you talked about our remote past but it must be understood that it is only a tiny fraction of our life. Now, it is important that we continue our story on Alma, our whole destiny is based on the expansion of our souls. Those who imagine that we have only one life are far from the truth. In fact, they are at the bottom of the heap and if they live in that belief, they are thus prisoners of their own great ignorance. Before leaving, Professor Lemoria, our solar avatar, founded our refuge, this magnificent palace where we are living. He showed us the importance of the expansion of our souls through knowledge of the spirit, to know how to live in the material world without being ensnared by it. Living a good life does not mean living as if in a monastery, but simply to live with modesty, to live off the fruits of the earth but remaining vegetarian, which is to say not to live off the flesh of animals."

"Because of negative karma which links us to the animal kingdom," added Evena.

"And also from the fact that this negative karma permits the beings of the shadow, the Luciferians, to control our thoughts until the day comes when we are at their mercy," said Adamos to make things clear.

"Yes, because they infiltrate our blood by humors originating from animal flesh particularly those of warm blood in order to influence us and take a directive role over our emotions."

"So the only means of putting things right is by spiritual knowledge obtained through educating our spirits. In the future, the human race is going to develop great knowledge of technology but if they lose the knowledge of their soul and spirit, they will use that technology to kill each other. The Luciferian agents, masters of their ego, know a thousand different ways to infiltrate themselves into their blood and their thoughts."

"We can overcome the demon spirits in ourselves and those surrounding us by the power of the will and by living in the truth."

"That's exactly it. I am now going to make you part of a program that Lemoria left us before his departure. In using the great map which he drew of Alma Gaya, he drew the great chain of mountains where we are towards the west and named the great belt of land, a continent connecting America to Asia, by giving it the name of his spouse Lemuria. He also named the place where we are now Muria." He then said, facing east: *"The great belt of land that we see bounded on the North and South by the two seas will be called Atlantis and will be managed by Atalanta, and as for you Adamos, you will take it upon yourself to organize Lemuria. Right at the end of this continent, there is another large one an even bigger land, extending to the South and we will call it Afrika because it is he who will be in charge of it. So also, the land which touches the extreme West of Lemuria will be taken by Zanga and his clan. You will be going from one summit to the other of the highest mountains at the four corners of Alma because in a short time, deluges of rain will beat down on the plains and flood them. There will be different kinds of catastrophes. Alma will pass through the same events that Mara lived through and that other planets experienced. It's all part of the changes and the cycles of life. Men have to pass through it as well, they also must experience life in the material universe even though it is an illusion. I will always be at your side. In all your difficulties, call upon us in your prayers. We are the Father and Mother of our creation and we remain in your hearts."*

The words of Lemoria were forever engraved in the hearts of each one of them. The teaching that he gave them was necessary consolation for their future and that of their children such as knowing that the world of matter is but a copy of the invisible world of the spirit. God divides himself in three: Shram the creator who himself gave birth to Shnu, who lives within his creation and maintains life in all its elements, finally giving birth to Shva who transforms his creation by creating the time and space which destroy it. One can also understand this truth in other terms: God divided himself in time as being the Father, who, thanks to the divine spirit became the Mother, who in turn gave him a Son, and continued his existence by self-perpetuation in all possible forms. Thus unity, filled with the divine, became diversity multiplying itself in complexity, then once created in space-time, form is destined for transformation and destruction. So man, caught in the vice of the material world, finds himself submerged by all his desires and by continuing to create things out of matter, loses little by little the sense of divinity.

At the beginning of time, with one foot in the astral plane and the other grounded in the material world, he still kept the consciousness of his divinity. However by the misuse of his limitations and, between other things, the distancing with time of his spirit from his heavenly parents and also with the dissipation of his divine consciousness, he materialized all his thoughts and separated himself from his divine substance. This great truth must be safeguarded so that the nature of man can be liberated and returned to its initial divine state.

Adamos formed the grand council. Then, with the help of Evena, he started to devise a plan of action to fly in the direction of the land of Lemuria.

"Over there, he said, are existing humanoid beings living in groups. Our task is to bring them our help. Evena who can see things distant in space and time, has seen images of disasters which are threatening them."

"It's true," said Evena, "their very lives are in danger. The same thing which happened in the past on Mara is going on here. Negative entities such as the dark Luciferians are going to attack them in a short time in order to make them into slaves."

"We shall embark in our astronef. I need ten men from among you. Evena who will stay here will keep in contact with me. All those who stay with her will get our news."

Adamos, with his small band of volunteers, departed in the *Gyrosphere* in a westerly direction. The craft flew silently over the mountains like a huge balloon in the daylight hours. It had to be done fairly quickly because in a few days the night-time would approach and last for seven days. Each of them was curious to know the humanoids and was imagining them in their own particular way.

On Alma it is the state of dualism which is dominant. The strong eat the weak, something which causes continual conflicts between created beings and darkens their existence. In the ancient past, there was an era when the great division appeared amongst men on the planet Lucifer. This gave rise to degeneration amongst the sons and daughters of the light, to those who succumbed to their ego in becoming sons and daughters of darkness, God in his infinite goodness said: "My children, sons and daughters of my light, by your will, by your wisdom, by your desire to serve me, by your pure individuality, by your eternal fire, by your beauty of being, you have become my angels. You can serve all humanity which is to come right up to the end of the ages which encompass a complete revolution of the wheel of existence. In this wheel of light, each of you represents the primordial qualities of life which he has chosen. You have become by your life experience, guides who work in the invisible. You are the extension of my right arm in my universal creation. It shall be as I have spoken."

Then he finished by saying: "You have become as I AM: Eternal."

So it is thus the will of God passed like an electrical current of infinite love amongst all those who experienced life in the human form at the beginning of the ages of time. It was because they kept their desire to serve God and offer Him prayers becoming the "Abel" of peace. God made of them angels and archangels, placing them on all the higher steps leading to divinity. The others, because they chose in the depth of their beings the left-hand path and the sublimation of their ego in causing evil, continued their lives under the influence of the black sun and maintained a spirit of ill will in a lower state of consciousness on all planes of existence. The lower astral became their sphere of activity. They were surrounded by all those amongst the human race whom they diverted from the good path into forms of degenerate civilized behavior that they were able to introduce into the human personality such things as greed, alcoholism, drug addiction, criminality and wickedness. Remaining trapped in materialism, the love of God lived on in them in its form of negative Maya, the domain of the moon and illusion. The world of duality became one of balance between good and evil. God gave freewill to man by the choice that he made between opposites. The new world after Lucifer became the world of duality. Lucifer before his extinction had become the planet Yin and Yang where the white and black were balanced and man was caught in the middle of this conflict. It had also become the means of knowing God in all His greatness.

The humanoids in their first phase of development, did not receive the spirit in their mental bodies because they were still in an embryonic state. It takes several evolutionary cycles of thought to reach that level of consciousness. However, such an awakening which is more or less slow can be speeded up by the presence of more advanced beings serving as guides. Humanoids are humans in their first phase of mutation going from the animal to the human, as from the astral to the physical plane.

"We are in sight of a settlement of humanoids down that slope," said Adamos pointing to a hill.

So it was, they were now flying over a large river and huts shaped like pagodas formed a small village. The people seemed frightened because they were making gestures such as covering their heads. They were scared and ran in all directions. This led the Marians to believe that they had already been attacked previously by other entities coming from the sky.

"It won't be easy to get near them," added Adamos.

They prepared to descend towards a forest glade on the hill. As soon as they arrived, each of them prepared to go out, but two of them stayed as guards on the *Gyrosphere*. Because it wasn't known what kind of welcome lay in wait, everyone was armed and ready for defense.

On approaching the village, Adamos decided to call a halt to see if the humanoids would come towards them. After an hour of resting and lighting a fire, they saw some hairy beings coming towards them and showing interest. Demonstrating patience, Adamos and his companions made it appear that they were eating something. This seemed to give the others confidence and, after a moment, the largest of them dared to approach. This creature started making bizarre gestures and speaking with a guttural sounding language. Adamos gave him a sign that he should come nearer and offered him a fruit. The humanoid took, with suspicion, the apple from Mara. Because the fruit was unknown to him, he made gestures to find out if it could be eaten. Adamos, smiling, cut the fruit into several pieces and ate one while offering them to the others near him. The humanoid took the piece and seemed reassured as he ate it. The other ones hidden behind the trees became more courageous and moved forward towards them. There were at least forty of them. The one who had advanced first was the biggest; overall, he measured eight feet in height and had a good stature, large feet and long arms. His face was that of an anthropoid. Children came with them as well as some old ones. They were all keen to start communication. The only means that could be used at that moment was telepathy and Adamos had this ability. He started to make gestures at the same time as he sent mental images to the one who seemed to be chief of the tribe. The latter understood the messages and responded in the same way. He invited the group to descend to their village and there, they set themselves in a circle at the middle of which were placed leaves and dry branches. Zanga with his lighter set it alight. Ankor who had brought his voice recorder made it play the music of the spheres which impressed a great calm on the surroundings. The humanoids were silent, their eyes wide open like those seen in the story of *"the Planet of the Apes"*, they didn't show any sign of aggressiveness. One old one came up to Adamos, who must have been the oldest in the village. His life experience and several incarnations lit up his eyes with intelligence. He tried to make himself understood with guttural sounds but he could not form mental images.

"Ankor," said Adamos, "you have brought along with you five resonators. Put them on the heads of three important humanoid males and choose two of their spouses."

Ankor placed the equipment on each of them, the centre of it on the forehead. An important conversation followed. The images which were now formed in the spirits of the tested humanoids created at the same time new nerve circuits in their brains. For several planetary hours, they were communicating in this manner. Adamos spoke to them: "My name is Adamos, I am the leader of this expedition on your world and we don't mean you any harm. We have come to defend you from your enemies. We know that you are going to be attacked and enslaved. We have come to bring order and to help you."

The large humanoid replied: "My name is Onuman, here are my family and my forebear. Our tribes have been attacked and made to suffer. It is our brothers become suddenly wicked who have broken up our families. We live simply. We had to defend ourselves against monstrous animals which share the world with us. We live on plants and their fruit. When our brothers were separated from us on becoming eaters of the flesh of animals, we had to defend ourselves from their attacks."

The old one spoke with dignity: "I am a forebear of Onuman. We wish neither for war nor discord. They forced these things on us and those who fell into their hands and have become their slaves must work deep down in caves to make weapons of war or other things of which we know nothing. They are directed by demons of a ferocious nature who have neither pity nor heart. They copulate forcibly with our women and their children become monsters."

Adamos replied: "We are aware of these things which are happening to you. We know that in this region there are still several villages and tribes who are going to be attacked. I want you to warn them very quickly that you are having a meeting here.

Communicate with them using your drums made from tree trunks, that is very important."

The humanoids of the tribe of Ondura did what Adamos had advised and the forest resounded with the varied sounds of their drums. These beings all had a type of intelligence which varied widely; those most intelligent took the lead and the others reverently followed them. They didn't wear any clothes and their bodies were hairy like those of the anthropoids. The male was head of the family and was obliged to protect it. As the spokesman had said, those families which had separated themselves from the clan had succumbed to degenerate activities in becoming carnivores. They became possessed by the evil spirits. Adamos and his companions recognized the Luciferian influence already at work on Alma. The Luciferian entities instilled themselves into those who were already at their mercy and used them as gaolers for their captives and for copulating with the women. These demons made to be reborn on earth those destructive souls coming from the lower astral. In this manner, there was a continual repetition of the contamination of good by evil in the evolution of human beings.

These humanoids were already spread out over the four regions of Alma in small groups and the mission of the Marians was to meet them so as to help them overcome the difficulties of their life in the physical plane and also in the plane of morality.

For hours, the drums sounded through the valleys and the forests. It was evident that the Luciferians were also alerted. However, since they didn't know the plans of Adamos nor his power, they could only laugh sardonically and maintain their own plan of attack.

It was now a case of setting a trap. Adamos had to devise a plan of defense. It was inconvenient that a fair number of the humanoids were under the yoke of the Luciferians and had gradually become wicked themselves. These were dispersed around the villages and were acting as spies. Adamos made use of them and with his power of suggestion acting at a distance sent them messages by thought transmission. Thus, he made them believe that their group was going to gather in caves on a hill above the first village, while in reality the group would simply return to the *Gyrosphere* because, from there, they could, thanks to their equipment, have perfect control over their assailants and it would be the inhabitants of the village only who had taken refuge in the caves. The Luciferians and their followers mingled with the villagers who were on the way to the great meeting. They were armed with machete type arms of all kinds: whips made with chains with spiked balls at the ends; they also had a sort of gun with a lance-pike which could pierce through a body from a distance of twenty feet. Because they knew how to forge iron, their triangular throwing knife was particularly dangerous. They had trained the humanoids to make war, an art in which they were experts. They had also trained dinosaurs for this task just as they had already done on Mara thousands of years before. They mounted them and directed them like battle chargers. Adamos, who was surveying the comings and goings of all these entities in the crystal sphere, said suddenly to Atalanta: "Hey Atalanta, take five men from your clan together with rapid radiation weapons and mingle with the humanoids in the cave. When the enemy approaches, they will want to speak to you before destroying you. Not knowing that we are hidden away from you, they will make you prisoners and thus lay themselves open, it is then that we will get involved. Don't use your weapons before I tell you, that's important."

"Yes Adamos, but when they capture us they'll disarm us."

"You'll have to hide your weapons because you are going to need them."

"If they tie our hands, they'll search us."

"Hide your weapons in your boots, I'm going to magnetize them before you leave. Their thoughts will be diverted from your boots."

"Very well Adamos, we'll make our preparations," said Atalanta making signs to his men.

The people of the village had all been warned about everything which was going to happen and they were afraid. They knew about the deceitfulness and the savagery of the Luciferians and even that of their own people once they were under the latter's control. Nobody was keen to fight but neither did they wish to be enslaved. They all had to make a decision on the matter.

"How are we going to fight against these demons? Their numbers are large and we have no weapons," they said to Atalanta.

"Certainly, you have your thoughts and your life to defend. Use your tools, stones, anything which comes into your hands and we will be right behind you to defend you. Above all, don't be afraid because fear paralyses all your actions and decisions. Tell everyone that."

"But we are not warriors."

"You are not warriors but you have intelligence and strength. At a time like this, you have your family to defend. You don't want to see them suffer at the hands of the demons and you have also your own life to save. You will all have to fight up to the limit of your strength and you must win this war because all your descendents depend on it. You haven't any choice and now get organized to receive the other tribes. You have spies amongst you and these must be arrested. When you arrest them, bring them to me so that I can deal with them."

Onuman bowed before Atalanta saying: "We will use all the force necessary and overcome the enemy."

"Onuman, have you any animals available for use in the war?"

"Yes, we have some dinosaurs which work for us and also buffaloes."

"It's good to have them. Make them dig a large trench around the village five feet deep. Fill it with straw, dead leaves and branches. In the middle set pikes of different sizes and cover everything with twigs."

While the villagers busied themselves with organizing their defenses, hundreds of kilometers away, the army of the Luciferians was advancing over mountains, jungles, valleys and swamps. A third of the army was mounted on dinosaurs carrying pikes and the rest marched to the beat of drums. They had placed the humanoids in the front. They came from their home in the iron mines and were intent on getting other slaves from among the humanoids and destroying those newly arrived.

Molox, their chief had had wind of their visit but his memory of the past had been diminished by a long stay in the astral hell and in his new incarnation, a thick cloud enveloped his consciousness. That is how heaven wished it. Now that his scouts were telling him that those he wished to conquer were trembling with fear, he was laughing contentedly, it all seemed so easy for him. Didn't he already have control over half the humanoids and as for the strangers who were hardly more than ten counted little for him. However, he had heard that they were traveling in a big flying machine and his masters in the astral had warned him of imminent danger. They had stated that he must fight and destroy them. That was why he had brought along with his army about ten red buffalos from hell and about ten flying dragons ready to destroy everything.

With a contented grin, he went forward with victory in his mind. About ten slaves transported him in his bamboo palanquin. His dreams were full of images of torture and suffering that he wished to inflict and of vengeance on his enemies. The spirit of Beelzebub in Molox was filled with negativity which he had to express, and that he had to revive, because in the remote past even when he also was human, he had chosen the left-hand path in living from one sensual pleasure to another and by the desire to take from others everything they had. He became a criminal, had no restraint and had become Cain. His conscience totally buried, he only listened to the voices of hatred because the stranglehold of the black sun had absorbed him. Like the others, he could have become an angel of light, but he had chosen to become a dark angel and now, again, he had a mission to block the evolution of the humanoids.

Chapter X

The battle of Kurukula

Now the town of Kurukula was in the throes of the fighting since seven villages had united and joined together. There were more than three thousand of them. Onuman placed his soldiers in different places so as to stop the shock wave of the Luciferians that they could hear coming from far off because to each series of drumbeats, they were responding by beating their spears. That was an intimidating ploy specially for inducing fear into their enemies. However, this time, they did not know with whom they were dealing. Molox, in this incarnation on the world of Alma, did not remember Lord Amos who defeated him on Mara thousands of years before, except at the last minute, when his memory was restored.

If Beelzebub had been at his side, he could have warned him, but that was not the case because the Lords of the brotherhood of light had not permitted it. It was necessary that the influences of evil be kept down for some generations to come, thus allowing a good start for human evolution.

Molox now deployed his army. He stood up to his full height and beat his breast which resonated in a muffled fashion and the drums beat rousingly. Sneakily, he advanced on the village but from behind. He had the trained scouts creep into it to take the inhabitants by surprise. These attacked quickly and took prisoners of Atalanta and his companions. Atalanta had come to set fire to the branches in the trench; something which made the shock troops of Molox recoil in fright. Atalanta was now in front of Molox the terrible.

"Who are you?" shouted Molox disdainfully.

"My name is Atalanta and I have come to protect these villages."

"You've got a nerve. Who do you take me for? Tie them around this fire. We'll grill them like sausages." Then he started imagining his pleasure. "As if you wanted to frighten me," and he started to laugh.

"Molox," shouted Atalanta, "I am giving you the order to go away and leave these people in peace."

Molox approached Atalanta with his sabre which he had made white hot.

"Atalanta," he said, "I'm going to make you suffer. You will be the first to burn in front of this fire, and he smiled while waving his sabre before Atalanta's eyes, however, the latter had taken out his weapon and he fired it at the navel of Molox who felt the fire entering his body. He gave a roar of pain and set off running across the fire. He slipped and felt into the trench then he emerged with his hair ablaze and shouted to his demons to attack."

Unfortunately, the humanoids were terrorized and did not move. The demons pointed their lances at Atalanta and his men but it was already too late. Each of them had his weapon in his hand and they were all blasted.

Molox had fled and had now returned to his general headquarters behind his army. From there, he gave his winged dragons the order to attack but Adamos had already called Sator to the rescue and a fierce fight started up in the sky. One of the dragons fell at the feet of Molox his eyes and head all bloody. "Help me Molox," it begged. Molox disdainfully cut off its head. He then ordered his fire-buffaloes to attack and the Luciferians lined up behind them seated on their dinosaurs. Several humanoids were crushed and struck down. Atalanta and his men tried to resist these monsters but their weapons lacked sufficient power. Then the voice of Adamos rang out forcefully. He faced squarely the chief of the Moloxians: "Go back to where you came from. You are not big enough to destroy us. I am warning you to stop this battle."

"Who are you?" shouted Molox.

"I have known you for thousands of years, Molox. You aren't going to win this battle," and he directed his negative green ray at the buffaloes which caught fire and went up in smoke together with the dinosaurs behind them.

"I know you also, I remember you," shouted Molox who had already beheaded several humanoids. He wanted to throw himself, his sword raised, upon Adamos when Sator, with a beat of his wing, lifted him into the air using his powerful claws. Molox struck him with his sword and cut off one of his feet at which point Adamos ordered Sator to let him drop and Molox then fell heavily on to his army impaling himself on five of the pikes which his men were holding straight up in the air.

"Molox," ordered Adamos, "you are going to return to hell for fourteen ages. Your work here is finished." Molox, stretched out on the ground, his body pierced through, bathing in his own blood, looked at Adamos, horrified.

"How can you command me? You aren't God," he said bitterly.

"No Molox, right now I am His representative. It is in His name that I speak to you and you have just, finally, spoken His name. That will count in your favor when you are reborn. In His name, I sent you his light. Tell your soldiers to return to hell. Alma is closed off from you at this time."

With a huge effort, Molox got up and made a sign to his men, then he himself disintegrated at the same time as they did and silence fell. The humanoids who had survived the carnage and who had obeyed Molox's orders threw themselves at the feet of Adamos crying out with fear and distress. The ground was littered with the corpses of animals. It was a smoking graveyard of humanoids and decomposing flesh.

"You have obeyed the orders of the demons, you will have to pay debts in the future. It is your negative karma. However, at this time you will have to help your brothers and sisters with all your hearts and all your strength. That will count in your favour in your future. We are going to stay with you awhile to teach you and help you to organize your lives. You have nothing to fear and I won't punish you," said Adamos smiling. "You will, however, need to change your attitude because your auras are stained with the blood of your brothers and evil has been rooted in your spirits."

The humanoids returned to their villages and, in time, order was restored. Onuman who had been seriously injured was treated together with other humanoids in the laboratory of the *Gyrosphere*. They were all quite astonished by the display of the Marian's technology. They, who lived such simple lives close to nature, had never imagined a world different from their own. They considered these beings from space to be gods. The fact of having lived through this war with the demons and having been saved brought an indescribable hope into their hearts. It was as if the spirit of the race woke up and gave homage to the Lord. For a long time they had known the animal kingdom, then that of the demons and now, in response to their misery and their prayers, the infinite universe of God's love had opened itself to their hearts.

Onuman had unlimited confidence in Adamos something which was necessary for humanity's future. Weren't they, after all, their own great brothers and sisters of space. Adamos did not forget the animals which had been sacrificed during the battle. Several dinosaurs had been wounded more or less seriously, in particular Sator who received another foot, his spouse and two other dragons. They all received special care. The surviving dragons placed themselves on the side of Adamos and Sator communicated his knowledge to them.

Adamos and Evena had worked out a construction plan for the city of Muria at the centre of an immense plain surrounded by mountains across which two rivers flowed down to the sea coast. The villagers were ready to help the group. Adamos had received a picture from the space brothers of the temple which he had to build having at its four corners lingam-obelisks. In the interior of the pyramid the three sacred lingams would be placed which corresponded to Shram, Shnu and Shva. The construction did not take very long because Adamos received the tools from the space brothers. Even though the great blocks of granite were immense and heavy, their cutting and placing was achieved thanks to the red ray and the ultrasonic antigravity waves which were used right up to the end of the construction effort. Then, Adamos consecrated the pyramid and addressing the humanoids said to them: "Shram, Shnu and Shva are the creators of this visible world and they are present in the whole of their creation. They are in you and you in them. In the final analysis, you are Shram, Shnu and Shva, and you have created the universe in which you are living and your creative thoughts by themselves continue to create it. You modify everything by your thoughts and actions, that is because you alone are responsible for whatever happens. The reason is that you are embedded in the akashic era and remain attached to it by your karma, however, you are not conscious of it. On the day when you become conscious of it, the world you live in will change, such is the law which rules evolution. Karma is the reward for your actions and thoughts. Everything that you have created has returned to you, you are living with it, it is part of you. The more you become aware of it, the more you master your creation, conversely, the less you are aware of it, the more you become enslaved to it. Yours is the choice between the two conditions.

Shram the creator visualizes and creates the world, Shnu maintains that creation by the will of being and Shva transforms it through time which destroys it. In reality, they are one god which is divided in space and in which unity becomes diversity but then again, it is only an illusion. Truth remains always within the primordial unity. I know that such truths are beyond your intelligence as it is at this moment. Your brains are missing thousands of neurons together with their connections. That is why truth is embedded in this pyramid for a long time in order that you will be permitted one day to realize it through meditation and that you will be liberated from the drudgery of the material world which is the domain of Maya, the illusion."

This small population of humanoids understood none of this deep and sophisticated philosophy. The images like the words with their sounds were unclear to their comprehension. Their intellect and wisdom were not awake but their heart was and also their love for their gods opened the pathways to their souls, there, where everything was understood. The majority of them now understood the brothers from space thanks to the image translator but they nevertheless still remained puppets guided by their senses. Their instincts were still their masters and responsible for the formation of their egos. Such was a normal part of the plan of creation. What was different in this case was the presence of a group of more advanced humans coming from Mara. What could be anticipated was a natural adaptation taking time and thousands of variations in form all included in the process. What was important, however was, that the dream had begun, progress would be continuous and could not be interrupted except by weather and cataclysmic events which alone were capable of slowing all progress by a return to the primary state of survival. Lemoria had mentioned: *"The human receives his body from animals, he evolves through them"*. If the human line comes from carnivores and predators he will be aggressive and murderous but if his line derives from herbivores, he will be more peaceful and wise. Lemoria at the time of his presence spoke to the soul of the animal world using a special ritual and said to him: *"Earth does not want any more big animals because its climate is going to change, the forms of the dinosaurs must change!"* Following that, the forms of the animals became smaller and smaller.

Lord Lemoria came to open the first golden age for mankind which was to last 108 000 years. Lemoria, before his departure, founded the city of Muria and consecrated the four divisions of the world of Alma in front of the sacred triple lingam. It was then that he blessed Afrika with his golden three-sided sword having the apple-shaped handle. Touching him on the head and shoulders, he said: *"You will establish yourself on the highest mountain on the continent of Afrika that you will name Mount Kiliman."* He turned to Atalanta and consecrated him touching him on the head and shoulders, saying: *"I bless you Atalanta, in the name of the sacred lingam and of our brotherhood of light. You will go on to Mount Atlanta in the land which will carry your name which shall be called Atlantis,"* then he did the same thing for Zanga, saying: *"You, Zanga, will go with your family to the eastern region of Alma to populate it and carry the good news, the large mountain in that region will be called Mount Evert. Mayax, you and your brothers will go to the*

138

north of Lemuria." When he turned to Adamos, he blessed him saying: *"As for you Adamos with your spouse and family, you will stay on Mount Machu and you will live in the city of Muria in the land of Lemuria. The spirit of your double will be with you and your kind. From here you will be able to overlook our great human family. You will thus become the first knights of the sons and daughters of righteousness, justice, love and truth, behold your appointed task!"*

For the transformation of humanity, Adamos and his people had extracted the genetic code from their own genes, which would give an unmatchable boost to the humanoid people. Only those who had the deepest desire for it could be inoculated and each Marian family would be able to take with it some of these humanoids to help them in their evolution. So it was that Afrika took with him a hundred humanoid couples on his long trip to Mount Kiliman. They were the first to leave and Adamos was the one who was going to lead them to their destination. They busied themselves in making their preparations for departure without further incident.

Chapter XI

A voyage to the heart of the African continent

While Adamos had gone to look for Afrika and his band on Mount Machu where everybody was waiting for news, Adamos's men stayed at Muria to teach the humanoids. The return of Adamos to the palace was joyfully celebrated. The war of Kurukula had left everyone in a state of anxiety, especially when they saw Sator flying off with his flock to bring aid to Adamos's forces even though it was known that they were well armed. Nowhere else did weapons as sophisticated as those possessed by our space brothers exist. The friendship was great among the Marians and their sense of unity was strong. That separation was hard for them but as Lemoria said, such a strong feeling of fraternal love is necessary to build good karma. Nevertheless, at the same time a form of detachment needs to be created with the understanding that each one is a part of God and that a separation is only another type of time-bound illusion in space which grafts itself on to the belief that one is separate from God.

A change in terrestrial rotation was under way: one day now lasted about 72 hours; if anyone was on the humid plain, they would be suffocated by the heat. Fortunately there were giant trees and dense forests which offered shade. On the mountains, with increasing altitude, things were more tolerable but shade was harder to find because the vegetation was less dense.

When they arrived on the African continent, it was necessary to get to work immediately and build a castle half way up Mount Kiliman. On the arrival of the *Gyrosphere*, a large cave was found close by to serve as a refuge and a place to store materials convenient for the major construction at the heart of the new African city. Those who had the talent to build with stone used disintegrator rays to cut huge blocks with the ease of cutting butter. Their atoms separated precisely under the influence of the rays, which used cosmic energy. The transport of the blocks of stone was accomplished thanks to the ionic transfusor. The humanoids needed to learn how to use these instruments. Gravity was systematically reduced and the blocks could then be placed on hundred-wheeled carts. If Lemoria was there, helping with the main task, he would lift and place the blocks where they should go regardless of their weight. These carts were made of reinforced planks which slid on posts over great distances. The work was done in this fashion to economize energy, because that was something which had to be concentrated for the elevation of the blocks one upon another. In that time, there were no cranes and they didn't want to use flying platforms for such work all the time.

In a period of one month, the castle was built and then they were already thinking of building the temple. Adamos was very busy organizing the work. "The temple will be a pyramid," he said, "with a special lingam dedicated to the earth energies which will concentrate the cosmic energy having the power to distribute it all around its central apex and the system will be maintained for 7000 years. This length of time will permit the family of the black race of Mara to be able to evolve in its new environment. The African region was the cradle of a thousand animal species whose roots of life go right back to the sea. All those metamorphoses acting on the entity and its milieu have permitted transformations which started from the ions of the minerals carpeting the ocean floor, to the unique characteristics of the vegetables and after that of the animals. In leaving the sea and living in the air, the beings, thanks to the principles of adaptation, intelligence and survival, have developed a great number of specializations in order to live and thrive in their environment. It was from these the humanoids descended of which one family did not follow its evolution and produced the anthropoids."

"Afrika," said Adamos, "I am going to stay here for another month to work with you on the construction of the solar temple and I will leave after its consecration."

"That's fine, we're ready to start. The days are very hot here, but as you said, the completion date for the construction has to be at the same time as the conjunction of the seven planets so we will have to work during the nights."

During the day, shouts and roars could be heard. Afrika bounded over out of the castle in the direction of the temple construction site. A dozen of the humanoids were being pursued by the worst of the dinosaurs a tyrannosaurus rex. One humanoid had become the victim of the monster who was preparing to devour him when Onuman cut off the tendon of its right foot. The monster, with a blow from its tail knocked him to the ground and Afrika intervened, his weapon in his hand, but another blow from the tail sent him rolling far away. Adamos who arrived at the site, and remembering Lemoria's teaching, started telepathic communication with the monstrous dinosaur telling it to: "Leave us in peace," however the dinosaur showed no response as it wanted to go after Afrika with gaping jaws, Adamos released his astral double which put itself right in front of the creature's eyes in order to distract it and then dodged from left to right. Adamos spoke to it again: "Go away and leave us in peace!" The beast, furious, paused a moment as if in reflection but since it was animated by the perverted spirit of Beelzebub, it returned to the attack, lifting up the humanoid who was already injured and cut off its head. Adamos concentrated and made another monster appear, a triceratops with immense horns which charged at the tyrannosaurus rex. For this purpose, Adamos was using the creative lingam of Shram. A fight to the death began between the two monsters. The tyrannosaurus rex whose right foot would not obey its commands was now at a disadvantage and the triceratops pierced it many times with its horns. Adamos made the triceratops disappear and killed the tyrannosaurus rex with his green ray. The humanoids surrounded it in order to cut it and eat its flesh.

"Don't do that," shouted Adamos. "The spirit of the monster will enter your bodies. It will turn you to evil. We came to get you out of this bad habit of eating flesh."

Many of the humanoids resisted the thought of Adamos especially those who had been trained by the demons to eat animal flesh. Then Onuman addressed them.

"My brothers, listen to Adamos and our brothers from space. They came to deliver us from these monsters and now, once again, they have saved our lives. Adamos, tell us why there are still so many dinosaurs when you told us that the avatar Lemoria gave the order for their species to become extinct."

"When Lemoria gave the order for extinction to all the species, he was then addressing their genetic system but in certain regions of the planet it takes time and here there were some exceptions. Since it has become law, it will be done. So don't eat your brother who has died. Bury him with a prayer so that his double can find its place in the light-filled causal plane. Onuman, you are capable of carrying out this task. Get your brothers together and form a chain of unity during your prayer."

In the days that followed, each of them worked diligently on the construction of the pyramid. There was no serious incident. Construction went on mainly during the night because of the great heat of the day. Those who were working on the geometric designs did so during the evenings. The men and women, together with their humanoids who were not involved in the construction work busied themselves with cultivating the soil and organizing the water supply. The method by which the pyramid was constructed was the same as the one used for the palace of Machu. Even Sator the giant flying dinosaur and his relatives, the dragons, who were saved from the sentence of Lemoria stayed there with them and helped to transport men and materials on the site of the huge pyramid. A large number of big elephants had come to join the group and gave extraordinary assistance in achieving the goal. It was touching and beautiful in a remarkable way to see such cooperation between the men from Mara, the humanoids and the animals.

The nights were not so long and the view of the sky much clearer. The light supplied by the *Gyrosphere* had become less necessary and the energy could now be advantageously concentrated on the cutting of the stone blocks using the disintegrator rays. Everything was now progressing more quickly. There were three large chambers inside the pyramid: one, the smallest, was used for psycho-spiritual initiations and was designated as the ionic and cosmic operations room for the healing of bodies. The other two, both larger, in the base of the pyramid, were used for the rapid mummification of bodies before transferring them to the tombs. (The humanoids were taught the necessity of this practice to keep the etheric double earthbound for a longer time in its astral aura for the purpose of helping survivors in many ways because a person could remain useful for the needs of humanity even from the world of the dead.) The last chamber was for deep meditation and had as its aim the exteriorization of the astral body. A greater pyramid would be constructed at a later time on the banks of the river Nile.

Adamos was satisfied with the progress of the project because a small kernel of the space brothers was on course to evolve in the African region. It was another pearl to add to the Lord's string and he prepared himself for the ceremony. For such an occasion the other brothers and sisters had to be brought from Muria including the triple cosmic solar and lunar lingam. He left the group, went on board the *Gyrosphere* and piloted the spacecraft in the direction of Mount Machu.

On his arrival there, everybody was ready and he was welcomed joyfully. Evena had prepared a special dinner and they were all in a good mood. On the next day, the group flew off to Mount Kiliman having been careful to take with them the three sacred lingams. It was that day when the planetary conjunction augured well, for a special ceremony on such a scale and those lingams had been created by Lemoria for this event.

The sun rose silently in the East and some of Evena's birds had just awakened and began a soft melodious song. The men and the humanoids gathered around in silence and the *Gyrosphere* landed gently near the wall of the small town which was being built. Everybody descended, silently chanting mantras of the light of day, to join the group formed by Afrika and his spouse. Altogether there were about a hundred men, women and children. They formed three large concentric circles around the altar at the foot of the pyramid on which were placed the three lingams. At the centre, Adamos traced a circle in the sand with the sign of divine creation, the OM, and with his companion sat down to await the coming of Lemoria and his double, Lemuria. After some time, a light descended from the sky towards the circle which, growing larger, made appear the avatar and his shakti in a gesture of blessing to everyone. They moved towards the three lingams which sparkled at their approach and emitted special colored lights: one was red, the other green and the last one yellow. Together they gave out a blazing white light.

Lemoria made his triple sceptre with three diamonds appear in his right hand, which he held close to the lingams. The rays of light penetrated the sceptre which shone and gave out jets of flame. He then directed the sceptre towards the apex of the pyramid which itself sparkled with light from its foundation and, all around, an incandescent whirlpool could be seen forming. Lemoria pronounced several sentences that were incomprehensible to those witnesses present and the scepter disappeared from his hand. He raised his hand over all the people present saying: *"I bless you all with the sacred cosmic light of the universe. If you do not stray from the teaching that I have given you, my protection will follow you throughout this world."* He lowered his arms and continued: *"Your existence on Alma is unique and by the fact that you are unique you are also a divine entity manifested in this world. You are not matter because that is only a garment which you are carrying during your passage here. Principally, you are energy, which is objectified in the form of a body. This body is subject to the laws which are present throughout all creation. You are under obligation to follow these laws so that your organism can evolve in the material universe. If you do not, you are putting your physical body into a difficult situation for its task is to preserve you up to the end of your terrestrial experience. You also prevent your body from following its*

145

own evolution at each level of its cells something for which you are responsible and which affects you personally but it is even worse if you prevent others from evolving because of the birth of negative karma which takes the form of punishment. Such a thing becomes a sword of justice suspended above your head.

When you become aware of your own divine reality, you are able to realize the marvellous being which you really are and glorify the Lord who lives in you. The Lord is never sick, neither is he sad or unhappy. He cannot suffer defeats or make mistakes. He lives eternally. He only wants you to follow his example. You can sense His presence in your meditation and through the good actions you perform every day. Thanks to a pure spirit, you are united with Him! Now, never forget, during all your incarnations, you will always have to resist the illusory world of matter which surrounds you on any planet on which you may be living, that is the task of survival in the imperfect situation which matter presents. Your task lies in reaching perfection in God's spiritual universe. The Lord created the imperfect world so that you can find perfection in Him. God always gives us the choice in each earthly incarnation, either to abandon yourself to the fires of the world of illusion or to return to the spiritual realm. The greatest problem for humans is their gradual separation from God. When man is taken into the unnecessary entanglement of the trivial affairs of life in society, he is hypnotized by his natural inclinations which become preponderant and leave his divine nature to one side. See why the return to God appears long-drawn-out, almost impossible for some. It is there that error fills one's spirit and he becomes the unconscious prisoner of the material world. Unreality becomes reality and the reality that he has forsaken disappears from him as if in a mist.

Before parting from you, we leave you with the following suggestion: Before sleeping, meditate on your day and place all the events you have experienced in the hands of God or at our feet. Lemuria and myself are beings realized in Him and we can receive your prayer. God manifests in each of you. Through us he is testing the world of His creation and we test it with Him. In the future which you are going to experience, your descendents who will be living in groups and in societies in the four different countries we assigned to you will fight amongst themselves because of their departure from divine truth. They will form religions as well as circles devoted to science and history.

Falsehoods in all their forms are going to appear because of the power they exercise on human beings and so it will always be necessary to return to the truth. Utopia created by ignorance will enter their spirits. They will not know how to calculate the time after the disruptions caused by different cataclysms that the Earth will have to endure because of the karma men have created throughout the length of days. They won't be able to count on the genetic mutations which you are going to bring to the humanoids present on Alma. These humanoids are subjects in evolution from the animal kingdom who must experience being men, coming from the anthropoid state to the human one because they will have forgotten that what happened had already taken place on other planets in the ancient past. Now, keep preciously in your spirits this sermon which we have just delivered to you for the future of humanity. Adamos and Evena represent us among you and through them you can always be with us. My spouse and I are ONE. We come directly from our mother the Sun which is at the same time our celestial Mother, the central sun of the universe. Her sublime soul is in our hearts, vibrating eternally and it is the same thing for each of you but you are not yet aware of it. We take on a body of flesh whenever we want (and it is different from yours in each new era of your planet) in order to connect all of the Earth's magnetic belts together to harmonize them so that your lives will be better.

Alma Gaya has its own karmic experiences to live through and it is affected by your actions and thoughts. You become the cause of karma for the Earth on which you are living. This karma affects the surface and all the vital elements. On account of your thoughts and actions, Alma produces and receives from the Cosmos vibrations which may be good or detrimental and which will reflect on its surface and also affect its crust. It is quite certain that the Luciferian influences which permeate you will try to use you to produce harmful results. It is for this reason that you must defend yourselves against them using the mental approach which I have given to you. Your thoughts, because they are creative, cause devastating winds capable of producing cataclysms and these have the same effect on the elements air, fire and water. Your thoughts followed by bad actions contrary to the laws of love and peace, disturb the harmony and have serious repercussions on the lands, cities and continents where you are going to live. They hang over the Earth in the form of dark clouds negatively charged which are invisible since they are in the astral but just as real as snow or rain clouds. You are responsible both as a group and individually for your destiny because of the experiences which you have created in your future. You may choose to neglect the functioning of all these interactions which are invisible to your mortal eyes, however, they exist and when you open your astral eye one day you will be aware of them and better understand the marvellous mechanisms hidden from normal life. All of that exists because your thoughts are creators like those of the Lord. When they are chaotic, they create an environment which is also chaotic since everything is reflected in the great ALL. Whatever is on high becomes that which is below. (As above, so below). Imagine for a moment that I am the Lord creator and I am dancing on your belly. If you send out thoughts of love and peace, my dancing will be soft, harmonious and positive and if you send out thoughts of anger or hate, my dancing will be turbulent and negative and you will suffer the consequences. If you persist, harm will accumulate, there will be damage to your health and your whole life will be affected. Finally, you will be sucked into a whirlpool of negativity and viciousness that you yourself will have created and you will have chosen the place where that will happen and again, at your death, you will find yourself living in the same type of world in the lower astral. It is therefore imperative that during your stay on Earth, you achieve a good control over the creation and emission of all your thoughts and actions.

There it is, we are leaving you to get organized building your homes. We will return for the blessing of the temples in Lemuria, Atlantis, Asia and the greatest pyramid of Egypto."

Lemoria and his spouse made a gesture of blessing to all, leaned against one another then disappeared in a ray of indigo-colored light. The time of their presence was quite short but everybody retained a deep respect for their words all of which were inscribed on the akashic records. It was very necessary to explain everything to the humanoids present. In such a little time, they had lived through extraordinary experiences and they realized it because their means of communication were very limited before the coming of the Marians. They did not have hieroglyphics or any other kind of writing and spoke to each other with guttural sounds not unlike the animals. The rest was done through mental images and by this means they understood, but always in a limited way. Their intellect was not developed neither were their mental powers which only functioned in the present moment. In contrast, that which replaced their intellect was their intuitive faculty. They were only functioning in a practical way in the present time guided by their instincts and by pure intuition.

Now the men from space, in developing their means of communication, were forcing the rest of the brains of the humanoids to develop. Later, they taught them writing, symbolism and the value of words, gestures combined with sound and mental imagery and also mathematics. It all took a great deal of time and a number of incarnations for each subject before any of them were capable of functioning on these different levels because the spirit when concentrated uniquely on the rational cannot imagine what may exist in the world of the abstract. Fortunately, there were men and women amongst the Marians capable of teaching and who loved that particular vocation. So it was that the humanoids were helped and guided by extraterrestrials. The time of arrival of the Marians on Alma was celebrated each year in springtime. On that occasion, Adamos gave a speech. The number of humanoids present had been increased. Since the changes had been made and the city founded, several hundred humanoids had arrived to join the group. Now a great number of them understood the Marian language and helped by interpreting to others.

Adamos thus began his speech: "You are living completely at the level of your instincts. That is why you are going to be living between paradise and hell. Paradise is when everybody is happy and we love and understand one-another. Hell is when there is dissention leading to hate and animosity. There are days when things go well and the next day, they go badly, and you live within the contrast of appearances that you believe to be real but is, in fact, imaginary. Still you hold on to it and restrict yourself to this illusory world in which your ego lives and cannot support the idea of not existing. The truth is to not believe in this illusory world of matter as being the only kind of existence possible. You can live in it without letting yourself play the game of the false reality which in fact only exists because you believe in it. If you learn to live in the illusory material world of appearances without attachment, you can gradually return to the spiritual world which is the pure essence of existence and that makes you the master of your emotions. The problem is that without wishing for anything else, you accept it and you are forced to give yourself up to the magnetic power of matter which keeps you a prisoner. Each of you has to live in the world without belonging to it. You can be serious about events which happen without really believing in them. Keep yourselves impartial about the things of this world but be completely in tune with the world of the spirit because you are before all, spirit not body! Matter belongs to God and depends on God, but it isn't God. For at last, if you firmly believe that you are this body, you become this body. It is your thought which makes everything and if you believe that you are a spirit and hence divine, you get out of your rut and at last realize that you are God and that your body is only an appearance. So, live in the certainty that you are divine and that you have taken on this appearance especially with the goal of having an experience in the world of duality, where diversity is king and everything except yourself is a paradox and depends on the state of your spirit. Now, in being divine, you have several levels of consciousness and always choice because that is part of your desire to be and if you want to increase or decrease your spiritual state, it will be in accordance with your desire. You have the choice to be free or a prisoner and that will also be in accordance with your desire. This deep cosmic philosophy was not able to be grasped by everyone though well heard, but once a seed is sown, it takes time for germination. Even if the brain has not opened all its capabilities for understanding, it gets transformed in consequence and, suddenly, clarity sees the light of day. It is only negative judgments which create obstacles to truth, and such things are the work of Luciferian spirits which remain in ignorance."

Formidable events often awaited our Marian friends almost every day, if not from the animal kingdom then from the forces of nature. Many distressing things were able to be avoided thanks to the extrasensory powers of the group of women led by Evena. They were seeing in the future things which could happen if the courses of events were not corrected. There is a difference between things which manifest on account of their karmic plurality and others which occur because events cause them and if they are known in advance, the consequences can be averted.

The Luciferian spirit has a task to fulfill and it can be done when an occasion is presented. Its destructive spirit is always grinding away, profiting from peoples' ignorance, naivety or viciousness. In each human spirit, a fight is going on between good and evil. Everything which concerns itself with the wellbeing of humanity is good and altruistic and everything which only concerns itself with the wellbeing of the ego becomes egocentric and evil because the personal ego, in only thinking of itself and its pleasures, distances itself from others, even from God, the great ALL and thus becomes isolated. It is in these moments which are often in accord with biorhythms and weakness brought on by karma that doubts, fears, insecurity and sickness make their appearance.

Together with Evena, there were eight women and the humanoids. In the pyramid, there was a separate chamber that was called the queen's chamber. In the middle of it there was an altar, on which a large basin was placed made of black stone like marble ten feet in circumference. It was filled with oil right up to the brim. In the chamber, absolute silence reigned. There was a total calm and nothing disturbed the surface of the liquid which was colorless and odorless coming as it did from the solar planet. Evena and her companions placed themselves around it, seated in the manner of the tailor, their eyes closed. They were in meditation and when Evena recited the solar mantra finishing with the lunar mantra, they opened their eyes and fixed them on the surface of the basin staying in deep reflection at which point the mirror of the soul opened. The most sensitive began to speak of visions which they had. These visions were generally premonitions of events which must come to pass but often it happened that the image of a deceased being who was dear to them formed and a contact was made so that the message given would materialize in the world. That day, images impressed themselves on the spirits of three mediums quite distinctly. They were seeing forms which were fairly hazy drawing themselves on a stone surface. Then the forms became more and more precise. Finally as in a cinema, an almost lunar landscape presented itself and a little farther off in an oasis of trees and flowers, a man was seated beside a small stream. He was wearing a white robe and his breastplate was designed in a golden circle with disc of gold at its centre as well. He lifted his head with a smile as he looked at them.

"You called me? My name is Andros. I am one of the rectors of the temple on Andromeda. I was asked to contact you to shield you from dangers which are threatening you. At this time, no cataclysm is possible, it's going to take a human generation before it arrives and you will be warned. Men are all equal on their path of evolution in the external world because they must live a material existence. That can change when they finally learn to live in the world within. I am seeing in a far future time a multitude of beings fighting each other in senseless wars caused by disagreements between egos and the lies they tell one another either in religions or in politics. Hypocrisy and hate make for the suffering of whole societies where greed and pride dominate their spirits in the entanglement of evil. All who remain faithful to their virtues and keep faith with the truth move forward spiritually despite all, as when a plant is made to grow wonderfully when surrounded by manure but each one must be alert so as not to enter the game or be influenced by it. A member of your expedition will leave you soon. He will enter the astral of the planet and wait for you there. Nobody on earth is perfect, everything is in a state of probation."

"Can one know his name and inform him, Lord Andros?" said Evena.

"It cannot happen just like that. The law doesn't permit me to do it but as I told you, everything will arrange itself for him."

At these words, the lord of the brotherhood of Andromeda disappeared from view and only stars could be seen on the screen.

Evena said to her sisters: "I remember, Andros had warned my spouse that we will always be guided by the lords of Andromeda."

Evena recited the mantra for closing the oracle and the opal-coloured light disappeared from the liquid surface of the stone.

Serah said to Evena: "Evena, what type of love is there between you and Adamos?"

"You would wish to know if our love is fulfilled by sexual activity Serah? Definitely yes because there are cyclic periods when planetary influences together with that of the moon are juxtaposed and then our organic nature makes itself felt by demanding a copulation. However, as you know, we haven't any children having not yet received any instruction for such an action. Our future rests in the hands of the ancient ones. When they decide, we will be able to become parents. It's different for you: you can procreate normally whenever your cycles are favourable. This goes for the man as much as for the woman."

"How then is sexuality for the humanoids?"

"As you know, copulation amongst the humanoids is purely instinctive and dominated by the use of force. They are dependent on their collective animal souls which still condition them to be half human, half anthropoid. With our arrival and our influence, a change is now under way. However, they continue to be dominated by a mating season and the males fight for a female, the strongest dominating the weakest and it often ends with a bloody battle. The antagonism between the two sexes becomes most strong when the dominant male forces his reproductive organ on a female who has not accepted his domination having herself a good supply of male hormones. In a combat of this nature, a male could have his organ bitten off. On the other hand, a female having more female hormones would be very much more submissive and things could end with natural copulation. It is during these singular fights that the character of the young ones is formed as much for the males as for the females, but passion doesn't exist between them like that which occurs in more evolved beings for whom love takes subtle forms uniting them as in a perfect unity. For these more evolved beings, love is a shared delight and the fight becomes a game where sweetness is based on caresses."

"That is more like what we feel, Evena."

"Yes Serah, because these two forms of sexuality are enormously different. It is on account of the fact that we are humans who are completely independent of our evolutionary path and become with time and experience, more spiritual."

"In other words, the more the thought and desire are aligned between the two sexes, the more there is accord between them."

"Yes, that's it. In contrast, the humanoid females who are attracted by our men coming from space have their curiosity increased tenfold and whatever concerns their sex only happens during their reproductive cycle. Then, their need having become more pressing, it happened that a humanoid had jumped on the back of a Marian and tried to have sexual contact. It was necessary to calm and soothe her, something that wasn't so easy."

"And their children, aren't they everybody's children since between one tribe and another there isn't much difference?"

"It is fine that way, they are accepted in their society and each one contributes to their education unless they are born with disabilities. In these cases, they become the outcasts of the group. Love for the handicapped doesn't exist. The ones with disabilities and the old ones get left out in the cold. They have to beg for scraps of food and some shelter. Often they become the prey of wild beasts. Mostly, they are abandoned in the forest where they die, bitten or stung by venomous insects. Very often the tribal chieftain has them get bitten by a poisonous snake which sprays its poison on the skin causing paralysis and death, then what is left is thrown to the scavengers."

"That really shows lack of compassion. They have no romantic love neither do they have feelings of gentleness; such things don't exist amongst them."

"Amongst ourselves, the Marians, we have very strong feelings one for another. Our animal sexuality is rather lacking and our conjugal life only requires a small amount of sexual contact. Our touchings are more of a friendly type and we are not driven to produce large numbers of offspring because we are too much used to continence."

"The humanoids are only covered by their hair and don't wear clothes like we do. So there is a big difference between our two species at this moment. They are attracted by meat and it is mostly those for whom it has become an essential nourishment so it will take a lot of time to break them off this habit. So much does the Luciferian influence still dominate them, that there are tendencies towards cannibalism. A great number of the humanoids were raised like cattle to be consumed for food."

"That's true! However, it was not in their nature to be carnivores. Once their vibration will be raised, they will lose the taste for animal flesh. It is still up to us to educate them."

Chapter XII

A death in the group

A group of Marians and some humanoids left Muria to explore the area round a volcano situated 300 km away. Zwaro was the leader and needed to keep Adamos informed of their activities. After traveling on their flying platforms over green forests where the reptilians gathered, they landed on a surface of blackened roots, bent over and tangled which grew out between deep crevices among the rocks.

"Let's place our equipment in a shelter," said Zwaro to his group and he took up his luminescent akashic camera to film the area.

They were wearing protective suits in order to approach the volcano which was active and at certain points was sending out puffs of burning vapour. The purpose of this expedition was to measure the activity of the volcano which was the nearest to their new city and to see if it could possibly be controlled. In this group of five, Zwaro and Zong were Marians and were accompanied by three humanoids who were there to carry their baggage which consisted of a group of measuring instruments. As the humanoids did not know how to operate the flying platforms, Zwaro controlled them remotely up to their point of landing which was accomplished without any problem.

Now, however, the three humanoids were fearful. They were startled at the smallest rattling noise or the tiniest blast of heat coming from the volcano. It was clear that they were ready to flee at any moment. Zwaro had come to the conclusion that it had not been prudent on his part to have chosen them to go on this expedition. Nevertheless, they advanced towards a mound up a slope where immense plumes of smoke were escaping from the volcano. Thinking that they would be able to install their instruments, Zwaro took with him the humanoid who was carrying a special instrument which measured molten lava and tapped him on the shoulder to encourage him. The latter, in a form of response, gave him a look which seemed to be one of terror such as a hunted animal might display. In jumping over a crevasse where a strong blast of heat was coming out, Zwaro returned to help his porter who was following him in his turn holding his equipment in both hands, but the humanoid, who was not wearing boots, had placed his feet on rock faces which had points and sharp edges. Wanting to press hard with his feet, he lost his balance at the edge of the crevasse and Zwaro, in trying to grab him lost his own footing and the two of them tumbled into it. A powerful jet of lava flowed over them; they screamed with pain and their mangled corpses fell prey to the flames. The others, coming close to the crevasse, halted there helpless, unable to offer any assistance. They were devastated at the sight of this sad spectacle, then it was over, it had all happened so quickly. They each returned to the flying platforms with a heavy heart. Two dear friends had been lost in a stupid accident which could have been avoided.

On their return to the camp, the funerals for Zwaro and the humanoid were held which were the first that the Marians would observe on Alma. The wife of Zwaro, Smirna, was overcome with sadness. There was in the *Gyrosphere* all the equipment necessary for survival and to speed up the healing of broken limbs and even limbs which were missing could be replaced in a very short time. However, in the case of Smirna's husband, there was no hope. These sophisticated instruments were designed to send messages coded in the format of the DNA to act directly on the organism's regenerative functions. It was based on the life code of each individual and was really the "open Sesame" of the genetic code. Also, thanks to the powers of the higher-dimensional light rays, one could make such body parts as hands, feet and internal organs grow but that was useless in the case of Zwaro and his helper Zo.

The same ray applied to specific places of the brain through the skull made the particular nerve connections around the master glands grow, especially the pineal gland, allowing the third eye to function. In opening the doors of the subjective unconscious, the powers of intuition were awakened and thus the awareness of the astral world which is invisible to the eye. The operation was simple and effective and the person became more sensitive to extrasensory perceptions. None of these procedures was performed on the humanoids seeing that it was not recommended to prolong their lives because evolution from one life to another is a natural process permitting transformations to happen progressively. In the view of the Marians, progress extends to infinity in the material universe.

A crowd had gathered in the temple of Muria around the jet of natural water which was in the basin filled with a thousand types of flowers by the magical fingers of Evena. In front of the half-moon shaped emerald table sat Adamos with Evena at his side.

"Dear Marian brothers and sisters, said Adamos, we have gathered here today to honor the departure of our brother Zwaro and his humanoid helper named Zo. It is an error of judgment which caused this accident. One cannot be too careful in the vicinity of a volcano but it was announced from Andromeda through Evena that a member of our group was going to pass away. It isn't therefore really an accident, it was a fatality which had to happen and we will, all of us, being mortal, be forced one day to leave the material universe. Let us now form a chain of unity around Evena's basin and call amongst us the avatar Lemoria and his spouse Lemuria."

Now they all gave their hands to each other around the basin and suddenly after they had chanted some particular mantras, a condensation of vapor could be seen in front of the emerald table and in a flash, Lemoria appeared with his spouse. As soon as they had finished materializing, Lemoria began to speak: *"Dear space brothers, here we are reunited to pay our respects to our dear departed ones. You have only to call upon us and here we are. By our chants of love to God, we can bring to ourselves all of the vital vibrations of the*

Cosmos. We are going to lead the chants, you have only to repeat them. These are all the ones beginning with OM only with different endings that we chant 108 times. Place yourselves in different polarities: one man, one woman and the children in front of you, holding your hands."

After the atmosphere had been charged positively, Lemoria moved towards the basin and lit at the centre a huge oil lamp which covered everyone with its light.

"Do not be sad at their departure," he said, "you know that death is only an illusion. You know that I can reconstitute their bodies but because of karma, I would be going against the laws of nature and that is something which should not happen. Zwaro has contracted a karmic debt from the war at Kurukula against the Luciferians. Whether you kill one or a multitude, it is the act itself which counts, not the number and he wanted to help his humanoid porter so he sacrificed himself for an inferior being. Thus he made the stain on his karma disappear for duty and for love. I am going to make Zwaro and Zo appear before you for one last time so that you will be able to greet them. After that, they will still remain close to you, but invisible, ready to help you in future circumstances right up to their next incarnation."

With his hand, Lemoria made a big circle and there appeared, fuzzily at first, the living forms of Zwaro and Zo. Everyone shouted with joy and Smirna went forward to embrace Zwaro for one last time.

Lemoria said: *"Those living in the astral world are close to you, each time you think of them, they respond in the invisible world. The vibrations given out by your thoughts link up with them. The whole world is closely linked. You think that you are separate but really you aren't. The instinctive will of the world forces man to become materialistic out of necessity and he becomes too deeply entrenched in this false view of existence. He loses little by little the real concept of his spiritual values and so becomes prisoner of whatever he believes in. That is also the beginning of the fall into ignorance. However, he can always get out of that situation by deep contemplation during meditation."*

With a gesture of his hand, he made something appear. It was the necklace of Zwaro's ancestors, a real family jewel, made of gold mesh circled with topazes numbering 108 that Zwaro always wore round his neck.

"You will place it on his tomb, it carries Zwaro's vibrations which will now be constantly with you."

At this, Lemoria and his spouse together with Zwaro and Zo suddenly disappeared from before the eyes of everyone. Adamos took the necklace and walked towards another building looking like a sepulchre. He was followed by the rest of the Marians. Inside the walls were tombs, hundred of them, ready for deaths which could occur in the future. Their vibrations for a long time were a kind of blessing for the survivors who came there for contemplation.

Adamos placed on the first empty tomb the necklace of topazes which Lemoria had left with him, the name of Zwaro was marked on the stone cover. So it was that he was the first to inaugurate the tombs. The humanoids did not have a place in these tombs, they normally left corpses to decompose in a clearing in the forest where scavenging animals came to devour them and their bones were scattered around. This unfortunate accident gave rise to a change of plan regarding research on volcanoes. From now on they would have confidence in Evena and her team in knowing the future during the absence of Lemoria who, regularly warned everyone whenever there was a problem ahead but not in every case, above all whenever karma demanded a major restitution. However, the avatar told them: *"Through me, you can reach the divine kingdom, follow my advice on the conduct of your lives and I will be there at the moment of your death to lead you into that kingdom."*

Another expedition was in the works for Atalanta in the days to come and everyone prepared for that. Adamos advised Atalanta to make a reconnaissance of the area around the place where he and his team would found the first city which would be called Poseidia. Atalanta carried with him the sacred talisman which Lemoria had given to him and which would serve to protect him. Since the distances were easily covered by the flying platforms, hundreds of kilometres could be traveled in one hour. They were able to go on a reconnaissance trip lasting a number of hours and return before sunset. This was a procedure they followed for several days but it was not possible to make a camp to rest and sleep in those places because of the new dangers which constantly threatened them. So they had to be content with several short journeys although each of these was very informative. At that time, they had brought with them parts of a parabolic antenna which needed to be installed at the top of the Mount Ara in order to survey the neighborhood. The goal of the Marian colony was to populate Alma in all its four regions and to stay in communication with the *Gyrosphere*, that gave everyone a degree of safety. On landing near a mountain lake, they saw some beings running away and hiding in the thick shrubbery. They looked human, did not seem hairy like the humanoids and were very much larger.

"I believe that these are the hominids of which Lemoria spoke and who live in this region, said Nastor. If they are hostile, we can try to frighten them."

However, the Luciferian spirits were still active in that place. As soon as the explorers had set foot on the ground, they were encircled by about thirty hominids who appeared to be warriors. They appeared curious and did not seem to want to kill the new arrivals. They showed signs of intelligence, because one of them advanced and made gestures while speaking in a language unintelligible to the Marians. Atalanta himself made a gesture that they were flying in the sky. The hominid seemed dissatisfied and scowled at them then gave a hoarse cry upon which other hominids grabbed the Marians by the arms with the intention of taking them somewhere. The welcome was far from warm. Atalanta said to his men: "Prepare to defend yourselves and cover one another." He had not finished speaking when he received a heavy blow on his head from a club and lost consciousness. His friends responded but these giants were very strong and held their arms firmly in their grip. Two of the warriors carried Atalanta and with all the rest, entered the forest. All along the way there were giant heads cut from stone, square heads which resembled those of the hominids, the smallest must have been 10 feet high; the bodies were smaller perhaps 6 feet high. It was learnt later that these effigies were made to resemble their chiefs and there were about one hundred of them. Their village consisted of about one hundred huts built with lava stones cleverly cemented with a mixture of powdered rock held in place by glue from a tree rather like a rubber tree. Their tools were made of stone but they knew about fire and how to use it, they were wielding picks having points made of flint and clubs.

They took the space voyagers before a huge bearded hominid with a large belly seated on a throne. The throne was made of crushed skulls arranged and cemented with the same product used for their huts. The skins of animals stretched or braided formed its seat. The hominids threw Atalanta roughly at the feet of this leader with a sly expression who rolled his globular eyes round and wide rhythmically with scowls and sniggering evilly. Two hominids served him blackened raw meat and, to drink, a skull full of greenish liquid. They began to bind our friends hand and feet on what strongly resembled a large wooden spit, one for each man, and then they took them to what seemed to be pits where braziers were burning. It was there that the females made them turn like joints of meat on a spit. Atalanta, had been awake for some time and on opening his eyes, quickly took note of this strange environment. There wasn't a minute to lose because this gargantuan chieftain already had his eye on him. Not being tied up, he quickly took out his paralyzing ray gun and, standing up, instantly immobilized all living forms around him. The chief, seeing that, started roaring and calling for help to about thirty prehistoric beasts like dinosaurs jumping around in a forest clearing. Hardly had they touched the ground when they were transformed into statues. Many fell down with their feet in the air. A great silence fell. The females, fearful, let go of their prey, Atalanta rushed over to his friends to save them. He was just in time because several of them were suffocating because of the smoke and heat. Our friends were now on their feet holding their weapons and heading towards the chief whom Atalanta had spared.

Telepathically, Atalanta addressed himself to the latter saying: "Is this how you receive visitors?" Then he pointed his weapon of Z vibration at the legs of his opponent. The latter started to scream, his legs felt as if they were on fire, he twisted his arms with the pain, his legs had become rigid. The effect of the paralyzing ray was to act on all the muscles except those of the heart, permitting the victim to remain alive. The person remains in a dazed condition, incapable of movement. Atalanta said: "I can kill you right away if you want to." The huge figure twisted its hands, now he had met his match and was ready to give in. Marzo and his men had gone to get the females and brought them before Atalanta with their children. There were about forty of them all trembling with fear. All of these types of hominids had suspicious-looking faces lacking in harmony and beauty. They threw themselves on the ground in front of Atalanta and the dazed chieftain. "Atalanta, what are we going to do with these hominids?" demanded Marzo.

"We cannot wipe them out, their nature is subject to Luciferian influences. We can only rule them by force, they don't know anything else."

"They possess a certain amount of intelligence, that is clear, but it is clouded over by the effects of consuming flesh. These are the warriors and they are hostile in nature. I even believe that they practice rituals of black magic."

"Yes, you are right, and it's my impression that they are not to be trusted, however, this is the region in which we have to build our city."

"When we build our first settlement, we will have to encircle it with barricades or walls. We'll put giant statues resembling them around it to warn them to stay outside."

"Yes, exactly, now we are going to revive them one by one. I am going to communicate with their chief and then we'll go some distance away and find a place for ourselves which is less dangerous," said Atalanta.

The chief had become more sociable and blushed as he approached Atalanta, however, he was giggling with pleasure when life returned to his legs so that he could stand up. He walked a few paces and seemed as happy as a child on which a good trick has been played. He stood before Atalanta and beating his chest with a fist shouted, "Atar". (That was his name) Following his example, Atalanta beat his own chest and shouted "Atalanta". The others put themselves in a circle around them and each shouted his name as he beat his chest. It was rather trivial but perhaps the beginning of an understanding. Before leaving, Atalanta said to chief Atar: "Chief Atar, we are now leaving you, but we would like to become your friends because we want to live here." "You will be welcome here," was his response.

How could an understanding be good between a band of bloodthirsty savages and the newcomers? That is something to realize because it was above all fear and respect for these new and powerful weapons which made the hominids more docile. Atalanta and his band got on board their transport in front of all this savage little group and took off for another mountain further away where they could build their tower. It turned out that about fifty kilometers away there was an ideal location where the giant trees were widely separated and it was possible to put down a foundation for the tower. Atalanta and his men came down to earth, unloaded their supplies and made marks around the area which would serve as reference points because it was there that they were going to found their settlement. They knew that it would not be easy and that great danger lurked in the vicinity. At the foot of the mountain, there was an ocean and its beaches. These were blanketed with trees, rocks and pebbles all regularly washed by immense waves. In these parts, reptiles were abundant and one had to stay alert, however, there was a place where a port could be constructed. On the *Gyrosphere*, there were plans for building a boat. It was true to say that on Mara, there were no more boats and that had been the case for a long time. Atalanta and his kind had never known them in their present life and they were delighted to have the chance to build one since Adamos had told them about the plans. Nobody knew how to swim and there was a lot to learn about navigation but really there was no choice in the matter. The surface of Alma was 75% water and two thirds was under ice.

It was easy to travel by air but the future had to be considered and boats driven by supramagnetic energy would be necessary for the transportation of large-sized objects. The place chosen by the shore of the ocean and at the base of the citadel was well situated for the construction of the city of Poseidia. There was a lot to clear, the trees were immense and the area abounded with giant reptiles. It was there that Atalanta and his friends saw for the first time a strange dinosaur. From its huge body, half submerged, extended a neck about fifty feet high ending with a head that looked like a lion surrounded by a large red-orange crown which appeared like a mane; others like it were swimming in the deep water and it was in their minds that they were seeing an immense sea-serpent. Its reptilian eyes were as big as Atalanta's head having at the centre a sort of golden diamond. Its jaw was ridged with enormous pointed teeth; there was no doubt that this creature was a carnivore.

Like Adamos and Lemoria, Atalanta had a strong active gland on his forehead between his two eyes (the level of a third eye) and could use it to send messages in pictorial form to all beings. Right away, he sent messages of friendship to the marine monster who had now seen the Marians. The latter gave a hoarse cry and lowered its head with the orange neck near to Atalanta as if it wanted to hear him speak but then it gave a horrifying scream which was a sign that it intended to attack. Atalanta, who was waiting for that, stepped back, held himself steady and then froze its body with his weapon. He left it with just enough mobility to move its head and made it understand that it was at his mercy but that he did not wish to destroy it using his selector of lower vibration. He sent short surges of electricity into the whole of its body. The very expressive eyes of the monster showed astonishment and pain, then Atalanta sent it a message of death. At this, the eyes expressed dread and fear. It gave vent to several roars starting loud and then getting softer as if it wanted to express pity.

Atalanta said to it: "If you want to be our friend, you must master your predator's instincts towards us and then I can let you live. I know your vital number and I can annihilate you whenever I like, even at a distance." The animal nodded its huge head to signal that it understood. "So I'm going to restore life gradually to the whole of your body," the Marian communicated to him, "but you must stay ready to give us service when we need you, understand?" The animal could now shake its head and roll its big eyes, it gave out another loud yelp to say that it understood. Then Atalanta and his men left it in order to carry on their work. They marked the slope again to take the material for the base of the tower. Steel ropes had to be fixed to support the tower which was more than 20 meters high. However, since it was not wide, that technique worked out well and the top of the mast with its instruments was put in place by being lifted vertically using the flying platform. The installation took little time. It was hoped that the animals would not climb on top of it. So they added a magnetic transmitter giving out hostile waves which should drive them away. Such things burn the brainwaves and being caught in that ray, causes the victim to suffer loss of memory, interest and desire. Certain animals start going round in circles as if disoriented when they get near it, then they quickly distance themselves. Using great precision, the Marians operated their weapons with the disintegrator rays over a huge square one thousand feet on each side. Everything disappeared from view as if swallowed-up in space. The five of them walked forward sweeping ahead of them with their rays everything which was visible. Some big trees were there. They pointed the negative green ray at the top of the tree and brought it down gradually to its roots and the whole tree just disappeared. If an animal was above or behind the tree, no matter its size, it was also disintegrated. The ray was completely effective up to a height of one hundred feet. For greater heights, they had to put two sets of equipment, one on top of the other and then they could reach a distance of two hundred feet.

The clearing was now totally cleaned and it was now necessary to cut tree trunks and build them into a huge barricade to act as a fence. The holes for the posts were easily dug using the green ray and in a very short time they had erected four hundred posts made from tree trunks which had been stripped, again using the ray. At this point, Atalanta announced that it was time to leave.

"We'll come back tomorrow to link other trunks to form panels and when that's done, our brothers and sisters will come to help us with the construction inside."

So it was that this small team of specialists, thanks to their unique machines and equipment, began quickly to colonize that part of Alma called the country of Atalanta.

Chapter XIII

The enslaving of the hominids

The hominids, who regarded the Marians like gods, had become their slaves. By this work, they learnt discipline and the mastery of their instincts. While using their physical strength, the Marians gradually instilled them with knowledge. They had much to learn: the techniques of construction with wood, the art of working with stone. Various worksites were now being constructed in the settlement which was going to be the future great city of Poseidia. For this activity, they were able to make use of the strength of certain animals. The Marian architects had good ideas. They wanted their city to be one of great beauty. When they knew well that this new land was being completely developed and that construction also meant destruction, it hardly discouraged them. They had the knowledge and that was the main thing. They wished Poseidia to be constructed by the hands of men working with materials from their environment and Lemoria had told them: *"It is up to you to go create and build your cities. I won't interfere with your work except in the case of temples which you'll build to the Lord. Then, I'll be there to help you."*

Everything went along fine up until the day when several men, women and children suddenly fell sick. It was a sickness which only lasted a few days and then they died. That was alarming. The immune system of the hominids was not prepared for the massive invasion of microbial agents coming from the Marians. Their sickness became like a pestilence capable of decimating their race. Their organism had no defenses and death resulted, accompanied by considerable suffering. The effect was even worse for the carnivores. If they were going to be saved, it was necessary to act quickly. Professor Zanga and his team had taken samples of blood and tissue from the sick. They were constantly at work researching in their laboratory and had discovered a vaccine that they injected into the Marians who then produced antibodies that could be re-injected into those who were sick, especially those who had not yet been infected. By this process more than half of the hominids were saved.

During the whole of this sad period, a hospice was built to nurse everyone, it was in this manner that the new city was inaugurated. Not all the people knew the reason for the sickness and did not understand what was happening to them. That was not helpful to them, because they were likely to panic and that would not be of much help. In certain cases, the Marian's technological equipment was used to cure them, and that resulted in a few miracles but not in all cases because the computers lacked information on the physical bodies of these people and too much time was required for a proper study. Since the hominids were very attached to the space people considerable harmony existed between people of a more advanced evolution and others at the beginning of the transformation of their level of intelligence and lifestyle.

Dr Zanga had just saved a hominid female whom he called Mariena and he decided to inject Marian genes intra-uterine having his own formula which would modify the physical form of the child who would be born. It would be the first child impregnated by the Marian race to be born on Alma. He was also going to be gifted because his genes came from the superintelligent beings of the planet Mara. The young woman was warned that a child was going to grow inside her. She thought right away that Zanga was going to be the father. He was not able to dissuade her too much since she seemed so happy. She did not doubt that she would be the mother of coming descendents who would be a new human race and she was not the only one. Other female hominids were chosen for the future, the spell was cast. The changes were under way to populate the world of Alma with a new race and begin a new era. However, the hominids, even those who were called "clear" having been born as a result of genetic intervention remained subordinate and were used as servants although they were treated humanely. The Marians came to colonize the world of Alma and it was an act of survival on their part. They were the stronger both technically and spiritually. The Marians were not ready to share all their secrets with these beings who were half animal half human and for those made clear in the future, classifications remained to be made before the Marian people accepted them as brothers. It was a question of intelligence, perception and consciousness. There were amongst them some who appeared to have better understanding and they showed these beings at their best.

With time, Adamos had ceased to use his electronic education system because it was found that forcing the membranes of the brain had consequences for the hominids creating a psycho-chemical reaction which disoriented them and caused them to fall into a dazed state. So instead of forcing nature, it was preferred to invite them to different classes of learning which all the Marians attended. These teachings were also transmitted each time to the colonies already set up in Africa and now at Poseidia, the first city of Atlantis. Muria the capital of Lemuria had become the capital of Alma, the nerve centre from which all the directives came. The laws were the same for the whole world and what was preached was exemplary conduct and the development of the primary qualities of love, peace and truth. Order and discipline became the principal means for transforming each individual. Wisdom was the art of using all positive objectives of intelligent behavior towards others in that society. The old ones appeared as masters and the younger ones owed them respect. This seemed a simple arrangement, however, history throughout the ages and the people taking part in it demonstrated the exact opposite. Egotism replaced love and hatred replaced wisdom. On a particular day, Adamos held the following conference.

"Dear brothers and sisters, here we are now established for several years on Alma and we already have good rapport with the humanoids that are here. We have brought them knowledge and hope but that is not all. We have to instil them with the fire of our spirituality so that they will open themselves to us and release themselves from the Luciferian influence. The majority of them are still living under the yoke of the erroneous saying "an eye for an eye, a tooth for a tooth", which holds them prisoners to thoughts of vengeance. In a short time, our brother Zanga, his spouse and his group will leave for Asia. There again, they will have to struggle against the physical world in order to survive. Nevertheless, each part of these four continents must know and teach the belief in the spiritual life. Those who are born on this world must know that life in the material universe is only a replica of life in the invisible realms. A replica which is fairly hard because of the sufferings that must be endured in one life and the others to come right up to when one is able to become detached completely from material desires and enjoy a continuation of life in the spiritual plane. They must learn that what is called cruelty in life, in seeing the animals devouring each-other, or men fighting each other, that the body is only an appearance of the idea of God manifesting Himself. The body is quite simply perishable and that only the soul, the spark of the divine, is indestructible and possesses true value. Thus you cannot destroy another person, you can only take on a debt that you impose on yourself and which you will have to pay. Whoever kills his fellow being out of hatred will have to live again with that person and learn to be loving towards him which is the opposite extreme of behavior, infinitely more beautiful and harmonious. These are the laws which came with creation and to which we must adapt ourselves. Each has the task of living in accordance with harmony obtained from the love for creation, the harmony of truth and the harmony of wisdom."

"Adamos," asked Zipho the Saturian, "do you believe that they understand the mysteries of reincarnation?"

"There are amongst them individuals who are open to the subtle teachings about the invisible world and if we can get through to them, they will be able in their turn, to teach their brothers and sisters. These truths must be known and we have no choice but to teach them."

"Adamos," asked Myrza, "can the soul of a humanoid return in the body of an animal?"

"Yes, because there are exceptions to the law of evolution. You advance by degrees towards new perceptions and in accordance with your desire for perfection. If the soul, seeing a loss of spirit in the being which it is occupying becomes upset, it will permit a retrograde step for the purpose of a lesson which needs to be learned. The more the being advances towards the light and perfection, the less there will be retrograde effects. In addition, the more a being advances, the longer will be the period between a death and the next reincarnation. It is the Lords of karma who decide on the time required."

"Is it the awareness of a being's virtues and the development of individual qualities which make a difference?"

"Very much so! In order that a being can have control over his future, he must first get control over his senses, his thoughts and his actions and he must be free of negative karma."

"The humanoids don't take time for reflection, they react directly to things."

"That is because their system is uniquely based on sensual reaction and it can take several generations before they are able to think before acting. Their evolution on this level is slower, they are not used to speaking about or discussing their feelings and we have to take that fact into consideration. However, in serving as examples for them, we are accomplishing our task."

"I wonder if the law of reincarnation has the same effect on the humanoids because we are now living on Alma."

"That's a good question Zipho, I'm happy that you brought that up. It is true that we have worked for thousands of years on our character, our thoughts and our actions but we are not yet liberated from attachments to the world of matter. Only Lemoria can give us that liberation and he does it by his grace. Many amongst us are on that path. By the fact that we have the desire to come to this planet, not just for reasons of survival but to help with the evolution of its inhabitants already makes us receivers of grace. However, it is true that we have contracted debts with the karma of the world of Alma and we have to keep that in mind. It is possible that if we make one of these humanoids suffer unjustly and with bad intentions that karmic justice will give us a lesson and make us live in a similar body in order to experience the same suffering."

"In the case of Zwaro, he was doubly blessed by his good action. Is it not?"

"Yes because he thought right away of saving his helper and he lost his life. During the course of a lifetime, one can choose certain situations and also accept or refuse propositions, but following our karma we have no choice in the kind of life we undertake. However, a certain choice is given to us before we reincarnate. This is the gift to certain people, by the angels of karmic justice who watch us closely. The purpose of our soul is to seek liberation from our debts towards the world and society. Then they show us pictures of the life which is being prepared for us. It is at this moment that we can accept or refuse certain situations based on the fact that we may not be ready for them. However, we cannot completely refuse to pay our debts. Once we are committed, events set themselves in motion with great precision in all their forms and the soul finds itself facing a fait-accompli. Payment is made by service and by suffering. Zwaro is now restored as an entity in the invisible astral; he paid by his death the karmic debt from the fact that he killed several Luciferians in the war. Everything was paid for by the resulting act. Whether you kill one or a multitude, it's the same thing."

"Adamos, do the humanoids have a group soul or, like us, an individual soul?"

"Both! They are still attached to the animal world and share a collective group soul. In a short time, because of a more pronounced individualism, they will become more personal, their ego will become more pronounced and their soul more individualized. This is because their consciousness will raise itself by one level. We also have a group karma in fact that makes us responsible as a society."

"By that fact, their responsibility will be personal."

"Yes, they will become like us taking account of their actions and bearing the consequences."

"And for those who are still flesh-eaters?"

"Those too, in taking the consequences because the blood of the animals devoured enters their bodies and causes them to suffer. The more they become conscious of their actions, the more they become aware. There are elements needed by the body that can be provided completely from the vegetable kingdom and they must face the fact that it isn't necessary to eat animal flesh. The tormented spirit of an animal can, for a time, haunt the spirit of the one who has eaten it! There are in nature forbidden fruits which shouldn't be touched and animal or human flesh is amongst them."

"Yes, I understand! Even in the vegetable kingdom, there are poisonous plants and others which cure sickness."

"Exactly, however, all animals are toxic for the advanced human being! When I say advanced, I mean one who understands well the role of life. Life has a wonderful cycle which begins at its conception. Life takes its birth in form, this manifests itself so as to express life. Whoever meditates on his form gradually takes control of his thoughts and is able to modify the form with a certain detachment from the external world in which form manifests. In taking control of thoughts, life can be manifested fully. The man who knows this secret can take control over his senses. He becomes a creator of form and acquires awareness. If he perseveres, with time, a transformation overcomes his consciousness and nature ends by delivering to him her secrets. He becomes a master of his life and then with unconditional love that he produces from his heart-centre to the infinity around him, he unites himself with the Creator who resides there. In uniting with his Creator, he becomes himself the creator through the love which unites them. Life, then, takes on a meaning and a reason for being. This transformation from one state of consciousness to another is called spiritual evolution and is absolutely necessary for each individual launched into the spiral of life. This is how he returns to the first source. That is his goal: to be totally aware of the love which fills him and expresses itself through him. His ego is thus transformed by a sharing with the whole of creation of the love in which it was given birth for the second time; it is the return of the prodigal son to the Father-creator. There he has completed a life-cycle and learnt to modify and then to master his consciousness with the help of his willpower. This is in order to leave the illusion of time and of being separate from the One, in the state of an ego until at last, he returns with love and understanding into the total unity as if nothing had happened. As a matter of fact, nothing has happened, all of the passage through the material state by the soul-spirit is only a dream that everyone lives through in their own way that is special for them.

Several amongst you have already asked me what it is that avatar Lemoria teaches us about life and the existence of God. Now, I am going to talk to you about the beginning of the divine manifestation. To begin with, it is useful to know that the non-manifested exists and that is "pure existence". It cannot be said that because a thing is not manifested in the state where we believe things exist that it does not exist at all! Quite the contrary, it is the source from which all things arise, the only reality and the only essence. It is the true stable state and is immutable! All the rest is just appearance in derived states. That state is pure and without any qualities since such are not necessary to it. There is no beginning and no end. It is Ain Soph (the ultimate positive) but also the total negative, the infinite power which remains unmanifest. One can imagine it being interstellar space, a Logos which has the aspect of a sun surrounded by its planets, or again, of suns which become energy beams. Everything is in the invisible, because manifestation only begins when duality makes its appearance and this we can call "space and movement". In this space, the energy of the Logos initiates movement creating two forces, the form desired by space for creating movement, then the desired force creating inertia in space. The desire for movement opposes the desire for inertia, becoming stronger with time but always slowed down by inertia.

See why there are no straight lines in the Cosmos, all movement gives rise to a curved trajectory returning to the point of origin in order to form, finally, a ring like a huge belt which turns on itself almost eternally and tends to communicate this movement to space creating the necessary tensions serving to bring into being other movements with other currents like a stone thrown into calm water forms waves which spread out wider and wider. When the biggest one reaches the same speed of rotation as the smallest and oldest, then that one finds itself attracted towards the second one. In these circles, the energy is manifest as being positive and negative, the greater part of the outgoing current being positive and the other negative. The current moves from one sphere to the other, from the positive to the negative, they attract and repel and that is what establishes the beginning of the Cosmos. From one sphere to another where the energy is manifest, a neutral ray exists with its derivation which could be called "the chaos, the barrier which cannot be crossed" representing the primary point of absolute rest which is the point of application of the manifestation of the cosmic force. That is the famous point of resistance which enables movement to take place. This sphere acts like a ring of energy which is the reaction to the primary force returning on itself to form the Cosmos and all the apparent forms of life which appear there. So it is this principal opposition that allows the Cosmos to come into existence."

"If we understand it well, Adamos, is it thanks to the principle of opposition that the cosmic universe was able to be born?"

"Yes, that allowed the conception of a secondary movement conforming to the laws of reaction. It is the secondary movement of energies put into action in opposing the first which established a state of stability creating the "finite" which is the limitation and which concentrates. It is the force of the "true negative" making an evolution possible. From this combined energy source evolution can get its starting point and, in summary, it is a pressure going from the circumference towards the centre. From these two rings of energy, the circle of the Cosmos submerges its aspirations towards the encircling sphere wishing to stretch the centre, it solidifies by contraction. It constructs in giving solid form to its growing force. It becomes the "true positive" which is then evolution. On the other hand, when it's rising, the ring of chaos doesn't belong to the sphere which it encircles like a serpent. It belongs to the space outside as if it was separated because it turns its aspirations towards space, wishing to stretch its circumference and trying to get back to the non-manifest whence it came. If it didn't meet any opposition, it would reduce to the "nothing" which it encircles. These two energies are the source of all force in the Cosmos."

"Is this the cause of all creation?"

"Yes! The cosmic ring creates solid forms. It becomes the creator of things whereas the ring of chaos does the opposite, it diffuses. We humans call one "life" and the other one "death", the being and the non-being, or again the light and the shadow, each being reliant on its respective ring. Now the class of humans is also divided into sons and daughters of light belonging to the first ring of the true positive while that of the sons and daughters of the shadow like the Luciferians belong to the ring of chaos. As for that which is called "evil" it has to be opposed by what is called passive-resistance. We don't give in to evil. We make a void around it, which is a form of neutrality therefore the opposition, limitation, concentration no longer affect it and do not encounter resistance. It will follow the law which rules its own nature and return to the movement of the ring of chaos. It goes to its own destruction.

To recapitulate, we have to conceive the Cosmos we are living in as being formed of three motions like spheres of energy turning within themselves. The first one gives birth to that one we see, then giving birth to two other motions, the ring of the Cosmos and the ring of chaos, limited in its circumference by the barrier-ring which may not be crossed! Nothing which exists can pass through this ring. These three motions are what is called "the trinity". The Supreme Being who is manifest there has several names. These three forces balance one another. The ring of the Cosmos is centripetal (pulling towards the centre) while the ring of chaos is centrifugal (pulling outwards). The ring which may not be passed maintains the equilibrium between these two forces by limiting extremes. Moreover, the ring of chaos belongs to the exterior space and to the non-manifest, constantly turning towards the past and its conditions, unable to construct anything, always dissipating. When the ring of the Cosmos, in circumscribing the ring which may not be crossed, finishes its first revolution, the Cosmos begins its existence and other motions are born in removing the excess force. The force gives rise to other forces, thus the first activity is motion, the second activity is light and the third activity is sound. All the whirlpools inside the sphere of the Cosmos become "the spiral energy rays". These give birth to the central sun, from which come the galaxies, with their currents of leaving and returning. Whatever happens in the great infinity is reproduced in the infinitely small world of the atoms. Thus, by the will of the Logos, a cosmos was born from space by motion and its energy, which, by its pressure forces, creates whirlpools transmitting force from one to another.

I will speak to you later about the evolution of a planetary or universal Logos but in order to carry over all this knowledge to man who is the fruition of all, it must be said that incarnation is based on the law of limitation which contains karma and its law of actions and reactions which are equal and opposite. Each soul which incarnates chooses its own material form and the collective soul of the race represents the Lord of karma to whom one prays or invokes regarding matters of destiny. He is the supreme self. The primordial task of man as spirit is to be loyal to the One, the undivided spirit. Apart from Him, there is no possible existence. He is the Logos originating from the unmanifest. The nature of the Logos-God constitutes the law to which we must submit if we want to live harmoniously in this manifestation. Lemoria tells us that all living souls take their existence from the non-manifest itself, but as man pursues his manifestation of being in the sphere of the sun Logos, he must follow the laws in order to operate within that sphere. That is an integral component of his existence. We are on a false track if we believe that we come from Satur,

Mara or the planet Alma because in reality, we come through the sun-Logos from the divine sphere of the unmanifested!

All men should know that by being evolved human beings, they have a huge debt to recognize with all respect to the earth which is in all truth their mother. Their bodies are built from her substance and live on that same substance. Not a single thing or thought exists on earth which doesn't have a link to the planetary being no matter how great and elevated or base and wicked it could be. This means that each one has a very great responsibility towards others and the earth's collective soul. That concerns also other forms of existence such as animals and elementals which all are connected to men. Throughout the whole length of our development across the ages, we take with us our bountiful mother and if we depart from the right path, we also force the earth on to the wrong path. Then, to see the degradation of the planetary being who nourishes and protects us is a painful experience, sad for nature and for life. However, the negative nature of man and his Luciferian influence hinders him from living a life of love and peace. The future will demonstrate innumerable wars, pillages and rapes of women that men are going to perpetrate before listening to reason and calming down! I am mentioning here what avatar Lemoria told us when he created the bowl of divination.

"I created myself pure as the origin of time. My creative power comes directly from Shnu the Lord of the universe and my spouse Lemuria has the same power which manifests itself instantly in the material world. She is my "Shakti" and her power is direct." The talk was continued by Lemuria: *"For him, yes, he is direct, my concentration is so great that as soon as the thought and its image is manifested coming from the divine spirit of my spouse it penetrates into mine, so the form appears in the material world because no barrier comes between the thought, its concept and me! Lemoria, myself and matter are completely united. Lemoria has the creative power coming from the higher astral of the universe and myself, Lemuria has the solidifying power proceeding from the lower astral of the earth."* Then Lemuria raised her right hand towards the earth and all of a sudden there appeared atom by atom almost instantaneously, making time stand still, the form of an

enormous cupola upside-down, made of marble, and containing a special kind of oil. Lemoria said to Evena: *"Thanks to this cupola, you will see images appear of the future and correct your destiny, on condition that you follow the divine laws and act according to the law of love and mutual aid."* Then Lemoria touched Evena's forehead saying: *"You Evena, will become the bond and guide by which the entities can be manifested. You will have to choose amongst the members of your group those and their descendents who will replace you in the future. This power is transferable up to the moment when a flaw arises and the Luciferians take control of it. May purity rest in your thoughts, gestures and actions."*

"A long time before, Lord Lemoria and his Shakti had caused a pyramid to be erected which was a sacred temple containing at its centre the three divine lingams of the creator of the world. These are the Lords Shram, Shnu and Shva. The three sacred lingams were the carriers of the three vital cosmic supra-positive energies coming from the sun as well as the sun of suns of all the galaxies.

During its consecration, Lemoria and his spouse had mentally and spiritually linked up this place on earth which was at that time situated at a strategic place on the equator where all these forces could meet and be concentrated. It was, in other words, the mouth of the world of Alma where everything could flourish and grow in peace and harmony. What was also needed was to have a place of exit on the opposite side which would become the place where the forces of negative energy would be able to leave and which would become a desert, that of Gob (Gobi). Thousands of years later, this arrangement would be reversed due to the rotation of the poles of the planet causing whatever is positive to become negative and vice-versa. This plan was part of the evolution of the planet. In this plan, the cosmic energy of the white sun full of power and light fills space with its force and directs it towards the black sun which absorbs it to overflowing during the millennia right up to the moment where the white sun is exhausted, burnt-up and then the black sun explodes because of its pent-up energy and becomes in its turn a white sun, emitter of force and energy, then the white sun becomes black. So it is that everything which finds itself and is manifested within this plan moves on an eternal carrousel.

In human life, from incarnation to incarnation, a man becomes a woman and a woman a man. In the plan of human consciousness, it leaves matter and becomes spiritual returning to the spiritual Father in order to come back into matter and again begin another cycle, going from an ion manifesting in the atom and from there to the mineral kingdom, the vegetable kingdom, the animal kingdom and finally back to become a human being. See why even the Luciferian devil will one day become divine. However, the Luciferians refused to return to the divine.

In the manifested world, the Father is time and the Mother is space. Time is only the measure of space, the two complement each other and are united in a metaphorical sense. In the final analysis, they are only an illusion which manifests from the divine will to be and to appear within the one as within the other. Even if one day, this knowledge and its concept sees the light of day in the spirit of man, there will not be any confusion. It is enough for him to continue to play his role in the divine plan and to abstain from anything which hinders it, all the rest depends on the self. In other words, he must avoid opposing his will to the will of God. If one opposes one's will to that of God, one ends up wanting to match Him in the plan of creative manifestation and then one becomes a fallen angel. In the plan of human consciousness, secondary manifestations are created which form new laws which are similar but which can be different in the sense of being in opposition and then, as the Luciferians have proved, one can be sucked into the black sun. The negative aspects which oppose themselves to the will of God and His divine plan are only another manifestation called Maya. Such things contribute to the formation of the ego which is only the negative imprint of the true self which wants to live according to its impression, which is based essentially on the lower consciousness connected to the world of the senses. One lives in the illusion that one is one's body and then one moves away from the divine truth. So there are two roads at the parting of the ways and it is up to us to decide which one we are going to take. The rule of the game is that you reap what you sow."

***

The city of Muria was already large and filled with beauty, the architecture of Mara was very much in evidence. The children had grown up and had become adults. They had been taught the ways of the Marian civilization since they were young. The courses of instruction had been given by incomparable masters using both sounds and images. The seaport already had two large ships 300 feet long constructed according to the plans of the Marian engineers. These were, however, of wooden construction. Later when mines would be dug, making use of the assistance of the hominids, iron would be extracted and refined and the boats would be of metallic construction using a special alloy whose secret they possessed. Thanks to the disintegrator rays, they could cut slices of all different thicknesses in stone, even in granite, with unbelievable precision. The sculptors used this technique to create the statues of religious and legendary persons and their inscriptions on the bases using smaller instruments won admiration. Around the major buildings and monuments dwellings were constructed with four floors. In the streets, displays, artistically decorated demonstrated what the artisans or merchants were selling, whether vegetables or fruits. There was even a currency stamped with M on one side and the number on the other.

On the plain of Muria, orchards were set up with fruit trees which had been brought from Mara in the form of seeds and which grew marvellously here. The hominids did not have access to the city and lived in the vicinity. They were not accepted into the Marian culture except under very strict and special conditions. The teachings were given to them in a different manner appropriate to their capabilities.

There was no wall around the city but electronic boundaries prevented approach thanks to a ray which could produce a burning heat in somebody still three meters away and could also cause death. Generally speaking, dinosaurs and dangerous animals kept away from the city limits. The entrance of Muria was adorned by two immense obelisks on each side of a huge arcade at the centre of which was a shining golden disc of immense size with a stone serpent carved on each side. On this massive golden disc, the letter M stood out majestically. There were also two huge golden lions with straight manes seated in front of the gate. The lion was fairly rare in this part of the planet and was looked at with curiosity, something which amused Evena. Gold was the precious metal which represented the Sun in being venerated for its vibrations. The temple of the Sun at the centre of the city had for a roof a dome of gold leaf visible from a great distance. From ships coming in from the sea one could see the temple from far away. A large number of trees around the port were used for the construction of cabins for the neighboring villages and for the interior fittings of the buildings. The world of Alma began to take on the civilized aspect of Mara. Close to the temple on a hill, an observatory had been erected from which the heavens could be observed and in the evenings, the marvelling children were shown with pride Mara, the planet which shone from afar.

In the great crystal sphere, they could see the terrible wars and the difficulties of survival which their parents had to endure on Mara before their journey to Alma. They were astonished to discover that there were no dinosaurs on Mara, the red planet, which had become almost barren so that Alma appeared to offer a great contrast in the worlds of plants and animals.

Muria was becoming a model city for the other cities planned by Adamos across the world and Poseidia was a copy of it. The Marians were the builders and on Alma, they really put their hearts into it. Mayax was the chief engineer and he worked for all the architects. He and his relatives were the men with bronze skin, heavily built, with black hair and eyes and a flattened nose. They had, moreover, a special language and a writing based on symbols. As for the rest, all the public places, the parks, the restaurants, the temples and the schools displayed the religious symbols of Lemuria brought by the Marians. That society had people more

183

literate than others, but the respect for one another prevailed in all aspects. Nobody was richer than anybody else and each had only thought for the common good. Samoe who had been nominated president wanted a harmonious regime. The priests, themselves, wished that the people remember the goal of earthly existence, which was not just survival in the primordial realm of matter but the return to the life of the spirit through detachment and the control of desires.

On the buildings and on the coinage the disc was engraved, which represented the sun Ra and at the centre a point which represented God with the letter M. On each side of the disc, whether red or gold, there was a serpent in the form of an S which represented the positive and negative energy used in creation by God. Every inhabitant of Muria was at the same time a soldier, a doctor of medicine and a priest of divine law. Each was both the brother and guardian of his fellows and children were regarded as the responsibility of everyone. In this family spirit, everyone protected everyone else, thus avoiding the Luciferian influences which, for their part, were looking for all ways of creating dissension and disorder either directly or indirectly. Spring water had been brought skilfully along stone conduits right to the city centre into a fountain from which filtered drinking water could be drawn and where other basins at the side served for doing laundry. The humanoids, under pressure to mingle with the men and women from space, started to be embarrassed by their nudity and thought of wearing loincloths as clothes, to wash themselves more often and to stop eating meat. The Marians had now chosen a great number of fruits and vegetables which were edible. It was about time, because over the years, the supplies which they had brought from Mara, even though these foodstuffs were for the most part in a dried form, began to run out and everyone was becoming used to eating the produce of the new world.

As they were busy constructing the conduits to bring water from the mountains down to the plain, Zanga's team were confronted by other problems because they were using columns of stone as supports and at one place, their plan called for passage through a huge swamp. There, two men up to their waist in water screamed with pain. They had been attacked by types of leech as long as an arm which attached themselves to their bodies and literally sucked out all their blood. These creatures had to be killed quickly before there was no blood left in the men's veins. That was done at once thanks to the electric charge of their rayguns. The creatures had their bodies completely immobilized and ended by releasing their grip but not without leaving a gaping hole in the flesh which needed to be closed up. It was then realized that these leeches had rows of teeth which were sharp and pointed capable of biting and completely emptying a body of its blood by suction no matter where they chose to bite. In the same place, there were also huge fish, which, on sensing their presence quickly attacked them. In the end, they placed a magnetic barrier around each worksite so that they could erect pylons and work in peace.

The insect world could hardly be described as more comforting. A type of gigantic spider, at least three feet across, could be lying in wait to jump on to a man in order to bite into his jugular vein and wrap him in a huge cocoon. She would then leave him to rot for a long time during which, under the action of an acid which she had injected into him, his flesh would turn to liquid which she would eventually drink. It was noticed that after a humanoid had become a victim of this creature, a space brother had passed some minutes before but had not been attacked. He thought that it was because he was carrying on him the pentacle of protection given to all the Marians by avatar Lemoria.

There were other flying insects to be feared because of their sting which could prove fatal. The worst was a certain hornet the size of a sparrow. About twenty of these insects which flew around in swarms would completely cover a warm-blooded animal and sting it to death. Large size ants would do the same thing and by operating in swarms, were voracious and destructive. However, the city of Muria, was protected at its centre by a barrier of magnetic waveforms. This was the case except for periods of interference which weakened the waves. The reason for this interference was not known but, according to Adamos, might have something to do with the phases of the moon. The full moon was also affecting the volcanoes and the tides and the winds. It was also causing violent earth-tremors. At certain places on the Earth, black pits of quicksands were formed, which, suddenly becoming incandescent and smoke-filled, would plunge deeply into the ground, swallowing up everything around by a descent into hell.

The expeditions of the Marians were rare during these times which, happily, were announced by Evena and her oracles. Adaptation to life on the plain and beside the seas was rougher than in the mountains. The climate was much hotter and extremely humid during the equinoxes. Descending from the mountains, one plunged into an ocean of mist where you had constantly to watch the road ahead, behind and on either side. Everywhere, there was a wild animal lying in wait ready to attack and make a meal of you. In the case of the Marians, having the third eye open, their ability to sense danger always warned them in advance enabling them to protect themselves but the others, less fortunate, had to protect each other at every instant. On account of the constant humidity, the vegetation alongside bodies of water was more luxuriant than high on the mountains. The contrast was great and so was the temperature. The cold in the mountains could be severe and lasting. The home and the temple that Lemoria had made for the sons of space were heated by channels of hot water coming from the heart of a volcano situated many miles away from that place allowing a normal and harmonious life in the whole of the city which was now spreading out gaining from this particular advantage. It had been named Tianaca and the large lake at the same altitude, Tiaka, from which the winding river Xingu descended right down to the ocean. This place was a little paradise on Alma. It was under the protection of the gods and it was also there that the divine teaching of the gods was offered.

Adamos had requested that a great sage Kethyr teach the royal way of the tree of life to all those who came to hear it, such teaching was preparation for the life within. He said: "The real purpose of life lies within and to wish to plunge body and soul into material things is a mistake. Materialism is the vehicle of the subtle and negative Luciferian power which keeps a man prisoner of his own illusions that he has created. In the interior reality, you have to work on yourself every instant because every instant is vital. Unconditional love is the weapon of choice against the enemy and if we have just built a temple, it is for meditation and offering to God what is due to Him that is the gift of the self. This temple which is really our body is also a monument which we leave to our offspring to remind them that the reason for being in the world is to worship God who created us, this God of whom we are a small particle. It also symbolizes our own return to the reason for our own reincarnation, something which could reflect on our own offspring. Generally, at the time of a reincarnation, we forget our past. Whoever prepares themselves for returning to the beyond and who throughout his life has followed a pure existence exempt from evil helps his passage through the astral purgatory and sets himself up for a road filled with love in readiness for the next reincarnation. This is an honourable thing because life is filled with fogs and illusions taking us through all kinds of hardships. Knowing all that, you have no need to construct an exterior temple to God because you should be looking after the one which you are inhabiting yourself.

Once you have understood the real mechanism which animates you, the tree of life is your temple and the whole organization of your body is an example of it. For example, there are several energy bodies around your physical body which cover it like an eggshell. It is in the aura of these energy bodies that the first man was formed. At the top of the first energy body of the aura is the crown which is also the principal origin of the life-force without which the body would not exist. It possesses a thousand rays like a sun and from this centre six other centres are supplied at different levels of the body. These centres are called energy wheels or chakras and are related to the body's organs which they animate electrically.

Below the head centre, the crown shines and sends down its rays to another centre between the two eyes. From this centre you are given awareness of other existences beyond your physical body and the world of matter which surrounds us. That is a world invisible to the eyes of the flesh, called the astral world and from this particular centre, the other eye, that of the astral, when it is opened as is the case for several of you, you are aware of the kingdom of the dead. These chakras are the points of entry for the other, subtle, bodies into the physical body. For each of you, the energies flow at different speeds in accordance with leading character traits and possess different wavelengths and affect different colors and vibrations. This place has a special relationship with the astral world and sends down another ray to the throat centre and following that to the heart centre. From there it goes to the navel, the solar plexus which is associated with feelings and emotions. The ray descends still further to the lower organs, those of sex and the other located at the coccyx which is the centre of the body's total vitality.

Further than the activities of the physical body, these centres have other functions which come into play only when permitted by the astral centre. These are the higher levels of consciousness which can be developed through the presence of an avatar or by the direct action of the three lingams. The force which is active at the base of the spinal column is the place where the mother, divine or earthly, drives her creation in the form of the physical body. We will call her Kundali. When she becomes active in the etheric and astral body, she increases the sensitivity at the level of the mind and of the senses, Thanks to her effect on the lower senses, she allows the development of awareness of the exterior world. Her efforts at the level of the solar plexus allow men to travel in the astral plane with full consciousness. At the heart level, she develops sympathy and sensibility to the vibrations of other astral entities, giving the ability to adapt and have better understanding. Instinctively, the awakening of the throat level gives the power to hear on the astral plane and that situated between the eyebrows will provide sight on the different astral planes. That is the power of perceiving the form and nature of an astral object. Simultaneously at the crown level, the pituitary and pineal glands can become the organs most sensitive to the astral plane, on all these planes there are different levels of vibration making different types of perception. These centres also function as organs of sensory reception for the astral which needs lots of information in order to correct and transform the physical world. It is the continual exchange between these forms which gives completeness and harmony. When you consciously enter the astral universe, it is these organs which serve you as organs of perception."

"Kethyr, is it the case that these centres of perception, the chakras, allow us to reach a higher level of consciousness and thus help us to control the material world?"

"Yes, it is an integral part of our spiritual advancement. The length of an astral life of a man following his passing depends entirely on two factors: those being the nature of his passing and his mental attitude at the moment of leaving his physical body. During his life in the world, he constantly influences the material progression of his astral body. He affects it by his passions, his emotions and his desires, that he allows constantly to take his directives, thus also indirectly by his actions based on his feelings including all the details of his life, his debauched acts, his acts of continence, his acts of propriety or of non-propriety, and everything which he eats or drinks. If by deliberate perversity along these lines and by ignorance he continues to introduce into his astral vehicle these gross and unfeeling elements, supported by low level vibrations, he will find himself on the lower plane after his death, supported by negativity and grief leading up to the slow disintegration of this form. On the other hand, if he maintains a life which is honorable and of complete integrity, the contrary effect will be produced. There will only remain for him to make in his attitude the domain of thought which he now must fully spiritualize. We must not speak of neglecting totally the material world, but of acting in a way so as not to be overcome by its illusions. This attitude must be held on to at the moment of death and immediately afterwards in order to be able to more easily dissolve the lower astral and attain the spiritual astral. Those who remain attached to the things of earth have a lot of pain in detaching themselves from whatever they are leaving behind. It is possible to embalm the body or to freeze it so that the ego can remain attached longer for some particular reason, but after a while, the astral etheric double has to disintegrate. Such a thing is necessary for its own spiritual advancement in the whirlpool of time."

"Is the astral world as natural as the one we are living in now?"

"It is, but it changes at different levels. Life continues over there, based on the same principles of existence of which one is the will to be and the other is the desire for something. In the majority of cases, a dead person arrives on the astral plane without realizing that he has died on the physical plane. He thinks that he must look for food, cover himself, have a roof over his head and look for work. He creates his own surroundings, landscape, house, furniture or even lives in surroundings already created by the thoughts of others. He possesses a great freedom in his environment and should spend his time helping others. That is why it is necessary to be useful to others during the earthly life on whatever planet one is living in order to take up good habits."

"Is a being always conscious during these changes?"

"No, when a man dies, his etheric form detaches itself gradually from the physical, that is something which can take several hours and the astral also detaches itself from the etheric form and that is what allows a man to introduce himself to the astral plane. He is unconscious up to the point when he detaches himself from the etheric and thus awakens on his new plane of existence. The exception is those who imprison themselves deeply in material existence. Such ones prevent this separation and still awaken in the etheric, but it is not a body in which it is possible to function. They are therefore for a time caught between two worlds. They are detached from the astral world by the shell of etheric matter but at the same time have lost the physical body and its sense organs. This results in a sensation of abandonment which creates the anxiety of being imprisoned in a thick fog, in which there are many other people but all unable to communicate. There are some exceptional moments when the consciousness can wander onto other planes but then fall back each time into that state without any outcome. During all this interminable time, the poor soul does not realize that in losing its grip on the material world, it will again fall unconscious and awaken to freedom in the astral plane!"

"Kethyr, are there other means of escaping this terrible trap?"

"Yes, they exist. The phenomenon in these people is similar to a type of auto-hypnosis of a confused and concentrated kind into which the person has fallen at the moment of dying: that being the instant of unconsciousness and half consciousness of the astral world and the fear of losing consciousness of the visible world. Now, very many of those who have left the earth for the astral become helpers in such cases and whenever they can, they persuade that person (who is in the confused state) to "let go" but it is only when the soul has the necessary faith and courage that such a thing can be accomplished. Otherwise, after a fairly long time, the cells of the etheric shell crumble and do not renew themselves and the souls then fall into a coma (which can be fairly long) permitting their awakening into the astral. However, those who remain in a larval human state run the risk of haunting those who are still living and absorbing their vital energy. The persons most likely to be affected are those who are psychically gifted such as mediums. These parasitical entities can be the cause of sickness to living people whom they are able to affect on account of their negativity."

"My question is: Can we modify, or at least protect, our astral by meditating on the psychic centres before the time of death?"

"Absolutely! The Lord Lemoria has explained to us how we can protect our astral, psychic and etheric bodies by putting them beyond the reach of negative entities from the lower astral which are active most often at the time of the full moon and at periods of a low biological rhythm."

"Can you give us more explanation about this?"

"Yes, that was my intention. You remember just now, I told you about the astral tree of life which each of you possesses and about its centres of perception. These luminous spheres with their spiral energy are governed by the vibrations of the different planets of our solar system. Whether their aspect is positive or negative depends on the correspondences and the karma of each individual at the time of birth. Certain centres are more functional than others absorbing too much of the negative influences from the earth and its own centre thus something which is particularly nourishing may become particularly destructive. If you pray during your morning meditation, the divine entities who rule these energy centres with love, act with enthusiasm on behalf of your harmony and your health, so much so that you even have no further need of the healing rays of our medical centre."

"These negative entities who suck up the vital energy from these invisible centres, where do they get this power?"

"This power, as you are saying, is our own which we give them. For sure, we are unconscious of it most of the time."

"But how can we give them power over us?"

"By our thoughts and our acts, depending on the case. Each time that we cause a disharmony around ourselves which affects others, we also weaken the harmony of our chakras. Each time that we fail to act in accordance with the cosmic laws of love, justice and charity, we create blockages and holes at different levels of these centres of consciousness and the results are reflected in the invisible astral body. From these holes both large and small, vital energy escapes and the "astral larvae" are attracted to these points and gorge themselves with delight on these energies to the detriment of the individual."

"Do anger hatred and a myriad of other sins also have the same effect?"

"Certainly. Sins themselves also cause blockages which act on the physical aspect of the individual in the long term."

"It is not only due to the kind of nourishment we take or what we drink?"

"No, everything which results in a loss of harmony in the spreading of life and its vital qualities causes all these problems. From one dimension to another, life is eternally renewing itself. Remember, however, that life is precious and we mustn't allow it to go to waste. Every human birth carries with it a particular mission to fulfill. That is something which everyone must know and find."

***

During this time on the Earth where there was haste to record the whole Martian epic, a lady named Oprah Winny well known for her altruistic programs discussing serious subjects and who was invited by NASA, had serious questions to ask. Knowing that communication was possible directly with the crystal sphere on Mars, she was put in touch with the sage Kethyr across time and space, and asked:

"Professor Kethyr, could you tell us, regarding the space epic that you have achieved and which for us on Earth appears in the remote past, it would seem that the black race is very ancient, does it originate from the planet Satur?"

"My dear sister, all the races are ancient. None is superior to another and the mixing between different human races has produced still other forms. Quite apart from skin color, the species is the same. Our knowledge of the black race teaches us that it originated on the planet Jupiter and it was amongst the first to emigrate from one planet to another when forced to by necessity. However, how far back that was in time, nobody knows. Certainly, the akashic records have recorded all episodes of life on all the planets and it would be interesting for you to be able to see all the changes displayed that there were since the beginning of time and all the developments of human beings since those times. Perhaps the avatar of your epoch will give you that chance when it may be permitted."

"In the future, will we, the people of Earth, have to leave the planet just as you have done?"

"Yes, because of the progressive distancing of the Earth from the Sun. In your case it will be, without doubt, a long way off. That is, unless you continue to destroy your planet by chemical and technological pollution as you are now doing, often because of greed and poor understanding which is, reduced to its simplest terms, a lack of love."

"Are you saying that it is possible to avoid this catastrophe?"

"That is the way things are. You need a world government capable of perceiving the mistakes and stopping them in time. Such a body would have full power and that itself is always dangerous. The antagonism between good and bad forces is a constant problem on Earth."

"What else can you advise us to do on that point?"

"Acquire the knowledge of mystical powers and of spirituality. That is the only possible way of renouncing materialism."

"Love should also be the choicest medicine!"

"You have spoken well! Love in all its forms and above all unconditional love, because this kind of love can wipe out the bad influences produced by egotism."

"People, when they become separated and divided become more and more egotistical."

"They also mix up vanity with egotism and do not hesitate to cause suffering to others. That is what provokes wars."

"This Luciferian spirit, is it constantly at work on the evolution of human beings?"

"Yes, its work is to put the whole world on trial. It is the marker of evolution. It allows a man to choose his destiny. It teaches us to reach mastery by the power of making good decisions."

"It seems to me that this spirit is perverse on account of its cruelties."

"That it is. There are different levels all included in the ladder of spirituality. An extreme situation can appear quite bad but overall, everything is an illusion."

"How do you explain the transmigration of souls?" "Has that to do with reincarnation?"

"It's different from reincarnation. The being which has its descent from an amoeba through the animal and vegetable kingdoms takes on all the various forms right up to humanoid and human. However, a soul which is living in a particular form on a planet in another solar system and which has evolved towards the light, may see in a dream life on the planet Alma, be dazzled by it and then may develop a strong desire to live here. So, as soon as this soul is free of its obligations over there, it transmigrates from its own solar system and touches down on the Earth like a meteorite crossing the atmospheric blanket. It enters into a body which is still being formed, let's say, for example, in a female humanoid. Once it has entered into this body, then, becoming a male humanoid, grows up and develops its instincts up to the day when, during the mating season, it fights another male and in a hateful act of jealousy kills him. In doing that, he attaches himself to the karma of the world of Alma and becomes a captive of his environment. With the passing of the years and several incarnations, he becomes a tribal chief. He is strong, very cunning and intelligent like Onuman. With time, he receives the wisdom that he already received a long time before when he was living in a different form in another solar system. This is a new awakening of his consciousness. It may be that he will begin to dream one day of belonging in another place, however, again that might depend on his degree of evolution. If his desires become more and more spiritual, he will live eternally beside the creator in the higher astral where it is no longer necessary to take on a body of dense matter!"

"How do these souls get to the earth?"

"When Lord Lemoria built the temple on Mount Machu, the pyramid of light, he also created a soul-transporter alongside the temple's central building where the three cosmic lingams are located. He made a large circle appear formed from granite monoliths several meters high at the centre, of which he made an open granite sarcophagus. At precise dates based on the alignments of certain planets, a young virgin woman desirous of having an extraordinary child is brought there. She is the first of all infused with the cosmic male energy of the lingam during a ceremony resembling that of the sun and the moon. The woman is placed in the sarcophagus, where lying down and in a hypnotic trance, she is induced (receives an incoming soul). Very much later, she will prepare for the birth of the child in the same sarcophagus this time to the sound of another ceremony in which she is surrounded by attendants and where the newly-born child will be born and subsequently baptized by the priests and priestesses. This process will be repeated at different places on Alma. The next will be in a giant pyramid in Egypto, which will be by far the greatest soul transporter."

"Why are you smiling and looking at me when you say that?"

"Because your questions are pertinent and you were already among us in the past. Now, you are here as a bright star for thousands of people. You know how to guide perceptively in your programs all those who are seeking, who are losing themselves or who are suffering in other ways."

"I thank you. So you have given us to understand that there are several forms of reincarnation to be taken account of in the ways of the soul."

"Yes, and states of consciousness too. The thoughts of the Creator penetrate the whole of his creation and if you want to know his thought, you have to climb the ladder of all the levels of consciousness going from the material to the infinite."

"There is still the question of the humanoid race which you helped in its evolution. Apart from their hairy ones, what are they like?"

"The continent of Lemuria, in a past epoch, was still very dense, its terrestrial crust only partly solid. That is why Lemoria wanted us to establish ourselves in the mountains which had just formed. Between the thousands of islands formed by these solidifications, there was a boiling sea surrounded by volcanic eruptions and the subterranean fires were opposed to the spherical wall which formed due to the progressive cooling of the Earth at the places more solidified. The humanoid lived in the middle of giant forests of ferns and giant reptiles. His form was still plastic, with a spinal column already solid but he had to adapt himself to deal with his environment. The longer arms like the anthropoids enabled him to climb the trees easily to protect himself. His senses of hearing and touch were well developed but not that of sight. The two lenses which he presently has are still in development.

During the period when the Earth was closer to the Sun, being part of the luminous mass, it wasn't necessary to perceive light and that changed due to the Earth's distancing itself from the Sun and changing its period of rotation. The perception of external light increased and the light caused the eye to grow. The language of these prehistoric men resembled the sounds of nature. They had means of communication and gestures were important. However, the environment seemed like a dream, their consciousness was not alert, the Devas (nature spirits) were their gods and in part, they still had a collective soul. When it was time to leave their bodies, they entered another body right away without realizing it. It is in this state that we first encountered them."

"Did they have the means of educating their children?"

"Yes. The education of boys was a form intended to develop their will, and which today, would strike us as cruel. They had to take part in fights and to endure pain. As for the girls, the development of the imaginative faculty was favored. By this, they were able to learn to keep their memories and they needed to resist feelings of fear. Memory was necessary to permit past experiences to serve as guides for future actions. The girls were thus able to know the difference between good and bad. In this manner, the humanoid women became the pioneers of their evolution. They were nobly and faithfully constrained to follow a life of virtue in order to assist in the education of their children."

"Are the egos incarnated alternately into one sex or the other?"

"Effectively, spirits finding themselves in a feminine body find it vital and positive open to spiritual vibrations whereas the male vital body is negative and more fitted to work with matter. We teach them about arts, laws, nature and science. Being close to the nature spirits and the angels who are cooperating with the evolution of the planet, they haven't the desire to do wrong which would place them in a situation of pure innocence. However, that is not a virtue because innocence is the daughter of ignorance, which cannot be maintained in the universe where the goal of evolution is the acquiring of wisdom and for that, the knowledge of good and evil is necessary, and as well the freedom of choice."

"This knowledge, transmitted by the female spirit, will it always exist?"

"Absolutely. When possessing the knowledge as well as freedom of choice, man places himself alongside integrity and justice. He can cultivate virtue and wisdom. On the other hand, if he succumbs to temptation and willingly does evil, he nourishes vice in himself and continues to do so and then he suffers the consequences!"

"Isn't that what causes negative karma?"

"For the man himself, yes, because God's plan cannot be prevented. Each of our acts becomes the field where the law of consequences is played out and one reaps what one sows. In the kingdom of God, only the good can endure. The thorns of bad actions carry with them the flowers of grief and pain. However, when they are washed with the tears of repentance and fall on a purified heart, the flowers of virtue begin to flourish."

"Is the descent into wickedness and the suffering which follows only temporary?"

"Because of the fog into which one falls, it only seems like a black cloud and one can once again contemplate the divine which is within each of us. Finally, if the woman was lacking in imagination, she would not be able to nurture the new body of the child which will be born and if the sperm didn't have the force of concentrated will of the man, he would not be able to achieve the impregnation leading to the germination and the continuous cell-division of the ovum."

"So are the twin forces, that is to say the will and the imagination, therefore necessary for the reproduction of bodies?"

"Yes, that's it! Only, following the separation of the sexes since they were androgynous beings, each individual possesses only one of these two forces. In the beginning, the androgynous being could not develop its soul. It had to separate itself in order to get to know about love."

"The nature-spirits and the angels, do they have the same sex?"

"The angels have no need of a brain to know and learn about the physical world. They have a vital etheric body. They do not have sexes and have no need to procreate. They carry out the will of God without hesitation. They do not mingle desire with their love and have no egotism. For them, wisdom is their gift. On the other hand, man, from the beginning of his existence, was obliged to perform the act of generation and to learn it painfully."

"Are the angels at the service of men?"

"Only partially and if he asks for it, they are at the service of God and nature. Man has the same powers, but he wastes his energy. The force which flows out with the purpose of creating another being is love. However, man has impeded it with ego-based restrictions. The angels give off all their love without egotism and without personal desire."

"Man, then, only thinks about sensual desires!"

"He only sends out a part of his love which becomes egotistical and sensual. The angels, however, don't mix desire with love. Man must go through the experience of feeling together with egotism but later separating the two and arriving at the state of detachment. The angels who have helped him build up his brain are then going to help him evolve towards the light of pure love."

"Considering what we have just seen about what happened a long time ago, man hasn't changed very much."

"Those who have changed don't come back to the planet any more unless they have a desire to help the ones who are still there. All these harsh voices which we are hearing in our time are coming from thousands of humans lost in spiritual twilight and who are running in all directions without knowing where to go. It isn't a case of denying God but of not having time for Him. These terrible voices are expressing blind passion, hate, anger and barbaric conflict and these are men who have never gone within themselves, having lost the consciousness of their origin with the divine soul. In order to liberate themselves, they must find the silence within. That peace which men have always been dreaming of will never materialize so long as they have failed to discover it within themselves."

"That was well said Kethyr. However, is there a radical means to achieve it? In our days, everybody is looking for ready-made solutions."

"It only needs meditation, the art of mental quietness. It is a case of withdrawing oneself in the silence from the external mind and its noises. In your times, take the time, one hour per day whenever you can and you will then have to leave aside some of the pointless tasks which are habits of yours. Too many people put all their attention on the pursuit of whatever is petty, banal or frivolous, when the real game of life is waiting to be played."

"Is it enough to forget our personality during such a time?"

"Yes, one tells oneself: I want to forget completely the world, society and my personality, my desires and my occupation. One does that each time with a little more intensity and determination. Do you see, there is a great secret in life that we don't know because we see neither the value nor the importance of a wise use of time. We will enter heaven after death only after reaching it while we are living! Now, I have finished my talk. Another time, we can speak again about these things."

"We thank you Kethyr for replying to our questions. Certainly, there could be more of them, however, as you say, we can talk again about these things."

Kethyr made a sign to Adamos that he had finished. The picture on the screen of the sphere changed its form. We had returned to the time when the world of Alma was still in its youth. Nature and its violent changes had things to say and men were forced to submit to them. The adaptation to his environment created for men quite a bit of suffering and very many obstacles to overcome. In the physical domain, nature performs miracles. Over a number of years, the laboratory team had constructed huge greenhouses resembling those on Mara when they could cultivate indoors a very great number of vegetables to feed the population. Amongst the most popular plants which they had imported with them were the "mays" (corn) and the "patata" (potato). These vegetables were well adapted for Alma's rigorous climate and in working the soil the aboriginal people began to grow them. They could feed themselves like the Marians, with fruits, vegetables, nuts and root crops. They detached themselves from eating animal flesh except for various eggs, particularly fish eggs. Their education also was going well. They were being taught mathematics, language and writing but they were not yet ready for higher learning. They were present at a great number of philosophy courses and that was what pleased them the most because there they received explanations that the influences of astral larvae and Luciferian spirits could contaminate their good intentions and their spiritual advancement. They learnt that such influences were particularly active during the time of the full moon and were able to open the door to the lower astral and cause disarray in their vital energy. The humanoids, because of their limited intellect, could not grasp the presence of God within themselves, they were inclined rather to worship an external divinity. It was hard for them to understand that their behavior during their present life, together with their actions, was going to influence the next terrestrial vehicle which they would receive for their next incarnation. The human being is like a flower which, before opening, must achieve its maturity, in order to give the right seeds!

Chapter XIV

The treasure cave

Adamos got the idea to search for metals to be used in producing new instruments and also for teaching the humanoids of Alma the art of metalworking. He spoke about it to Evena: "Evena, can you make a search by divination of the planet's mineral wealth in this region and communicate with the entities who control access to the mines?"

"When the sun reaches the zenith, we will gather together and put the question to them," she said.

At the stated hour, Evena and her divination assistants gathered round the oracle and after performing their solar ritual, she asked the Lord of the mineral world to be present. He came without delay. A sprightly-looking reddish person appeared in the stone mirror. He seemed astonished.

"You called me. I am King Yul, governor of all Alma's mineral resources."

"We thank you for being present. We need your services. Adamos needs to know the location of a mine where we can obtain copper, gold, silver and iron ore and one which is the nearest and most accessible from Machu."

"There is a mine that the Luciferians were operating in the past and which contains all the minerals. The entrance is through a huge cave. However, you will have to make a trip there and then I will guide you."

"That will be fine, King Yul. We will get ready for an expedition starting tomorrow at sunrise. Come and join us."

The next day at sunrise, a small fellow was there in the centre of the palace. It was King Yul. He was dressed in a suit glittering with gold sequins and wore a hat decorated with multicolored jewels. He was smiling in welcome.

"I am happy to meet with you," said Adamos.

"So am I. You are really different from the Luciferians who were using us like slaves. I heard that you decimated them and made them leave. All nature here is happy for what you have done for us."

"Very good. We have amongst us some humanoids who worked in these mines but they no longer remember the cave's location. We are ready to be shown the way there."

"Perfect. Follow me."

Then he started moving with a hopping gait. They crossed several forests, water courses and mountain trails taking care to mark the route as they went. Finally, they arrived at a huge cave.

"See, there it is. Inside there are still stone staircases and nothing has changed but deep inside there is a monstrous creature that the Luciferians left to guard the mine. I cannot follow you but you know how to contact me. If you need me, call upon me."

"Yes, if it's necessary, I'll call you, Yul. Onuman, follow me with three of your men, let the others stay in the cave and remain alert, ready to lend us a strong hand if needed."

Adamos, followed by these hominids, went down a large stone staircase at the back of the cave and it was like entering a threatening shadow. Adamos stopped to listen. "I sense a presence around us," he said, "something strange brushed against me as if a sticky creature was following me. Ah! Over there, shine the lights in that direction."

Then they saw a human being completely naked and without hair either on his head or his body. He had large green eyes and thick lips and seemed fearful as they approached. Adamos adjusted the portable language device for sending mental images which he carried on his belt and sent messages to the strange being. The latter replied in the Marian language saying: "I am Slam, guardian of this place. I know your language having learnt it from the Luciferians. You want to visit the iron mine. I am going to lead you there" and he went down some other stairs. He seemed to be very fearful of the light and signed that they should follow him.

Adamos said to Onuman: "I don't trust this Slam. To me he seems dishonest. I hear him sending strange signals to another creature. Warn the men to be on their guard."

They descended into the depths of the earth and saw huge machines for the extraction of minerals, abandoned there, scattered over a large expanse and there were tunnels which went out from this chamber in all directions. Slam operated an instrument to which many wires were connected and large light turned on at the centre of the chamber. He made them a sign that they should follow him down one particular tunnel which gave off a bad smell. They had hardly walked two hundred paces when Adamos, who was in the lead, fell into a crevasse which suddenly opened beneath his feet. Slam had operated a lever hidden in the wall. Onuman had barely reached him when a huge jet of fire shot out in front of them enveloping Adamos. Onuman threw himself on him to put out the flames. They had just fallen into an ambush since a monstrous dragon advanced upon them opening his immense jaws, still smoking. As it had a long neck, it bit off the left foot of Adamos whom Onuman was holding by the waist in order to lift him up. Seeing this, Mayax, who was just behind him, fired his weapon at the dragon's eye. There was a jet of green dazzling light which passed through the monster causing it to collapse. Its head fell into the crevasse where there could be seen a pile of skeletons, doubtless those of previous victims. Unfortunately, it carried off Adamos' left foot in its jaws. Mayax made an emergency tourniquet at the ankle and communicated rapidly with the *Gyrosphere*. Right away, doctor Zanga's team got ready to take off in order to go to the cave, something that was done without difficulty thanks to directions to the place which were now available. On their arrival, they brought the transporter down to the ground and took Adamos on board, who was still conscious, but in a meditative state, and in record time brought him to the laboratory of the transmigrator rays. There, a tissue sample from his knee containing the DNA and the RNA from the cells was processed by the magic eye and the brain of the computer. Adamos' left leg was then placed under the triple rays of the cellular transmigrator and an astral halo could be seen forming at the site of the missing foot. At the end of a miraculous instant, the left foot formed itself. Starting as a blue astral light, it became first red and small then small and white. Adamos could already move his new toes. He wore a satisfied smile when he got up. Everything had gone well, above all because he had not lost very much blood during the crisis. Onuman, the faithful humanoid, had saved his life.

The watchers, at the time of consulting the oracle, had seen what had happened but the images had become hazy as if an invisible operator wished to hide the information from them. Without doubt it was the influence of the Luciferians who did not want the Marians to be able to get a preview and thus be prepared for a sneak attack. So it was, they had found the huge mine, but there was a price to pay. Adamos had not forgotten Slam and his deceitful attitude. He told everybody about it as an example. "In situations like this, he said, you can only count on yourself and the help of your friends. Onuman himself is also a faithful friend and I am fully aware of it. Soon, we are going to be able to start the work of extraction and we will be giving courses on metallurgy and afterwards on art. However, we will have to block up and make inaccessible the tunnel where the corpse of the dragon rests together with all connected galleries for a long time. In addition, nobody should speak a word to Slam if they see him because he is an agent of the Luciferians. We cannot have the slightest trust in him. He was the one who fed the dragon and a great number of humanoids perished in this sad fashion. The world continues to turn and we also are turning a page in our own history."

Mayax interrupted Adamos saying: "Master Adamos, I am ready with my wife Maya, my children, and a party of humanoids to go to the north of Lemuria and found a Marian colony."

"Yes Mayax, it was also my intention to ask you to do that. Our years on the Earth are shorter than on Mara and there is still work to do, but this will take a month of preparation. We are going to request a consultation with the spiritual beings who are guiding us and Evena will help us with that. I have seen on the screen that there is a mountain near a volcano where you will be able to establish a settlement. However, because there are areas of dense forests to cross which are particularly dangerous, we will take you there in the *Gyrosphere* together with material to construct your first building which should be of stone. You can tell your men and your family to get ready for the next lunar cycle which will be a time more favorable for this trip."

"Thank you Adamos, but since I am an engineer, I will request the right to build a boat of smaller dimensions for this expedition. I find that it would be important to help us to know that environment better."

"You have a good idea there and I encourage you to follow it through. We are going to help you build your boat, and later, we'll be able to send you the necessary materials for the construction of your city over there just as soon as you have found an ideal site for it."

So the group prepared themselves for another exodus to populate the world of Alma following the plan which had been conceived by the avatar Lemoria.

Chapter XV

The presence of God in the universe

The Marians, after their first experience of life on Alma, had no more need to be reincarnated. Lemoria had promised them that. They could continue their existence on the higher spiritual planes. Only those having a deep desire to come back to help humanity progress upwards in their spiritual ascension could return. Generally, this would be during the incarnation of an avatar for the purpose of helping him in his work of unconditional love for the world. The goal of all life must be respected because it is essentially spiritual.

Adamos had formerly mentioned the importance of living for and respecting life. He said: "The Lord Lemoria places very much emphasis on spirituality. You cannot live only by your instincts, because they keep you fixed in the physical experience and hold you prisoners of your senses and your desires. You have to follow the path of your heart especially that of the love which you have for God who is in everything and present everywhere. Society is going to create common laws and religions, approaches which are still based on instincts and which lack spiritual value. So then, you need to search for the truth, right there, in the depths of your heart, because it is there that may be found the centre of your divine reality. That done, your mind will follow."

With time, a great change had happened amongst the children of the hominids. This showed both physically and in their character. These were the children which were inoculated with the Marian genes. The change could be seen in their body and their bearing. A new human race was in the process of coming into being. Their intelligence compared to that of their parents had taken a magisterial leap forward. They even had difficulty understanding their parents and were now preparing for a future which was very different from theirs.

From the Earth, some influential persons had fairly pertinent questions to address to Lord Lemoria. Evena, who had come aware of these messages, put her attention on the oracle in the pyramid in order to contact Lemoria. After a few moments, the images of the avatar formed. The transmission of his sermon was carried directly to the Earth at the NASA centre.

"You called me and I am here to answer your questions."

"Here is the first question," said Evena. "The religious leaders want to know where God is located."

"Look at it this way," replied Lemoria. *"The goal of existence is the search for God. So, in order to live in Him, you have to cultivate love and share that love with the whole world. You cannot give more to one than another since we are all alike. That is part of the universal assembly of faith which at the same time is the principle of the life within. It is also the way of universal love, the path of righteousness with the need to love which is an obligation. God is to be found in everything, his name is carved on everything. Each drop of liquid or an atom contains Him. In developing your intelligence, you can realize the presence of God. Each man who develops his higher consciousness can realize his unity with God, and in knowing himself as divine, he can be aware of his mission on this planet which is one of perceiving divinity in everything, even in the non-existent."*

Evena continued: "We have come here on Alma in order to continue this experience of life in the material world, because on our planet, human life was becoming practically impossible. We are before everything spirit and soul, since we are not the body, that one is only an accessory. So, even with our adaptation to this new planet and its physical environment, the material existence remains secondary. If we separate ourselves mentally from God's divine principle, we fall into a multitude of traps led by our personal ego. It is thus that we get dominated by the negative including unsatisfied desire, resentment which leads to hate and jealousy and becoming tormented by pride and vanity. In all this despair, only the divine love can save us by replacing errors with understanding."

Lemoria resumed his discourse. *"God is love, therefore one must immerse oneself in love in order to merge at last in Him. He is beauty, then we must bring beauty into ourselves. He is totally compassionate so compassion must be the driving force of our lives. Love within us should develop like the bud which will become a flower and each of us should become such a flower. God says: "I am the seed of every being." This seed is the immortal essence, so if the seed of the grain is immortal, the plant, the tree, the flower and the fruit are also immortal. In fact, God cannot be limited by a particular form, with its own name, or its own category, or by a religious belief, because He is residing in everything, no matter whether humans, humanoids, monkeys or other animals. When you see God everywhere, you set in motion a massive expansion of your consciousness. By the renunciation of desires, you are going to experience immortality. Our requirement is pure consciousness. One should not cause division by criticism and, even worse, by judgment. In the whole universe, God is omnipotent, meaning He is all-powerful. He is also omnipresent, meaning that He is in everything which exists. He is omniscient because He is all-knowing. I am repeating all that for your benefit but I know that really, in the depths of your being, you know it. However, in the future, a number of different circumstances can monopolize your thoughts and forgetfulness of reality will intervene. Whatever happens, don't forget that you must serve as examples to others by your wisdom and also to the humanoids who are still affected by a lack of knowledge. The tendencies of people in the future will be to become more and more egotistical. They will think "me first, the world afterwards and God last" while it is the complete opposite which should be followed: God first, the world afterwards and myself last.*

Even if in your life, you are constrained by thousands of disappointments which combine to give you hardship, never abandon love towards others. Concentrate the whole of your attention on the source of love and the supreme goal of life, God! Love yourselves because it is God who lives in you. Love your neighbor knowing that it is God who lives in him, residing in his heart even if he knows it not. Just the fact of recognizing that God is in everything will transform you. Later on, in the future, thousands of beings will recite the divine names while rolling their rosary beads between their fingers while others will do breathing exercises, gestures and poses in a learned fashion. Combined, all these contortions are really beautiful, but if the people doing them haven't a pure heart and reject living in the truth due to their abandoning of unconditional love, they will be insulting the reason for their own existence. Passions, bad impulses and worries, degrade human nature from one planet to the next. Only love can rein in the negative which is born from anger, jealousy, hate, pride and malice. God is to be found in your heart. You who live now in the world of Alma are our future. At this time you don't have to fight to protect yourselves from ferocious animals like dinosaurs but your problems are the same, they only change in their outward forms. The most important transformation is that of the heart. Do you still have other questions?"

"No and many thanks to you. We understand you well. The battle between good and evil only changes in appearance from one era to another, but it remains, and humans are affected by it right up to the day when each wins the fight and obtains deliverance."

After several weeks of intense effort, the boat of Mayax and his group was finished. They were ready to undertake the voyage. The boat made from balsa wood was light, was one hundred feet long and was propelled by a magnetic jet of ionic energy. On the prow, could be made out a large lion's head. They had decided not to use the *Gyrosphere* for this trip. These pioneers did not have all the resources that the Marians had brought along on their interplanetary journey. They had to live from day to day with whatever type of fortune nature handed out to them. Nevertheless, they were able to communicate with their base at Machu. They were following the bank of an immense river that they called Pacifica. At times, it opened up to something like a wide sea, at the side of which gathered large numbers of animals. Navigating this took several days. Seeing an extensive stretch of quiet beach, they went ashore to make a fire and start cooking some vegetables. Everything seemed normal when all of a sudden; they became aware that some heads of giant lizards hiding amongst the trees were watching them. Seeing that they were discovered, they gave out cries like those of monkeys then all at once spreading out huge red ears in the form of umbrellas, they attacked the group. However, guardians had been put in place in preparation for any attack. The jet of fire from the red ray guns touched about ten of the lizards causing them to melt immediately. After this setback, those following them fled in all directions without waiting for more. When he approached the smoking corpses, Mayax observed: "These monsters have the teeth of carnivores; they move around quickly and are very dangerous."

Having said that, he traced a large circle of fire around the group. "With this here, he said, they won't attack us any more." In fact, the luminous vibrations produced by the circle prevented the lizards from approaching again by inducing in them intense heat which increased continually. Everyone ate silently, but they did not have much of an appetite.

Following this event, another surprise awaited them in that beyond the circle of light, four figures appeared resembling teddy-bears, giving out piteous cries and making signs to attract their attention. Maya, Mayax's spouse approached them to speak to them in the language of mental imagery. They begged her to have pity on them saying that they had been attacked by the lizards who wanted to devour them. About ten of them had already been killed and they asked for protection. She opened the protecting circle to let them enter while making a sign and saying a mantra. These little fellows very much resembled the Ewoks from a well known story and were speaking in small bass voices. They hung around Maya like children. It was learned from them that a band of them were living in a dense forest nearby and that they had constructed huts in the trees at a good height, out of reach of carnivorous animals. They invited Mayax's band to visit their village. They called themselves Kirouis.

Following this incident, Mayax devised a protective entity using creative thought. This entity looked like a bat and was ordered to survey the whole area to warn them of all possible dangers. This was a visible entity but had the ability to disappear whenever danger threatened. Mayax had learnt this technique from Adamos.

Such a creation had a temporary life, needed a daily recharge of energy and could prevent a sneak attack from the rear. Thanks to it, the team was saved several times from the approach of malevolent predators because it was able to warn them in time.

The Kirouis let them to their elevated village. They had a large assortment of plaited creepers with which they had made bridges by entwining from palettes of wood, balconies and huts, all connected together. They lived mostly on fruits and nuts and a few vegetables. They had agile fingers with which they were able to fashion a number of useful objects for the maintenance of their lives but since they were not aggressive, they did not have weapons to defend themselves and only depended on their intuition. Because they had soft bodies, they became easy prey for the giant lizards who pounced on them as soon as they set foot on the ground.

Mayax, who had been presented to their king, undertook now to counsel him to establish a system of defense and armament against their assailants. He showed them how to kill using a bow and to make poisoned arrows with the sap of several plants and from animals. They stayed several months with the Kirouis to help them and when they departed, the Kirouis had become the Amerindian Pygmies of that continent. At the time of their departure, the king and his relatives made them a feast and since they were beings who had become very attached to their new friends, they showed great emotions. Mayax made them understand that his group would remain on good terms and would come back to see them. Meanwhile, after showing them the power of communication using drums, they departed. The Kirouis, very interested in their ship, wanted to know all about how to construct one and Mayax showed them how, by hollowing out a tree trunk, they could use it as a boat and he showed them how to make what was needed to propel it. He explained to them that his people wished to settle in the area, but high on a mountain, just because of the wild animals which foraged on the lowland plains. Then the King asked if Mayax would agree that he and his little people might come and join them. Mayax, after a short conference with his team, accepted this proposal and the king seemed very happy and gave them five of his people to go with them. At this point, the Marian voyagers re-embarked on their boat, weapons in hand, without further incident. After several days of navigation, between several altercations with other monsters on their way and having to negotiate some streams, they arrived in view of a high mountain. There it was, following the plan of Adamos, that they were going to found their village at the level of a plateau surrounded by forests at the middle of which ran a watercourse. They called it Vilcamba and from there, they could divide up and emigrate very much later to the north. Mayax reported to Adamos via the communications tower of the *Gyrosphere*.

"Adamos, we have arrived at our destination without the loss of any person and we are now getting ready to build our village."

"That's great Mayax. If you are short of anything, we'll send it out to you on a flying platform. Here also everything is going well. Some serious incidents have occurred in Afrika, but as for Atalanta, things are also going well with him. I'll let you have other details later."

"Same here Adamos. We've met some strange beings called Kirouis who have a friendly nature and want to join with us for their own safety. We'll send you other details soon. That's it, out."

So communication was well established amongst the Marians between their central headquarters at Machu and their far-flung colonies on Alma Tierra. After having made an immense circle of protection around Vilcamba the Marians hastened to construct a boundary wall. A large number of Kirouis had come to help them. Faithful to their tradition of living in the trees, they constructed at Vilcamba, among the tallest trees another village of that type, which was not really necessary but it gave them the confidence to feel at home.

A great friendship grew up between the Kirouis and the homoids, the latter much bigger and stronger played the role of protectors. It happened that a male homoid felt sexual desire for a female Kirouis and thus they started a household. Since all the hominids who accompanied the Marians had been inoculated with

Marian genes, the line of descent showed itself as being unique, above all on the side of Zanga's people having slanted eyes similar to Mayax and also having a yellow skin. This region was going to be the motherland of their race.

Later, Zanga and his spouse, in their turn, departed from Machu and the continent of Muria to head westward in the direction of the sacred mountain Evert, where they established another centre of Marian activity, all part of Lemoria's plan. Thus it was that the four lines of this great Marian family peopled the world of Alma for the future. They were all derived from the same source, that of human beings. Whether they were homoids, hominids or humanoids, Saturians or Marians or even mixtures with the Kirouis, it mattered little because the divine spirit of their souls was perpetually aflame with experiences which were new and even sublime so much so that the Luciferian spirit of discord did not appear to shoot its venom into the order of things for a long time.

There was a particular day when frightening noise was heard around the fortification wall of the new city which attracted everyone's attention. Near a large rock, fighting for its life was a huge mammoth around which circled a giant sabre-toothed tiger. The tiger was trying to jump on the mammoth's back so as to plant its sharp teeth into the nape of the mammoth's neck. It was not succeeding and was roaring in fury as the gigantic elephant beat it with its huge trunk. Such huge animals were unknown in that region and all were astonished, trembling with the notion that these monsters would be capable of breaking through the barricades protecting their city. Seeing that, Mayax concentrated his mental powers on the mammoth's forehead and gave it the perfect idea for its own defense. So, suddenly, the mammoth with the end of its trunk picked up a large tree branch from a pile of chopped-down tree-trunks which were serving as barriers and lashed the tiger's head with heavy blows. The latter, taken by surprise, was forced to retreat and the mammoth overcame it using its heavy front feet to crush its head. The battle now having ended, the solitary mammoth, went away along the mountain trails and was lost from sight.

Maya went over to her spouse and asked him: "Mayax, it was you who gave the mental suggestion to the elephant to take the big branch and overcome the tiger."

"Right, Maya. It was preferable for us that the mammoth was able to defend itself. It's very dangerous to have such a tiger hanging around where we are."

"Perhaps there are others," she added.

"It's possible, however, we are going to reinforce our circle of protection and create invisible guardians to protect us and avert all possible dangers."

"What if a herd of mammoths come and break down our barricade?"

"That couldn't happen, because the vibrations of the circle vary according to each particular case and will amplify themselves to the point of causing death. Even a herd of mammoths will retreat."

"There are some monstrous animals on this planet of which we are not fully aware of. How could we have survived up to now without our means of defense?"

"A good question, but consider this, the humanoids and the Kirouis have as their means of defense to escape to their place of security. With regard to one of these monstrous dinosaurs, remaining immobile and out of its reach protects you, because they do not see well and their sense of smell is mediocre."

"Why has the Lord created such monsters?"

"I have considered that Maya. However, I recall that the Lord Lemoria told us once that these monsters like all beings of the light are His creation and thus part of His divine expression of being. He can take all possible forms where and when He wishes. When one monster devours another, it is still He who devours and allows himself to be devoured. The Luciferians, who themselves also have the power to create in the world of matter, use their gifts to make all kinds of creatures which please their desires. They won't be able to create angels of beauty and kindness; such things don't fit in with their state of consciousness which remains at an inferior level. On the contrary, their desire is to destroy whatever has been created, so their thoughts cause a tiger to be born, or a similar monster with wings possessing all the means for destruction. They are the opponents, the artists of ugliness, that is their domain. The Lord Shva gives them their rights; he is the opponent of creation because he destroys it, though he is also at the same time the creator Shram. He is only the opposing aspect. Amongst ordinary human beings, there are those who create beauty, those who maintain harmony and those who destroy it."

"So, we need to understand by that, Mayax, that this phenomenon is present in the whole of creation and in all the planets of all the solar-systems in the universe."

"Yes Maya. Everywhere there is good and evil, beauty and ugliness. With exceptions, for sure, as Adamos tells us, in Andromeda or in other galaxies. There, highly evolved beings have departed from the duality of nature and their semi-physical bodies are purely spiritual, being like those who are living in our sun, the avatars. They don't suffer from the rules of form, rather they create them. When they are on the side of good, by their love, they create beauty and love in all forms. However, when they are in opposition, that is to say associated with the black sun, they create destruction and the apocalypse. They become the Luciferians who worship the beauty of the black sun."

"So, there will always be a confrontation between good and evil on this world even after changing the planet."

"Yes, it cannot be otherwise. It is the formal decree of the Creator and lasts up to the moment of deliverance. This deliverance only arrives at the moment when we no longer feel the need of living and reliving the experiences of the material universe, in other words, we reach a saturation in our spiritual selves."

"So then, it would be preferable not to bring any more children into the world."

"We can call souls into the terrestrial life but only in a very responsible fashion. Let's not forget that very many souls have to come back here to pay their karmic debts; so we must be ready to receive them. It is essential that we teach the truth to our children. So their education must be for survival and adaptation to the environment. This is because our society depends on it and they must learn, above all, the reason for their existence. To bring children into the world is a task of great responsibility and they must be properly educated."

"What is the return to the pure state of the soul preparing to return to God?"

"This is how it is. For all of us, the experience of living in this body, in the material illusion, is no more than a game of going and coming back. When we stay blocked in the cycle of reincarnation, we are imprisoned by the errors of judgment and the insatiable desires of our ego to keep surviving in the material universe. There are many who believe that living is limited to occupying this body."

"So, as to the spirit-soul which commits lots of errors when incarnating, that is due to its state of consciousness".

"Exactly so. The spirit-soul, having passed through its experiences in the worlds of mineral, vegetable and animal sees itself one day becoming a homoid. This soul climbs up through the different grades of the states of consciousness of the physical world but once it becomes human, it needs to return to the pure spiritual state by transforming the self."

Mayax and his people decided to construct a stone pyramid which would serve as a temple and around which other buildings would be constructed. Their education and their religion were following the path traced out by Lemoria and they remained in contact with the mother city where all the decisions were made. The place they had settled was yet another part of Alma where a new Marian generation was starting out.

During this time at Muria, another of Adamos' conferences was transmitted concerning the necessity to remain in communication with the divine being within, so as not to fall under the shadow of material illusions. Such a philosophy of life was necessary to keep a rational balance in the evolutionary process, as much for the group as for the individual. Adamos used to say: "The more you concentrate on the needs of the physical world and the more you fall under its shadow then the more you will become its slave because you forget your own reality and its divine essence." Then he gave as an example: "There exist other solar systems that I remember where life is lived on two planes consciously at the same time because the physical plane hasn't crystallized in the thoughts of the inhabitants. A material body which hasn't crystallized can disintegrate easily and reintegrate itself a short time afterwards in a different place. For the spirits of these people, the stability of atoms is not necessary; it keeps the power to transform itself instantly, even though in the spirits of the inhabitants, it is known that the stability of form is non-existent. It is illusory and can transform itself continually with the result that, in these beings' philosophy, reality is not physical but purely spiritual. In contrast, if people continually materialize their thoughts and concentrate their attention on that approach believing it to be the sole reality, they crystallize that form and make it become hard. The atoms solidify themselves leading to the complications of life, such as the shaping of things, wear and tear or getting old, the whole situation becoming more and more temporal. Such an action changes one's philosophy of existence, necessitating new laws putting good and evil in continuous opposition, creating the law of opposites implying that of Karma with its causes and effects. The final result, now apparent, is the thoughts of man fixed in this illusion of a material life in which he embeds himself more and more right up to becoming a prisoner down at a low level of his consciousness. Man creates by his thoughts but can also, by such means, create his own misfortune!"

Then someone asked Adamos: "How can man free himself from this illusion?"

"It is with the help of the higher consciousness that he can free himself from the yoke of the world of illusion and it can also be done by meditation."

"What happens when he dies?"

"Once he dies to the physical world, the man and his spirit returns to the astral state where he can create instantly in the illusory world of the astral. There he realizes that in the creation of forms which he can shape at will, it is only a game of the spirit and that the reality of the physical world is only an appearance despite the solidity he perceives when he is living in it."

"It is really paradoxical. We live in a manifested world where we have to follow the laws of survival, of pain and misery in order to realize that it doesn't exist, that it's only a fantasy of our spirit and that of the creator."

"That's right, and forms change together with their laws from one planet to another, from one world to another indefinitely, and from one life to another."

"And you have to become the creator to realize it and to be able to liberate yourself, isn't that so?"

"Yes, because this knowledge is liberating!"

"So you must consciously raise yourself above the forces which control the world of senses and instincts. You have to spiritualize yourself totally in order to arrive at that point."

"Perfectly correct, because when we thus raise our level of consciousness so as to dominate the world of cause and effect and our Karma, we receive the key to our liberation, we become God once again. We continue to hold on to life because we are life but we leave behind the stranglehold of forms. It's as if we are a butterfly emerging from a chrysalis. We liberate ourselves."

"However, in this allegory, we liberate ourselves from one form in order to become another."

"That's true, but when we raise ourselves through higher and higher levels of consciousness up to God then we share His consciousness. It's no longer necessary to take on a form and thus our liberation is complete."

"Can anyone fall back into the illusion of self despite that and again start a new cycle of reincarnation?"

"According to his deep desire and love for humanity, as Lemoria said: *"You called me and I came…! From one era to another, your spirit having become mature through suffering calls me and my love for you forces me to incarnate so that I can bind up your wounds and bring you hope and sympathy."*

"Amongst the enemies of the human spirit brought by the Luciferians, there is laziness and indifference. In order to make peace with the difficulties of the physical world and in dealing with them, a man develops his intelligence and arrives at a status-quo where he becomes lazy, preferring to enjoy an easy life. He protects himself from the rigors of existence once he has tasted the pleasure of inactivity."

"You are right. Indolence is a subtle enemy in man's evolution but it has a positive side permitting him to sit in a peaceful setting where he can follow the lead of intuition which can bring him to spiritual experiences. This makes him discover the temple within of which he becomes the preacher and the listener creating a mysterious state of soul which makes him aware of his double nature. It is as if one half of his being is watching what the other half is doing, then, thanks to the absence of thought by a conscious cessation he is permitted to encounter his pure awareness and receives an experience of unity. Once in this state of conscious-suspension of thought, the total truth of being, hidden by all activities, such as desires and thoughts reveals itself in all its spiritual grandeur."

"One can say that, such a situation appears when the spirit has voluntarily eliminated all its ideas and that a total vacuum remains."

"Yes! One has to stop, momentarily, the torrent of ideas in order to contemplate the thinker while resting the intellect, all the time watching attentively that space that has been created in the consciousness. This level of consciousness resembles the situation in a deep and dreamless sleep, without the problem of forgetfulness because it is a state of perfect lucidity. It lifts the veil of unconsciousness which envelops deep sleep and one discovers heaven on earth. It is only in this sublime state that thoughts are momentarily suspended; as in deep sleep, they cease altogether. Nevertheless, one remains in full possession of consciousness even when thought is absent."

"The higher self, of which you are speaking, is difficult for most of us to understand."

"I know. So, let's take an example, the theory of the electron. It resembles the higher self, because it represents the atom as being like a universe in miniature with its solar system. At the centre of the atomic system, there is a positive electric charge around which circle a cloud of negatively charged electrons. These energies are balanced one with another so that the atom doesn't break up. One can see the positive charge remaining stable while the negative charge moves in orbit round the centre. The point of absolute rest round which the electrons move in orbit corresponds to the higher self which is pure and all the electrons which depend on it correspond to the intelligence, the emotions and the physical body but the supreme self is unchangeable."

"If I understand you well, to recover one's soul is to return to the original state?"

"Effectively, we were all in an infinitely distant past going from one planet to another in the Luciferian époque, purely divine beings not yet hobbled by the envelope of the body nor hampered by thoughts. Angels, in other words, divine beings we still are, but by reason of this gradual thickening due to egotistical thought-forms, we have forgotten who we are, so when we manage to pierce this layer by deep meditation, we finish by perceiving our true self, the higher self. This self is totally different from the personal ego because the latter is egocentric."

"So we should stop acting as though we are prisoners of the body, captives of our thoughts and slaves to our passions. Our pure consciousness is completely bound up by these chains and we are like caged birds."

"The whole art of meditation and its concentration consists of lifting off the chains and becoming free spirits. That done, with the spirit fixed on this unique goal, we can always penetrate more deeply within ourselves and discover a great peace and a feeling of ineffable well-being which will lead to the ecstasy of a perfect union with the higher self."

Now the goal of these conferences was to keep the spirit balanced with its own divine qualities in spite of all the daily pitfalls and confrontations with nature that human beings had to encounter. However, these teachings were not a religion. There is no need to run after different divinities when one has accomplished perfect union with the self! When each one has different levels of consciousness to experience, it is necessary to remind everyone of all the laws and principles and further the mental and physical processes which intermingle and balance themselves in life. It is true that without their technology and the help of avatar Lemoria, the Marians would not perhaps have been able to establish themselves easily on the world of Alma. But how will they escape the perils of cataclysms to come and of a thousand other dangers which abound down here?

The Earthlings who were now receiving all this information knew it well since they were there as the proof but at what price? There had been so many dark periods in human evolution on earth as demonstrated by history that one asks oneself why all these trials?

Now, the crystal sphere continued to show fantastic images of the Marian epic with the developments in Lemuria and Atlantis. This will need another book to describe. To satisfy the curiosity of the Marians, Lemoria had projected before his departure, on the large wall of the huge palace, images of the future and he said to them: *There will be times both hard and happy in the history of men. There won't be an end of the world because there is always the end of a cycle or of an epoque. The world is continually changing but the laws remain the laws. The actors change but their soul remains the same. It is a truth which perpetuates itself across the ages and I will always be with you to guide you. That is important, with time, under the Luciferian influence, the ego and its distinct personality is going to raise up obstacles to the impersonal self of the soul wishing to keep it a prisoner of the illusory world of matter. Then you should always be asking yourselves what is this body visible to the eyes of flesh? Is it really the only existence? Then, finally, you will know the truth and the truth will set you free.*

A long silence ensued, then there was heard the nasal voices of the small Marians, guardians of the planet. "Men of the world of Alma, listen carefully! From time to time, we travel around your planet to check on the progress of humanity in the material plane. We are the guardians of your race and you have given us the task to perform of looking after your physical evolution and we are doing our best. However, it is Lemoria, the solar avatar who has total control of spiritual evolution. We are only here to maintain the world in a manner that life can be experienced so that your souls can live through their experiences going from the ages of mineral to the vegetable, from the vegetable to the animal and from there to the human. It is, however, the work done on yourselves with your consciousness which will lead you to becoming the superior and divine being that you will represent."

***

The Marian transmission continued to supply the computer of NASA with information on the fantastic past of the Earthlings who came from the planet Mars and their amazing epic on Alma Tierra, our world. Their adventures and exploits will be told in the next volume *The Atlantean Archives*, always on the same theme with the same heroes of our tale and their descendants.

Table of contents

From the same author, books to be published:

The Atlantean Archives

The Egyptian Archives

The Oriental Archives

The Tibetan Archives

The Sathya Sai Baba Archives

The Secret Archives of the Ancient